DRAGON CROWN

Sea Dragons Trilogy Book Two

AVA RICHARDSON

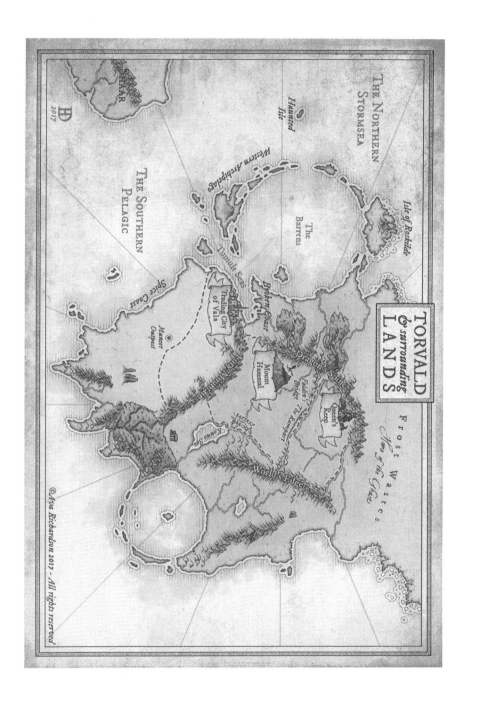

CONTENTS

Sea Dragons Trilogy — vii
Copyright — ix
Dragon Crown — xi
Mailing List — xiii
Blurb — xv

PART I
Chapter 1 — 3
Chapter 2 — 10
Chapter 3 — 15
Chapter 4 — 28
Chapter 5 — 36
Chapter 6 — 48
Chapter 7 — 61
Chapter 8 — 70
Chapter 9 — 88

PART II
Chapter 10 — 109
Chapter 11 — 118
Chapter 12 — 130
Chapter 13 — 138
Chapter 14 — 150
Chapter 15 — 172
Chapter 16 — 186
Chapter 17 — 203

PART III
Chapter 18 — 211

Chapter 19	225
Chapter 20	239
Chapter 21	250
Chapter 22	282
Chapter 23	296
Chapter 24	315
Chapter 25	329
Epilogue	349
End of Dragon Crown	353
Thank you!	355
Sneak Peak	357
Other Books by Ava	375

SEA DRAGONS TRILOGY

Dragon Raider

Dragon Crown

Dragon Prophecy

This is a work of fiction. Names, characters, places and incidents either are the product of imagination or are used fictiously. Any resemblance to actual persons, living or dead, events or locales, is entirely coincidental.

RELAY PUBLISHING EDITION, MAY 2018
Copyright © 2018 Relay Publishing Ltd.

All rights reserved. Published in the United Kingdom by Relay Publishing. This book or any portion thereof may not be reproduced or used in any manner whatsoever without the express written permission of the publisher except for the use of brief quotations in a book review.

Cover Design by Joemel Requeza

www.relaypub.com

DRAGON CROWN

MAILING LIST

Thank you for purchasing 'Dragon Crown'
(Sea Dragons Trilogy Book Two)

I would like to thank you for purchasing this book. If you would like to hear more about what I am up to, or continue to follow the stories set in this world with these characters—then please take a look at:

AvaRichardsonBooks.com

You can also find me on me on
www.facebook.com/AvaRichardsonBooks

Or sign up to my mailing list:
AvaRichardsonBooks.com/mailing-list/

BLURB

In order to embrace her true nature, a young Dragon Rider must accept who she is—and where she came from.

Lila knows her people's way of life is dying, but trying to get Raiders to become Dragon Mercenaries is no easy task. Although the world around them is changing, many among the Raiders still cling to the old ways of piracy. When a desperate message arrives from the West Witches, Lila and her new friend, the eccentric, unseasoned magician Danu, must risk a mission to the island of Sebol to learn what they can of the new danger they face, a threat that menaces all the Western Isles.

To face it, Lila must leave her Raider past behind and become the leader Danu knows she was born to be. Knowing the crown of Roskilde holds the key to her destiny, and perhaps the key to defeating the deadly threat that is upon them, Lila must seize it. But to do so, Raiders and dragons will have to learn to trust each other—and Lila—as she leads the charge. Can Lila let go of fear and doubt and face the future, or will the only life she's known be destroyed?

PART I
The Haunted Isle

CHAPTER 1
LILA, ON SPRING'S DARK TIDE

"Senga! Adair - Pull up!" I shouted as the two Raiders clutched onto Kim, their sinewy Blue dragon, as she hurtled towards the sea. "What is wrong with them?"

The Blue that they were riding awkwardly flared its wings, shrieked, and tried to slow its descent. It was embarrassing all-round, as Kim scraped her toes along the choppy blues, the small form of Senga was thrown forward, and Adair was flung from the Blue's back, plunging into the Malata bay like a cannonball.

"Sweet waters," I swore, turning to look at Danu at my side. We stood on the rocks above Malata harbor, trying our best to coordinate what few Dragon Raiders we had. Just learning how to talk to a group of dragons all at once was also a learning curve. Danu could hear them and talk to them with his innate dragon ability, and, through their excellent hearing, the dragons could hear my voice. Or I could convey our instructions to Crux and hope that he would get the right message across. But these techniques were taking time to simplify. Some situations called for Danu to mentally 'shout' at all of them, and sometimes it was easier to just holler at the dragon that we wanted to listen – if they did! Del and Vaya were on Thiel, another Blue and Kim's brood-brother, whilst older Martov was on the stocky Green Porax, and half a dozen other younger Raiders were still waiting on the shore for their turns on Retax, Holstag and Grithor, Ixyl, Viricalia and Lucalia.

"It's not going well, is it?" Danu said, blinking his eyes as if he had been dozing and not paying attention. Great, I thought irritably.

"What's wrong – are we keeping you up?" I sniped at him. I knew it was unfair, but I was in a foul mood, and Senga's and Adair's antics weren't helping improve it at all. Danu had been complaining of bad dreams recently, and he was always awake and looking pale when I encountered him in the mornings. I put it down to his highly-strung nature.

All through the long storm-lashed winter, I had been encouraging the Raiders to take to the dragons that now regularly visited our skies. I hoped that their appearance meant that the dragons were willing to bond with our Raiders – or at the very least that our Raiders wouldn't reach for their spears every time they saw them! Ever since the battle against

Havick's forces in the fall, Malata had been locked down by the fierce winter storms that swept around the Western Archipelago. There was no raiding and only a little fishing near the in-shore waters, but that hadn't stopped some of the dragons of the Western Isles from taking an interest in us. *I spent years dreaming of this day and got into a lot of trouble sailing to Sym's island just to be brushed off by her hatchlings,* I thought a little ruefully, *when all I needed to do was to get into a fight with Havick!*

Of course, I knew that wasn't entirely true – there was a whole lot more going on that had made the dragons come to our aid. But when I was in a bad mood, it at least felt good to have something to grumble about.

Thank goodness someone was taking an interest, I thought, frowning as Danu's eyes glazed over once again.

"Danu! Come on – we need to get them ready before…" My anger failed me as my words trailed off into silence. Danu's eyes snapped into focus once more, shadowed and worried as he nodded. He knew as well as I what was coming. With spring would come not just fairer weather – but Havick's return to terrorize the southern half of the Western Archipelago – the Free Islands of which Malata was but one.

"I'm sorry." Danu shook his head. "I don't know what is wrong with me today…"

You're spending too long out on the harbor with all the other of my dad's sailors, I thought but didn't say. But it was true. Over the winter we'd all had our fair share of work to do

— there was the wreckage on the Bone Reef that needed sorting and clearing from the battle (we'd had a lot of good bits of salvage from that!) as well as general defenses that needed replacing after the fury of the winter's waves and before the Roskildean fleet returned. Father had his dock teams working from break of dawn until after dark, rebuilding the walls, re-caulking the hulls of the boats, and making a thousand other minor repairs — all of which Danu threw himself into, often staying for the harborside bonfires afterwards.

If I didn't know better, I would have said that he liked this life.

"Incoming!" Senga shouted from above, howling with laughter as Kim swooped low across the bay and extended her back legs just like a fishing eagle, to snatch Senga's spluttering idiot brother from the wave tops.

"You have to admit, that was a good move." Danu grinned.

It was. But I wasn't going to let a chance maneuver spoil my bad mood. "They're doing this on purpose. They're just playing about!" I said, incredulously. Even Kim appeared to be enjoying herself as she whistled and called to her brother Thiel to join them.

"No, wait!" I waved my hands at the other Blue, but it was already too late. He roared in his young, bullish voice, letting out a puff of flame as he and the two humans on his back dipped even closer to the bay. Thiel trailed his foreclaws along the waves, sending up huge plumes of white water over his sister.

"Bah! Right, that's it!" Senga laughed indignantly, pointing for the Blue dragon underneath her to do the same.

"Not with Adair underneath you, for heaven's sake!" I groaned, watching as Kim dropped Adair in the harbor waters with a *plop* and circled back to antagonize her own brother.

"This is ridiculous," I growled at the spectacle. "I'm supposed to turn them into fighting fit Dragon Raiders, not children messing around on the backs of dragons!"

It wasn't as if we even had enough Raiders or dragons wanting to fly together. Although Sym's brood visited our skies, only the younger dragons took an interest in the day-to-day life of the Raiders, despite my cajoling. And of the Raiders? Only those around my and Danu's age showed any interest in dragons, ever since the battle for Malata when they had seen just how devastating an angry dragon could be.

But it wasn't enough, I thought. We couldn't always rely on Sym to decide to fight our battles for us, the Raider part of me thought.

"Why claim that tomorrow it will rain?" Crux's reptilian voice breathed soot into my mind.

"Huh?" I said.

"You humans. Always borrowing trouble from tomorrow, when you have enough today!" I could feel the mirth in his words. *"For now, sister-Sym fights with you, until we can find the witch who attacked the dragon newts. You have the same goals as her."*

Almost, I thought, not wanting to disagree outright with

Crux, the Phoenix dragon I had bonded with and that Danu and I rode. (Who *does* ever want to argue with a dragon?) But still – I knew it wasn't enough.

"Lots of my people lost their lives during the Battle for Malata," I murmured, my eyes wavering towards where the shell of my father's flagship, the *Ariel*, was still shackled to the harbor wall, undergoing repairs from the barrages of cannon shot that had rained down on it.

"And many dragons were injured!" Crux replied indignantly. He, too, still had a ragged hole in the leather of his wings that had only closed-up a little, and still gave him trouble in strong winds.

"I know that, my dragon-brother." I sat down on the boulder feeling frustrated and useless. Danu still stood in front of me, staring glassy-eyed at the horizon as if he was asleep standing up. *Maybe I'm not the only one who is being useless,* I grumbled to myself, turning instead to Crux. "And believe me, I never want to see any of your kind hurt for us – not you, not anyone. But I'll be asking the Raiders to fight Havick's fleet – maybe not just his fleet, but also his armies as well. I don't want to ask that of any who aren't bonded."

There was a moment of silent regard from Crux, which could have meant anything. Finally, he spoke. *"You are wise to want to rely on yourself, Lila Wave-Rider, and not just the good wishes of sister-Sym. But you should let the dragons of the Western Isles come to their own decisions about when and with whom they will fight. They might surprise you."*

And with that rebuke, he was gone from my mind, leaving me feeling even more stupid than before.

Just great. I really *had* annoyed a dragon.

"Woohooo!"

My grumbling thoughts were broken by another plume of water thrown up by the antics of the young dragons and few brave human Raiders on their backs. I scowled.

"Don't be so harsh on them, Lila," Danu said lightly, rubbing his eyes as if they hurt. *Oh great, I forgot about that,* Danu can hear and speak to all dragons, and only when Crux has chosen to speak to me alone are our conversations private. But Crux didn't have the same notions of privacy that I had. Where I might have a private word with a crewmate if I wanted to tell them off – Crux would just blare it out to every dragon (and Danu) that could hear it. "At least humans and dragons are having fun together?" Danu said. "That's, uh… more than you could say four months ago."

"Four months ago we were fighting for our lives, Danu," I muttered back, wondering how to get through to them all that this was serious – it wasn't a game!

"Urk." The sound that Danu gave was very slight, and for a split second, I thought he was just going to yawn – until his body thumped to the grass at my side, out cold.

CHAPTER 2
LILA, MESSAGES FROM AFAR

"What's wrong with him?" I asked, looking at my mother, Pela, through the gloom of the chamber.

Danu lay between us swathed in blankets with the curl of sharp, pine incense heavy in the air. We had brought him here to the Town House where my parents lived, Crux carrying us on his back before settling in the gardens outside. It wasn't much of a house, more of a colonial mansion at the top end of town, dating back to when Malata was just another outpost for the empire of Torvald.

This room was the healer's hall, which must have been some servant's rooms originally, as it was below the ground floor, with lots of draft and open, sterile stone spaces with stairs and windows leading to the outside. Since us Sea Raiders get into so many scrapes and fights, my mother had ordered it turned over to the Malata healers, and at any given time there was usually a score of people down here on beds, being tended by those with what skills we had.

Danu was murmuring and sweating in his blankets, and I moved to take them off of him.

"No! Leave them, child," my mother said sharply, rapping her knuckles against the wooden cot edge of the bed. "He looks as though he has a fever, and you have to sweat a fever out of a man."

"A fever?" I felt fear grip my stomach. Heaven knew how bad some of the fevers could be that swept through the Western Isles. My foster parents, Pela and Kasian, had lost their own natural-born child to the Blood Ague, just such a fever that had killed one in ten.

"No one else is sick?" My mother looked at me sharply. "None of your…." Her eyes flickered to the high windows, in the direction of the harbor. And the dragons. "You don't think…?" my mother said cautiously.

"Mother, don't." I shook my head. "It's not an illness caught from the dragons, I promise," I said desperately – although I knew no such thing.

"How can you know? You've only been flying around on that Crux of yours for a couple of seasons," my mother said sternly, but not altogether unkindly. I could see the worry in her eyes as she scanned my face, looking for any sign of weakness.

She's probably terrified of losing me like she lost her first born, I thought, grinding my teeth. "I feel fine, honestly. And none of the others have complained of being ill. If the dragons *did* have some sickness, then I would be the first to get it, wouldn't I?"

"That's what I'm worried about…" my mother grumbled.

"Not sickness." There was the sudden heavy thud and thumps as a concerned Crux landed in the lavender beds outside. Through our connection, I could sense the *shape* of him as he stalked quickly to where the windows of the healer's hall showed just over ground level. His shadow eclipsed them, and we could all hear his snuff.

"Get him out of here!" my mother almost shrieked. "If he has brought this fever—"

"Mother, no!" I said quickly.

"Not sickness! It's magic!" Crux huffed once more, louder against the glass. I relayed the information to my mother, who did not look convinced at all, but stopped her shouting.

"Crux can sense magic," I explained. "Whatever is happening to Danu, it is something to do with his magic…"

"Mgnhhuh?" Between us, Danu moaned and thrashed his head from side to side.

"Crux – can you do anything?" I begged of him, and for a moment almost regretted that I had asked him as he pushed his mind fully against mine. I tottered where I stood, marveling at the enormity of the dragon's soul. He had been holding his mind away from me this whole time! I realized suddenly, as I could feel the scales on my – his – body, I could hear the cries of gulls that were many leagues away and even smell the larger marlin that swam close to shore.

"Let me see..." Crux was using my senses to examine Danu, and I felt myself sniff and snuff the air. *"Oh. I forget that your nose is so small,"* he grumbled as he took in far more subtle information from the room than I could. He could smell my mother's fear, he could smell the family of mice that had made their home next door in the wine-cellar – and he could smell Danu's *mind*.

Joined with him as I was, I could also feel the fierce, glowing stubbornness that was Danu. He was angry and upset, but he was fighting whatever this was. A pall had been cast over him, trying to force him to do something, to open his mouth, to speak…

"What is happening to him?" I gasped, as Crux withdrew from my mind, leaving me feeling like a fish flopping out of water.

"A bit like what I did to you just then. Although we have a bond, which is why we can choose to share thoughts and feelings, sights and sounds," Crux told me. *"Danu does not have a bond with whoever – whatever is doing this to him."*

"He is possessed?" I cried out in alarm, earning a low moan of worry from my mother across from me.

"Not quite. More…used," Crux said as words started to spill from Danu's mouth.

"H'gmah...ugh..." He coughed and his body shook. His eyes rolled white. *"...You must come...Great danger..."* Cough, shake. *"...ugh. We are besieged....mgh...Zanna. Zanna seeks to end the Western Witches....Come to our aid, Danu and Lila!"* A sudden coughing, spluttering fit, and Danu's color once again returned to his cheeks. He blinked, his eyes bleary, but at least they focused once more on mine.

I felt, through Crux, an echo of that magic draw back from the room like a tide receding from a rocky beach, and in its wake, Danu was groaning and trying to push himself up.

"My head…" he said.

"Danu? Are you all right?" I rushed to his side, seizing a hand. He felt cold as if he really *had* a fever.

"I…I'm fine, I think." My friend shook his head weakly, before looking at me with startling ferocity. "But Sebol isn't. Chabon and Afar are in danger. I think they've been trying to get through to me for a long time, for days…"

"That would explain your strange weariness…" I nodded.

Danu's hand gripped mine suddenly, fiercely. "I saw them, Lila. Havick's fleet. He's surrounded Sebol."

CHAPTER 3
DANU, ACOLYTE OF SEBOL

Lila was still looking at me with worry through her shaded eyes as I brought my things to the lookout rocks above the harbor, where the dragons had made their home on Malata.

I didn't blame her, though, I had to admit – my knees still felt a little weak and shaky after the witches' strange magics had flowed through me. I didn't even know that Afar and the others could *do* that – to speak in my mind as the dragons did.

"Not as we do!" Crux breathed ash and fire into my thoughts suddenly, making me stumble. He was annoyed, clearly.

"Okay, sure, I get it, my friend…" I coughed weakly, heaving my saddlebags to the floor and mopping my brow. I still felt a little feverish. I wondered how long the after-effects of whatever spell they had cast would last.

"You are ill because your witches are using magic they do not fully understand." Crux raised himself up on his paws to regard me with his great green-gold eyes. The stare of a dragon was an uncomfortable thing, and I looked at my feet in an echo of embarrassment for my mentors.

"They were only trying to reach me," I said quietly, as Lila looked in alarm between me and her dragon. It was barely a few hours after my strange 'collapse,' but I had managed to convince Pela and Lila that they should let me ride to Sebol, to scout what this trouble was. Pela had forced me to sit and eat bowl after bowl of stew before declaring me as ready as she could make me. Lila, on the other hand, had gone to rally the Dragon Raiders.

"Your witches were trying to talk as we dragons talk. But they do not have the"—Crux cocked his great head and sniffed the wind delicately as if searching for the term—*"right organs for it. Not like us dragons. That is why you hurt."* Crux huffed a puff of smoke in condescension at our apparent human stupidity. *"They should have just asked a dragon to relay the message."*

"I don't think there *are* any dragons on Sebol," I pointed out.

"There used to be…" Crux shook out one of his wings and started to preen the bits of dead scales from underneath it. This intrigued me enough to want to ask him about the previous

dragons – but there was no time, as Lila was clearing her throat loudly.

"You done?" she said to me in an annoyed tone.

Why was she annoyed at me? I thought in dismay. I was the one who had been apparently possessed by the Western Witches somehow. *I* was the one who had been ill.

It seemed that my innocence, however, was not about to stop the daughter of the Sea Raider's chief from being annoyed as she rolled her eyes at me and carried on talking. "We have Senga and Adair on Kim– and heaven's strike me down for admitting it – but they are the ones with the strongest bond to their dragon, Stars save us." It was clear that was a fact that she wasn't pleased with. But there was nothing that we could do about it.

"No other Raider?" I nodded behind us toward the hillside, where Thiel was snapping at some old mutton, and a few of the younger Raiders were trying to feed their own dragons hanks of meat.

"No." Lila shook her head. "I'm loathe to even take Senga and Adair – but Father said that if there was a chance that we were going to face any Roskilde forces, then he was going to send a ship with us unless we took more dragons."

I nodded. Chief Kasian had become defensive over the winter, after the battle against Havick. He had only barely got out of the melee alive, and now he walked with a pronounced limp from the wound he'd received struggling to swim out of the sinking *Ariel*. "He only wants you safe," I said as I fixed the tags and ties on my saddlebags.

Lila sighed heavily, as she looked out over the harbor, doubtless to where her father was overseeing work teams of Raiders trying to work on his beloved flagship. My friend lost some of her angered look, and instead, I was struck by how much she had grown since I had first seen her, rising from the waters of the dragon atoll. She was a little taller, and although she still had that slight frowning brow, her eyes were clear and unwavering as she calmly assessed the future. She looked more like a queen, I realized. Less like a pirate.

"Spring's here," she said softly. "There is no safe for any of us, now."

With those dark words, she gave a small shake of her head and turned back to her preparations, waving at where Senga and Adair were collecting small throwing-spears, and telling them to mount up.

"We fly before sunset!" Lila called in a loud voice. "I want to get some sea beneath us and leagues behind us before we have to stop for the night!"

She gave commands like a princess, too, I thought as I hefted my bag of provisions.

※

Despite the dread and foreboding that hung over our mission, it was hard to deny the exhilaration we all felt as first Crux, and then Kim leapt from the lookout rocks and took to the air. It is hard to describe the fierce joy that one feels when the land falls away beneath you, and you feel the pull and stretch of such a mighty creature's muscles throwing you higher, higher into the skies. The island below us became smaller and smaller, throwing its coast into sharp perspective: the encircling reef of Bone Rocks around Malata, the scurrying Raiders in the harbor or about the town growing smaller and more insignificant as we soared.

There were only two other times I had felt this sensation of freedom and joy; either being on a boat at full speed, with the wind in the sails and the ship skipping across the tops of the waves with the future ahead like the horizon– or when I had been in the thrall and flow of magic.

But not like the magic Afar had used. I was shaken from my good mood as I remembered the psychic ache and fevered limbs it had given me. I had felt my mentor Afar's magic before, of course – the witch was considered a harsh tutor by other acolytes' standards, and so I had experienced first-hand the mighty invisible shoves of her magic as she tried to demonstrate a particular charmed word or cantrip.

None of that had felt like what had happened to me. Witches, as a rule, always abided by our ancient Matriarch and leader Chabon's famous maxim "only use your power if you have no other choice" and so, more often than not, their magic was usually subtle and discrete: strange dreams, visions, prophecies, or the calming touch of healing.

But what I had experienced just this morning? It was unlike anything I had felt from the Western Witches before – and certainly from Afar. Did that mean she had discovered more ways to use her eldritch powers? Or that what I knew was just the tip of the iceberg? Or could someone else have been using magic to contact me? Someone whose magic *felt* different to me?

I worried and fretted as we flew, trying to pay attention to the horizon and the distant blurs of islands and check for signs of Havick's patrol boats, but time and again, I found my thoughts returning to the strange powers of the witches. *My powers,* I had to admit.

There was so much that I didn't know! Even after all these years training! The Western Witches had been gathering knowledge under Matriarch Chabon for decades, generations even. How many times had I been told that during the reign of the Dark King Enric, Tyrant of Torvald, the only light of knowledge and wisdom in the world had come from Sebol – what the Islanders call the Haunted Isle?

There was also Ohotto Zanna to consider, I gritted my teeth in frustration. She had apparently been working with Lord Havick for years, giving him the power he needed to raise whatever strange darkness had been part of his assault on Malata. Though Chabon Afar was the Matriarch of the Witches, she had been weakened and unconscious for near to a year now, and Ohotto was one of the senior-most witches who could succeed their Matriarch in ruling Sebol. And as a senior-witch, Ohotto knew more of these hidden magics than I did – and somehow, I had to find a way to defeat her.

"Land!" Lila called, breaking my thoughts. She waved a hand to Senga and Adair and pointed at the spit of an island in the distance. It had grown dark in our furious flight, and the stars were appearing over our heads like a silvered blanket. The warmth from Crux had made me forget how cold it must be, but I knew that Lila was right. We must land, eat, and plan the next stage of our mission: how to get through Havick's blockade of Sebol.

"We made it to Batash, then!" Senga said, grinning even as she collapsed onto the cold grasses gratefully. Behind her I could see Adair climbing down a bit more gingerly from Kim's shoulder, jumping to the earth beside his sister before his own legs wobbled and he sat down with a thump and a groan.

"That was the longest flight, yet!" The rakish Adair grinned wearily, proud of their accomplishments.

"And you managed not to fall off," his sister Senga quipped back, earning a good-natured growl from her brother.

"Good grief," I heard Lila mutter, already clearing some of the land where we had last encamped here, and the blackened fire circle could clearly be seen. "What do you think, Danu? Can we risk a fire?"

I winced. Batash was the nearest island to Sebol – not that we could see it in the dark. It was also a custom for petitioning fishermen to build high bonfires here, to attract the witch's attention before they sought their aid.

"We could…" I reasoned. "The witches will know that the fire is a sign for them, but if Havick really is there…?"

"We have the dragons," Lila pointed out. "The dragons will be able to sense the Roskildeans before they see us, and the dragons can move faster than any boat too. We can be away before any Roskildean bilge-boat sights these shores."

I nodded. *She thinks like a leader, too.*

"Crux, my brother?" Lila said, approaching the Phoenix, who was busy stretching his forelegs and extending his wings from the long flight. The dragon snorted smoke at her, but then did as she asked, and shot a jet of flame on the damp pile of wood we had left here from before. The dragon flame took to it as eagerly and easily as if it were seasoned ash.

"Useful creatures." Senga laughed, patting Kim's large talons, who mocked a snapping bite at her. Lila looked alarmed at the way that the twins mocked and rough-housed with their younger Blue, but I could sense no resentment or animosity coming from the dragon, despite the provocation. *Maybe the twins are more like dragons themselves,* I thought wearily, remembering how we had seen the young newts chasing and play-fighting with each other on Sym's dragon atoll.

"The younglings that are now missing," Crux said and

shook his neck and shoulders, peering into the northeast darkness, as if he might be able to see the far-off home of the distraught Sinuous Blue; Sym. Maybe he could.

"I know, noble friend," Lila said, and I realized that Crux hadn't needled his thoughts to me alone but had shared them with all of us. His comments had not only troubled Lila, but Senga and Adair, too, fell quiet with the memory. We had told them what had brought the dragons to our aid – the chance of revenge against Ohotto Zanna, who we believe had taken the newts to power her dark magics.

"That is one of the reasons we are here," Lila said gently, moving to Crux's shoulder to stroke his scales. "The Western Witches have much lore written down. They might know why the newts were taken." I watched as Lila's eyes hardened, and her voice went cold and small. "And if Havick is at Sebol, then there is a chance that Ohotto is also."

"Skreych!" Kim let out a jet of flame into the air, her mighty tail swishing against the edge of the rocks of the cliff beyond. I had forgotten that Sym's newest brood were also Kim and Thiel's brothers and sisters. Dragons don't have young often, and so it was quite possible for brothers and sisters to be different in ages by decades or even centuries.

"Can you sense her?" Lila suddenly turned to Crux, knowing that the Phoenix dragon had senses that far outstripped any of our own.

"No." Crux scratched at the ground angrily, sending up

huge gouts of dirt and rocks. *"The isle has magic about it. My dragon senses cannot penetrate it."*

"So, you do not know if there are *any* ships blockading Sebol?" Lila confirmed, muttering a curse against our bad luck.

"We'll find Ohotto, I promise," I said, knowing that far more rested on going to Sebol than finding out what was wrong with the witches. They had collected more lore and history than anywhere in the Western Isles. They might be able to help us figure out how to defeat Ohotto's magics. But as well as that, there had been a great injustice done to Sym's brood – and the dragons were eager to exact their vengeance.

But first – we needed a better plan that just to 'sneak into Malata.'

"Last time we were here," Lila spoke for the twin's benefit, "Danu had us fly in low, through the fogs to the back of the island."

"We could do that again." I nodded, remembering that it had worked well for us before.

"What about that witch with your mentor?" Lila asked.

I frowned, trying to remember. "Calla?" I said. She had been one of Ohotto's students, who had appeared to still be on the island and stirring up trouble.

"Yes. She met us with Afar, remember? She might know the route we took. If the witches know we're coming—if Afar's magic message was somehow sensed or intercepted—" Lila shook her head, looking at Senga and Adair as they watched us, their eyes wide. "I don't want to throw you into a magical battle so soon, when we haven't even practiced combat drills, yet…"

"Lila!" Adair snorted. "We've been fighting since we were ten years old, as well you know!" He turned to pat the stack of short fishing spears that he had brought with them. "It was my idea to use these – we can throw them from Kim's back!"

It was a good idea, I had to admit, wondering why we hadn't thought of that. Instead, Lila favored her bow and I had my magic. But the short spears that the Raiders used out on the Bone Reef to bring in small catches of fish were perfect to use as javelins.

"Still," Lila said heavily. "*We* have more experience of this." She nodded to me and Crux. "And *your* lives are in my command at the moment. So I want you to keep out of danger."

"What?" Senga kicked her heels against the ground, her eyes as sparking bright as the fire.

"*To start with!*" Lila snapped. "Listen up, for once, the pair of you!" I was shocked by the fierceness in Lila's tone. I hadn't heard her speak to the twins like this before. She must really be worried, I thought. I didn't blame her. If Ohotto was out there somewhere – then there was no telling what strange magics that she could summon.

"We might not be on a boat anymore, but I'm still your captain, got it?" she snapped as if we were all back on board the *Ariel*. "I want you two, because you're both quick, to be our scouts."

Senga raised her eyebrows. "Really?"

"You all heard Crux, right?" Lila said. "Their dragon senses are dampened around the island, so we're going to have to do this the good old-fashioned way. You two, on Kim, will fly high and far – so high that I want you to be no bigger than a fishing hawk on the wind, and you will scout what you can see of the island. You'll swoop closer, and Kim will relay to Crux – with us – if you see any boats in the harbor or sense Ohotto's dark magics."

Lila then turned to me. "Meanwhile, Danu… You and I are going to go back into the fog, on Crux."

"But I thought you said that you didn't want Calla to remember our route?" I pointed out.

This was where Lila grinned. "And I thought *you* said that Chabon lived at the far end of the island, on her own. And Afar told us, last she saw us, that she was going to try and protect Chabon at her enclosure, didn't she?"

"We might be able to sneak straight to Chabon and Afar without alerting the surrounding blockade!" I realized what it was that she was trying to do.

"Exactly." Lila nodded. "We sneak in, we talk to the witches, we carry who—or what—we can out of there – all under the Roskildean's noses!" She looked, for a moment, content with her plan.

I just hoped that it would work.

CHAPTER 4
LILA, CAPTAIN

We moved before first light, the dragons leaping silently from the cliffs to swoop low over silvered waters. The skies above were ragged with torn clouds, and so the stars shone dimly, or not at all.

"The sun will arrive before long," Crux informed me, his voice sounding tight and small against mine. I had asked the dragons – and their riders – to keep all of our chatter to a minimum, not knowing just what strange magics that Ohotto had at her disposal.

"Thank you," I whispered as I flattened myself close to Crux's neck, allowing his warmth to fill me. At our side I saw a shadow of movement, and, like a great monstrous bat, the shadowy form of Kim rose on powerful wingbeats higher and higher into the skies. I studied their flight critically as they circled—to my surprise, they had lost all of their previous awkwardness and clumsy maneuvering.

Maybe that was all that they needed; a mission, I thought with a small sigh. Senga and Adair were good sailors, very good sailors – as they had been brought up in the life from cradle to young adulthood. And like all Raiders, they got a bit excitable and antsy on dry land. It was our natural frustration at being cooped in— stranded, I thought – and maybe that was what all of their antics had been evidence of.

Either way, I was glad that they would be up there, and not down on the island with us. Not that I didn't trust them or wouldn't put my faith in them to guard my life with their all when the time came, as I would for them. But it was strange to have their lives in my hands. More so than last year, when I had been the first mate on the *Ariel*. Back then I had a network, of sorts, around me. The sailing master, the quartermaster, my father the captain. If I messed up, then they would probably growl and spit at me – but my mistakes wouldn't cost someone their life.

They would here, and now. Is this what my father feels like, all the time? I wondered as we skimmed just a few feet over the dark waters, towards the heavy fog bank that always seemed to cling to the Haunted Isle's shores.

It was strange, realizing these things now. I had spent my entire life training to be the next captain, the next chief. To be as respected as my foster-father Kasian, or to be as strong and fearless as my foster-mother Pela. I thought that was what my life was meant to be – until Danu had found me and told me about the prophecy. It had been scryed by none other than Chabon, the Matriarch of this place– I still wanted to say *'accursed'* whenever I thought of the Haunted Isle – and it revealed my true parents: the assassinated Lord and Lady of Roskilde, who were the Sea Raider's natural enemy.

All I had wanted was to raid with my father and to teach those arrogant Roskildeans a lesson. But now…?

I didn't know exactly what it was that I wanted – not for myself. I still would like to captain the Sea Raiders, of course – but that goal seemed small compared to the prospect of captaining a cadre of Dragon Raiders! I wanted to put an end to Havick's evil and his brutal attacks against us Raiders, as well as his devastating tyrannies against the free peoples of the Western Archipelago. He had destroyed whole villages and ports when they hadn't managed to pay him his taxes. He was a monster, and he had to be stopped.

But was I good enough, brave enough, tough enough, to lead both the Sea Raiders and the Dragon Raiders?

"You ARE a leader, Lila wave-rider," Crux broke his silence to whisper into my mind. *"These friends follow you, as Kim and Thiel follow Sym. They look up to you. They trust you."*

I accepted his wise words with a bow of my head, feeling

humbled, hoping I could live up to them. No time to fret now, however, as the dark wings of the dragon swept us into the heavy fogs, and as we were swallowed whole by the indistinct greys, it felt as though I was closeted alone from every other creature.

"Crux? Can you sense what is coming?" I whispered, holding the tines of his neck and shoulders in a fierce grip as I peered into the grey. I thought the dawn had broken the sky; there was a lighter area of fog to our east – like a golden haze, but the strange mists and vapors around the Haunted Isle still refused to budge.

I didn't like it.

"Now I know what it must be like to have a human nose," Crux grumbled in the back of my mind, mourning the loss of his super-sharp dragon senses.

"Really? Nothing?" I said in alarm as a shadow swept towards us out of the fog. "Up!" I rolled in my blanket and leather saddle, and Crux flapped his great wings to pull us up and over the spire of rock that emerged the murk. Just like the last time we had come here, I recognized the ghoulish carvings of giant faces with sharp, gnashing teeth.

"Well, I don't think I would **ever** have as bad senses as you," Crux indicated. *"I can still hear Kim, far above, and I* *can smell the trees and sands, the kittiwakes and fish nearby. But I can't see them!"*

I ignored the insult. To him, it must be like being blinded. Another shape loomed on our right, as another, half-submerged head of rocks broke from the fogs.

"We're nearing the eastern edge of the island," Danu whispered. "I remember those rocks."

Good, I thought, scanning for any sign of enemy boats.

The water beneath us was disturbingly placid, apart from the steady waves that pushed towards the unseen shores. It was as if there was a dead zone around the Haunted Isle; an area of waters that were as unnatural as the Western Witches themselves. It filled me with an unnameable dread. Even though Danu had told me on many occasions that his magic *was* natural, was as natural as the dragons' power to breathe fire – to me, it still seemed strange what the witches did.

"It isn't like what we do," Crux confided in me. *"But it is similar, for those – like Danu—who have the gift naturally."*

"And for those who don't?" I couldn't resist asking. There was something about the creepiness of this place that was like a hurt tooth – making me want to prod it and see just how terrible it had to be. I looked over to Danu to see if he felt any of the same that I did. He looked worried, but I didn't think that he shared my Raider's sense of unease at the witch's strangeness.

"Then they must be like the witch known as Ohotto." Crux

coughed a small spark of flame into the fogs as his temper bristled. *"They steal dragon power. They become darkness."*

I shuddered. Maybe I didn't want to know about it after all.

"Cliffs!" Danu called, and Crux once again slowed his flight and swerved, flapping his wings to climb as the fogs ahead of us parted to reveal walls of slick yellow-grey rocks, deeply cracked and draped with hanging vines. We climbed the small updrafts at the base of the cliff, and I was glad to see that there were no answering shouts or warning bells as we crested the top, swooping low over dense forests.

I felt a buzz in the air – like the sort of sensation you would imagine a heat haze, or a water mirage to have if you walked into it, and Crux was turning, flapping his wings.

"What is it?" I asked quickly.

"Kim and the others, above us. They are over the island, and they say..." There was a moment of what I assumed was silent negotiation between the dragons, unheard by us. *"Ships are moored in the harbor of this strange place. Tall ships. With many masts, and many men."*

A sudden rush of anger beat out of the dragon's heart, in time with his wings as he roared in his mind.

"The witch known as Ohotto? Is she there? Can you smell her, sister-Kim?"

Crux and Kim were not siblings, I knew, but I was starting to see that all dragons – once they were friends, regarded each other as brothers and sisters under the Brood-Queen, whether they were blood relatives or not.

If only human society were that accepting, I thought.

"Not accepting, necessary. If we are in another queen's territory, then she is in charge of our safety." Crux's words in my mind were taut with frustration as he waited for the younger Blue to relay what information she could sense. What little good it would do under these fogs, I thought.

"Skrayr!" Crux growl-shouted, cutting off his booming voice before he gave our position away. *"Kim says she cannot sense the witch we came for."*

"But that does not mean that she isn't here," I said. "The fog dulls your senses."

"I know. I would have us fly to attack the ships right now – but Kim says that there are many."

"Enough to form a blockade?" Danu wondered.

Below us, the forests of Sebol were broken by the walkway avenues that slivered through the trees, made up of stilted wooden platforms dotted with the occasional strange, standing lanterns like glowing orbs at odd intervals. Here and there several of the avenues met in clearings, where a cluster of rounded huts, their walls made of wood and daub under angular roofs, sat together.

"Where are all the witches?" I asked in alarm. The sun had just broken, and surely that meant that even here they would have morning chores to do?

"I don't know. But I don't like it," Danu said behind me.

"Chabon's hut is at the far eastern edge of the island, ahead of us."

"Then that is where we will go," I said, and, before I could even ask it, the Phoenix dragon beneath us was dipping one wing and turning on wing tip to swoop back towards the cliffs, as silent as a hunting hawk.

CHAPTER 5
LILA AND THE WITCHES

"*I smell magic,*" Crux informed me as we flew over the last rise of land to a wide clearing just under the rocks. Large trees, dripping with vines, encircled the area, revealing an elaborate hut-platform surrounded by smaller ones built out from it like bubbles, and more of the strange standing glowing-orbs.

"The House of Chabon," Danu said reverently.

The large, central structure was as wide around as my father and mother's colonial mansion. Its roof and those of the attached buildings were a dizzying collection of wooden slats forming complex geometric shapes, with lots of small, peaked windows letting in the dawn light inside.

No sooner had the hut come into view, then a large group

of witches rushed from the largest hut. They were all women, and they wore a variety of costumes; dresses, trousers, jerkins or robes – but each one held a staff of different types and materials. Some were bone white, others barely bigger than walking sticks, some were made of dark-colored wood.

My hope that they were merely coming to greet us was burst when they all raised their staffs towards us.

"Danu...?" I said through clenched teeth as Crux hovered on massive wingbeats in front of them, his chest pumping like a bellows as if he were preparing his dragon fire at them. "I don't like the way they are pointing those staffs at us..." I growled.

"Afar! It's me, Danu! We have returned!" Danu clung onto Crux's spine with one arm and waved the other at the witches.

It was then that I realized the witches were pointing their staffs *past* us, and, strangely, each witch was drawing her staff down to the floor at her feet in a steady line. The air above the clearing shimmered—they must be doing something not to us, but to the clearing itself.

"A protection ward," Danu said. "The witches are lowering it for us to enter."

"How did I not sense it?" Crux was irate as he whipped his tail, powering us down into the clearing on steady beats to land in front of the large platform.

"Ready? Raise it again!" a familiar voice shouted, and, as I slid from the shoulders of the dragon I saw that Afar herself –

tall and fine-boned – was directing her coven to raise their staffs in unison, and, as they did so, the same crackle of invisible energy passed overhead.

"Afar? Are you well? What has been happening here?" Danu said, scraping down the other side of Crux to land with a thud on the dirt floor beyond and cross to the nearest stairs up to the witches. I hesitated, still feeling unsure around them. I didn't like how easily Danu could rush into their company.

"Danu, my friend – thank the stars you have come at last." Afar looked wearier and older than the last time we were here as she leaned on her curving staff of bleached bone. It has only been one winter, I thought.

"At last?" I heard Danu say.

"Yes. I am sorry for being forced to use that magic to reach you – it is not something we like doing," the proud woman said, earning a ripple of agreeing noises from the mixture of old and younger women around her. "But I feared all other attempts to reach you had been intercepted or lost."

"What other attempts?" Danu said.

"We sent birds. And then Sister Moira, in a boat," Afar said heavily. "You received nothing?"

"I knew it," spat a small dark-skinned older woman with the sandy-colored pelt of some dead desert beast wrapped around her shoulders. "It must have been that Havick."

"Sister Moira?" Danu said weakly. "She was kindly…."

"She was. But now…" Afar's voice was heavy.

"When did you send these tidings? How many moons

ago?" I called out. Everyone knew that sea passage during the winter months in the Western Archipelago was dangerous – but that was usually why we used relay systems, sending a bird or a messenger to the nearest island, where someone there would be paid to take it to the next, and the next and so on. The Western Archipelago had been using that system, or bonfires and watchtowers, for generations. Why didn't the witches just do that? I wondered, feeling more than a little annoyed that they might be so reckless as to send any living creature all the way across storm seas straight to Malata.

"Six weeks ago, we sent the first bird – a skua," Afar said. "It was ensorcelled, not to deviate from its path until it had found Danu."

Both Danu and I shook our heads. "We have received no such messenger," my friend said.

"And then we sent a tern, similarly ensorcelled," Afar said sadly. "And last of all, two weeks ago, we sent Sister Moira."

"Many things can happen to birds and boats out on the dark waves," I said hesitantly. But I knew already what the answer probably was.

"And I fear that a lot of things *did* happen to them." Afar's tone was a little sharp. "But no matter. You are here now, and I have terrible news to tell you. Six weeks ago, the navies of Havick managed to find a route through the fog banks to our harbor. At first, it was only one boat, but then, as the weeks drew on, more joined them. They have brought tidings from our 'sister.'" Afar's lip curled on the words, "Ohotto Zanna."

"Skreyar!" Crux suddenly roared from his place behind us, causing half of those assembled witches here to flinch or step back in alarm.

"What does *she* want?" Danu growled.

"She has sent us an ultimatum. Or, as she calls it, a negotiation," Afar said. "But that is only half of the terrible news I have for you both. It is Mother Chabon."

"Chabon?" Danu suddenly quailed, and an anxious worry settled over the crowd. They really cared for this witch that I have never met.

"She is ill. Worse than before. We fear that Ohotto is working her dark magic against her, which is why…" Afar raised a slim-fingered hand to the skies above the clearing, at whatever invisible warding spells they had cast there.

"Afar," Danu shook his head. "This is much bad news to start the year on. Tell me everything that has happened. Everything that Ohotto has said."

"I will, but it is probably better for you to come in and see for yourself." I thought that Afar was just talking to Danu alone until she raised her sharp eyes to regard me as well. "Lila, please – she may not be aware of it, but Chabon would be honored to have you in her house."

Honored to have me? I wondered, incredulous. I was just a Raider's daughter. Only I wasn't at all, was I? The other witches were looking at me now, with wide eyes.

"This really is her?" said the one with the animal pelt,

regarding me with wide eyes. Everywhere I turned, the witches nodded gravely at me.

Danu cleared his throat. "This is Lila of Roskilde, the rightful Queen of the Western Isles, the victor of the Battle of Malata, and the one who was foretold."

"My lady," said the animal-pelted witch, bowing deeply.

I felt unsettled by their reaction. The last time I had been here, only Afar and Danu had known of my real heritage. Now, it seemed as though I was something of a celebrity.

"Of course, Afar, it would be an honor to join you," I found myself saying, as I stepped up onto the platform, as the crowds parted before me.

Inside was a cool antechamber, a workroom of sorts, piled with heavy cloaks, blankets, and tables with a variety of implements as useful as knives and ropes, to arcane-looking bottles and bowls. These witches were at least a practical bunch.

The air was heavy with the scent of incense, and an open oaken door revealed a much larger chamber beyond, split into quarters by heavy tapestries hung from the ceiling. As Afar led us forward, a hand pulled one of the veils back and a thin-looking witch with thick dark hair emerged, bearing a bowl of water.

A look passed between Afar and Chabon, and the other shook her head sorrowfully.

"Come," Afar said. "Even if it is just to pay our respects," she said darkly as she stepped aside to usher Danu in first, and then me.

The chamber of the Matriarch of the Western Witches was less like a bedroom, with chairs pulled up around her bed and many small, wickerwork tables that held scrolls or more of the strange powders and herbs. Her bed was large, with knitted patchwork blankets over heavier, patterned wool.

And in the middle of it all was the small and mounded form of Chabon. She looked ancient, her skin almost translucent and a knot of wrinkles as her breath rattled through thin, cracked lips. Her hair was long and surrounded her head and shoulders like a shining, platinum halo.

"Oh, Mother…" I heard Danu whisper, moving to kneel at her side and tenderly hold one of her shriveled, claw-like hands.

"Ach…" Chabon murmured in pain, and Danu snatched his hands back, looking at Afar in worry.

"The work of Ohotto, we think," Afar murmured. "Every moment of wakefulness seems to bring her pain, but we can find no natural cause. She should not be in such pain as she is now, even with her grand age…"

I was moved by Danu's tenderness and the emotion that emanated from the usually austere Afar. "Is there anything we can do?"

Afar looked at me, her eyes dark. "There is. But it is not your gift to give."

"What do you mean?" I said.

Afar opened her mouth and then closed it again, shaking her head. "No. It is too great a request. And it is not something that Chabon herself would approve of."

"But Master, we have to try!" Danu hissed the words under his breath. "Chabon has always been the heart of the Western Witches. No one else alive in the entire islands and the Three Kingdoms beyond knows as much as she does!" Danu frowned at his mentor and then looked pleadingly at me. "And Chabon can help us, too. She is powerful. She is the one who first saw the Prophecyof Roskilde. She could counter Ohotto's magics."

"Zanna..." at the words of my friend, the older woman spasmed, as if in great pain, and her eyes flickered open, closed, open.

"Mother?" It was Afar, moving to her other side. "Is there something you wish to say? To tell us? We have brought you guests."

I watched as the old woman licked her lips, shivered, gasped, and Afar herself damped a cloth and gently patted her lips. A soft sigh, but I couldn't tell if it was one of contentment or more pain.

"Mother?" Afar said gently once more.

"Zanna... The Darkness. She brings back a terrible darkness…. That, that…" A serious of hacking, painful coughs wracked her small form. "Swallows us all…."

"What darkness, Chabon?" Afar leaned closer, but the old woman's eyes fluttered closed, open, and closed again, and her wheezing eased down a notch. For a moment I was terrified that she was going to die right here in front of us – until her breathing grew more steady and regular. She was asleep, or unconscious.

"What does she mean?" Danu whispered into the dark, and Afar's jaw twitched in shared frustration.

"It is like this now. It is hard to decipher what are true visions and what could be the pain…" Afar laid a gentle hand over Chabon's brow and murmured under her breath. The frown lines around the old woman's eyes seemed to ease a little, and the light grew a little brighter in the room around us.

"She will sleep a little easier now." Afar shook her head, turning to address not Danu, but me. "I am sorry that you did not get the proper opportunity to meet her, Lila of Roskilde. She would have liked you." A ghost of a smile. "You are as stubborn as she is."

I nodded my thanks, saying nothing as Afar led us back out of the small chamber and into the wider room beyond, where some of the other witches were already pulling seats by the raging hearth fire.

"Please take a seat and share what food we have," Afar said as another brought in bowls of dried fruit, bread, cured meats and cheese.

Senga and Adair are still above us, I remembered, taking only a bit of bread and cheese. "Our friends are waiting for us," I said. "We cannot stay long too for fear that they might be caught."

"There are more of you? Enough to defend Sebol?" one of the witches exclaimed, a hopeful look on her face.

I winced. "I don't know. How many ships are there? What is it we might face?"

"No," Afar said with certainty. "Our enemies are too great, and our first priority is to secure what we can before it is all lost."

"Really, Afar?" Danu said angrily. I could tell that he was still annoyed with his mentor over not revealing what 'gift' could possibly cure Chabon.

"There are four galleons in our waters, probably crewed with between twenty to fifty people each," Afar said. "They will receive no messages from us, they will not answer our hails, they just sit there, blocking our only port."

"We might be able to do something about four ships…" I said carefully, thinking of a diversion, perhaps. Draw one or two off. Give the witches a chance to escape?

"And besides that, all of the witches around the harbor are loyal to Zanna. That was her ultimatum that she sent to us, by way of a black arrow loosed from the deck of one of the ships. A note that said that the witches were to accept *her* as their leader, and to overthrow the ailing Matriarch – and if we did not, then she would take the island by force," Afar said in horror.

"That is insane!" Danu cried out. "What right-minded witch would do that?"

"You remember the last council meeting we had, Danu? Ohotto and Calla had already convinced half of the congregation that Havick was the only chance that we had to hold back some great evil," Afar explained. "Now, Ohotto claims that she needs our entire support. As soon as we heard the news, I and the other loyal witches came here, to defend Chabon..."

"But not without taking a few precautions..." the animal-pelted witch beside her cackled.

A grim smile from Afar. "Yes. That is how I know that Ohotto is not here. *I* cast an enchantment on the library of the witches before fleeing, knowing that the others would seek to use that knowledge against us, no other witch than I, Ohotto, or Chabon, is strong enough to break it."

"Then – the lore of the witches is safe?" I asked.

"For now. But Ohotto's blockade has stopped any aid from reaching us. We are trapped, and it is only a matter of time before those other witches loyal to Ohotto manage to break our wards and protection spells."

"And in this library..." I said. "Is that where we will find more information about the Darkness that Chabon warned us about?"

"I don't know, but it is where all of our lore is kept." Afar pursed her lips in worry.

It seemed to me like we had no choice. "We will help." I nodded. "We will help you retrieve your library and break the blockade."

There was a ragged cheer from those assembled, tired witches around me – but from their tired tones, I could tell that they were as much in the dark as I was about how we were going to defeat half an island full of witches *and* four galleons!

CHAPTER 6
DANU, SNEAKING

"Danu – are you good with this?" Lila looked at me through those shaded eyes of hers. We had stepped outside of Chabon's hut as the rest of the Western Witches still congregated inside, Afar marshaling them all to their respective duties in our hastily-constructed plan.

"Of course," I said casually, turning to walk out over the walkway that climbed up the last rise, to the broken clifftop above. The wind was high as it always was at this end of the island, but it was still chill, and the fog banks still heavy below us.

"Danu," Lila said warningly as she followed me. "Something's up, I can see it in you..." she said in a quieter tone.

Whumph! There was a clash of wings as Crux lowered himself over us, hanging in the air for a moment as he enjoyed the updrafts from the cliff. I allowed the sudden, awesome appearance of the Phoenix dragon to hide my concerns.

"Come on, Lila – if we're going to do this, we have to get the word to Kim and the others quickly," I said, but she was still frowning at me. She could sense my unease.

"Danu, if you think that this is a mistake – if I'm putting you in too much danger, then you only have to say…" She didn't move.

"What word to Kim?" Crux turned his serpentine neck to us, as he reached casually with his claws to grip the edge of the cliff, flaring his wings for a moment as the winds buffeted him and then settled.

I said nothing, ignoring Lila. It wasn't that I was scared or angry at her at all – but there was something that I needed to know, and now was not the time for it. We had enough on our plate!

"Danu…" Lila, apparently, was far more stubborn than I was.

Okay then. I sighed. "It's Chabon. How ill she is – and what Afar said, that there was something that we could do to help her. A gift."

"I heard," Lila said.

"I want to know what it is! I cannot understand why Afar wouldn't tell us," I said in frustration. Afar was my mentor. Or she *had* been, before. She might not tell me everything, but she had always trusted me. "It seems *odd*," I told Lila. "The only reason why Afar *wouldn't* tell me what it was, would be because she thought that I wasn't ready for that information."

"Okay," Lila said, taking my concerns in her stride. "But maybe she is just too upset with this blockade? She needs time to think about it, time that we can buy for her."

"I guess," I said, but it still felt like a betrayal. Like she didn't think I was worthy of learning the secret, I thought. Because I was only an acolyte.

"And Afar herself said that Chabon wouldn't approve, so maybe we don't want to know, either?" Lila shrugged, and with that, she seemed to regard the situation as solved. But it wasn't for me. It was the same way I thought about Ohotto and her magics. There was more lore in the library, and within Chabon's fragmenting mind than I knew. *And I needed to know it if I was to become a mage.*

"Crux, we have a very great request to ask of you, my friend," Lila started, as she explained her plan to him. It was a dangerous one, and she was asking him to take on most of the risk, after all. I could see how worried she was – far more worried about Crux than she was about me or my concerns – not that I minded, but it made me realize that she didn't see Sebol in the same way that I did. She didn't see that this place could have all the answers to all the secrets we had ever wondered about.

Lila moved to Crux's maw to rest her body for a moment against his snout, hugging his long face. I heard a churring, wittering noise from the dragon in response, before they broke apart.

"Have no fear, little humans. It will be a pleasure to rip the wood and sail of my enemies apart!" With that, he lifted his snout to make a keening sound, high-pitched and mournful into the air. We waited for a moment before there was the sound of whirring wings, and the flashing, spiraling form of Kim bearing Senga and Adair appeared low over the forest, rushing to join us.

"Lila! Danu!" Adair waved excitedly.

They're both still on her back, thank goodness, I thought as they landed with less grace than Crux did, but more gratefully, it appeared, as Kim folded her tired wings together and bumped snouts with the larger Phoenix in greeting.

"We thought you'd forgotten us up there!" Senga laughed, sliding down from Kim's shoulder with ease, staying at the dragon's side to pat her flank.

"No such luck," Lila teased, pulling the covering from the basket she had hauled up with us, filled with cheese and bread, and flagons of fresh spring water. The twins hungrily took their fill as Lila explained the situation.

"We need to break the blockade, but we also need to get to the Library of the Witches," she said. "Which is on the other side of the island, under enemy control."

"We get to fight?" Adair said eagerly. Nothing, it seemed, dimmed his enthusiasm – not even circling high above an island for hours in the cold airs!

"Well. Hopefully *not*," Lila looked at both of the Raiders seriously. "But I will be asking Crux to join you, just in case."

"Skreeyit!" Kim coughed a small burst of flame into the air and rattled a hiss at Crux. In return, the Phoenix only opened his mouth and panted, lolling his tongue as if he were laughing.

"Kim believes she can fight without me," Crux teased.

"Please, dragons!" Lila held up her hands in a calming gesture. "If this is to work, then we need both of you mighty and brave creatures."

Kim inclined her head at the gesture. The way to a dragon's heart was always through its pride or its stomach, it seemed.

"I will be helping protect the witches on the ground," Lila said.

"And I know what it is we're looking for in the library," I said, nodding to Lila. Her plan had originally been to have me riding Crux with Senga and Adair on Kim above, driving the blockade boats away – but I had kicked up a fuss until she had agreed to let me go with her on the ground. Lila was by far the better fighter than me, of course – and I could see why she wanted to be able to use her martial skills to protect the witches – but I wanted to be there when Afar gained access to the library. That way I could find out what this Darkening was, and search for the mysterious 'gift' that might save Chabon.

"But we will be fighting our way through to you," Lila said pointedly to Senga and Adair. "As soon as we have made it past any enemies, I'll call Crux back and join you in the air to help you against the boats, understand?"

"We won't need your help!" Senga laughed fiercely, but Lila only shook her head.

"It's that kind of bravado that could scupper the whole plan," Lila said severely. I saw a shade of Kasian in her then, in her forward-looking, direct stance and tone. "Promise me you'll accept Crux's lead. You'll follow his decisions in the battle."

Is that any safer? I wondered in alarm, looking up at the large male dragon grinning back at me, his scaled chest puffing proudly.

"Don't worry, Lila." Adair sighed. "We get the idea. Just work to distract and lead the boats off, pull back if it starts to look too hairy." Adair cocked his head to grin at his sister. "Just like we're raiding, huh. Hit and run?"

"Yes!" Senga clapped her hands, and that was it. The plan was set.

"And Crux?" Lila turned to her bonded dragon last. Once more the dragon lowered his head to make the wittering, chirping noise at her, before he launched himself backward, spinning in the air as he did so to unfurl his wings with a snap like sails, and swoop out, high over the fog bank, and circling higher and higher above our heads.

"Woot!" There was a shout as Senga and Adair scrambled for Kim's shoulders, barely having time to tie their ropes and belts about their middles as Kim jumped from the cliffs after the larger Phoenix.

"Great," I said to Lila. "Do you think that they'll listen to a thing that I just said?"

"Not a chance," I said, feeling worried myself.

※

Afar was as good a commander as I should have expected, and within moments she had organized a team of five of the best-prepared and most-fierce witches to join us in retaking the island. They included Gamba the lion-pelted, Helga, the black-haired crow-maiden, Mellia and Katya; all of them senior witches who looked as though they had been in a fair number of scrapes before.

"The rest of you split into two groups," she ordered of the loyalist witches. "Half will stay here and protect Chabon, and the other half will follow us." We waited (impatiently) as they did so, with not a little arguing over who was to go into which group. Witches are very good at arguing.

In the end, though, and to Lila's ever-increasing agitated sighs, she had a team of fifteen witches ready to follow us, and twelve who would stay with Chabon.

"Okay. You lot?" She talked to the those following on behind. "You make for the outskirts of the village, and then to the Great Meeting Hall. There, use what enchantments you have to lock all doors and subdue all left who oppose us. By then, I hope we will have broken the worst of Calla's core followers."

Do you? I thought in alarm, looking at our small band. Either Afar knew something that we didn't (which was much, I thought with a little rancor) or she was putting a lot or faith in her team of five. And us.

"And those staying?" Afar's tone faltered. "If we do not come back, or if we have failed, then you will know about it. May the stars shine bright on your deeds."

It was a farewell speech, I thought, feeling slightly ashamed for my earlier suspicion of my own mentor. If Afar didn't come back, then she would have failed, and the remaining witches would be left to fend for themselves.

"Okay. Ready?" Lila gave Afar the nod, who returned it gravely. My mentor stepped aside, and Lila smoothly took her place to talk to our five "combat" witches.

"I cannot hope to know what you are capable of," Lila started by saying. "But I ask that you listen to me, first. I have fought in more sea battles and been in more brawls and practice fights than anyone here, I think – so I might know a little of what it is we have to do." She looked at each in turn, but it was Gamba who surprised me by responding.

"You are the protector of these islands, Lady Roskilde," she said quietly, earning an agreeing nod from the others.

"Uh, right," Lila blushed and stumbled for a moment before her confidence returned. "I am. So, follow my lead. We'll sneak in. We will not engage until we have to. And, because our numbers are so small, then we will fight as Raiders fight – we will seek to disable, outpace, and capture, not defeat in open battle. If you face greater numbers of soldiers or witches, then you pull back, seek a different target. Understand?"

"Aye, princess," one after another witch said, and I was amazed at how ready they were to respond to Lila.

I could feel it too, though. She had a presence that came out of her when she assumed power. It was naturally confident without being overbearing. It was strong and resolute without being cruel or demanding. *She is a queen in waiting for a throne,* I thought, suddenly remembering the prophecy.

It was happening. The prophecy was really happening – right before my eyes!

"We move!" Lila waved her scimitar in the air, earning a ragged cheer from the witches behind, and we set off at a jog, our feet pounding the walkways that crossed the island.

※

We made good time – Sebol was not a particularly large island by any stretch of the imagination, but because of the small population of witches, much of Sebol was given over to the deep woods and rocks. By the time we came up to our second break from jogging, Lila gave the nod for me to take the lead as we had discussed, and lead us off the walkways, to pick through the tree roots and between the hanging vines.

"We'll be much slower," I whispered to Lila, who was looking at me steadily, her sword still raised. "But they won't hear us on the boards or see us coming."

Lila nodded, and we picked our way between the vegetation. The sounds of the forest grew around us—the harsh calls of the birds from above, the rustle of the island's pigs out in the green glooms.

The growth ahead thinned, breaking out into open spaces, and, beyond that – hut shapes. The edges of the small township that the witches had raised, I knew. It wouldn't be much further, I thought. The other witches were huddling behind us against the bowls of trees and rocks, looking severe and determined. *Right. We can do this,* I told myself, about to take a cautious step out until—

"Skreyargh!" The sound split the skies, causing an explosion of birdlife around us.

"Crux!" Lila gasped and pushed past me to crouch at the forest's edge, looking up into the sky with worried, searching eyes.

"Lila – wait!" I hissed, moving to her side to see what was happening.

The dragons had timed their attack perfectly. Even though Crux's dragon bond couldn't penetrate the magical enchantments that surrounded the witches isle, the dragons above must have still been able to smell or sense us in more mundane ways, waiting to attack the blockade as we arrived to do our secret work as well.

With ear-splitting screams, the dragons swept down from the skies above, low over the forest on the other side of the island. The witches' township sat as many of the island residences did; around a small natural harbor. Ours was a simple curve of shingle beach, fenced by rocky outcrops at either end.

And out there in the grey waters, sitting on the edge of the sea fogs and forming a line across our harbor, sat four black ships, whose sails were tattered and torn as if the dragons had already attacked them.

"I've never seen ships like those," Lila whispered, and I could only agree. They weren't the high galleons of Roskilde, that was for sure. They were wide, with tall prows that rose, arching like the necks of miniature dragons. Along their gunwales were the roundel shapes of shields, and from their bodies sprang nests of oars.

But it was their wood that was unlike any other that we had seen before. Blacker than mahogany and darker than aged pier-wood dipped in pitch. It was to these strange vessels that the two dragons came screaming towards, dropping lower and lower over the harbor waters, about to strike—

"No warning bells," Lila muttered, an instant before Crux, in the lead, grabbed the topmost crow's nest of one of the ships. He clutched it as his momentum shot him forward and then kick-released it behind him as he flung himself back into the air again. The ship wobbled, the mast creaking loudly so that we could hear it even from the edge of the woods.

But still, there were no shouts from on deck. No answering arrows or cannons.

"What is going on?" I said in alarm. Something wasn't right here. Where were the crews of those boats? Where were the other witches?

"If they're too stupid to fight back, that is their problem!" Lila said hotly, taking a deep breath and looking to the huts beyond. "That one is the library?" She nodded to the next largest hut to the main meeting hall where we had been before

"Yes," I said, readying myself from my crouch as Lila was already moving.

"Gamba, Helga, go!" Afar said behind me, and then we were running, crouched low to the ground as we pelted over the stubby grass of the clearing and bounded up to the walkway.

"Hss!" I heard a snarl – but it was no dragon. Their shrieks and calls came from behind the buildings that now obscured the harbor from our sight. This sound came from in front of Lila.

But there was no one there.

"What?" Lila skidded to a halt on the boards, her sword up, her face a picture of confusion. "Someone was here a moment ago. A figure—" I whirled to look around us. There were huts standing on either side of the walkway platform, and more behind them. The entire town was raised from the damp grounds in this way. There would be many places for a lone assailant to hide.

But why should we be worried about a lone attacker? We were five of the best witches of Sebol, plus an acolyte and a Raider.

How little I knew, as a shape materialized on the other side of the hut from Lila, stepping out of the shadows as if it had been made of them. It raised a broken broadsword and bellowed as it charged at my friend…

CHAPTER 7
LILA AND THE DEAD

"Ah!" I gasped involuntarily as a hand grabbed the collar of my shirt and pulled me back from the attacker.

Woosh! The blade held in the man's hands skimmed the air before my nose as I stumbled back.

But there was something else that had made me shout. Something even *more* wrong than being attacked out of nowhere, by surprise. It was the attacker – there was something terribly, terribly wrong with him. Through a hole in his cheek, I could see clear to his yellowing teeth.

"Root and Star…?" One of the witches gasped as she came bounding onto the platform beside us. My attacker swayed from one foot to the other, hefting a sword that was broken but still almost as large as my scimitar.

"What's wrong with him?" Danu said – and it was undeniable that there was, definitely, something very wrong with him. His skin was naturally pale, but its white-blue sheen was unnatural. And then there were his eyes: dead and cloudy, like a fish that has been out of the sea for too long. His jerkin and trousers were ragged and pocked with little tears, but still, he moved with an uncanny grace and speed.

He grunted – or snarled – making some strange clicking noise through his mouth as he lunged towards me again.

The threat of violence made me unfreeze from my fear quickly, as I parried his strong, clanging blow and returned it with a double-quick lunge.

Thunk! My scimitar hit home, chopping with a heavy thud into the man's shoulder.

The man grunted, not in pain, but rage. My blow might have pushed him back a little – but it didn't even slow him down as he kicked out with a half-rotting boot, forcing me back.

"Lila!" Gamba hissed in worry and alarm, and her shadow passed me as the other witches fanned out in front of the strange dead things.

But my eyes were glued on what was before me, and what was even worse. "He's not bleeding," I said, stumbling back. *A man who doesn't bleed? What can I do against a man who doesn't bleed?*

"Imperis Ata!" Afar shouted, thrusting her bone staff forward at the strange half-man thing. A ripple of energy shot past me as tendrils of blue light exploded from the curving tip of her staff and slammed into the man's chest, sending him flying back against the wall of the hut. He slumped to the floor, his jerkin smoking afterward, but as I watched in horror, he shook his head from side to side and slowly pushed himself back to his feet once more.

"Sacred waters!" Afar said in horror.

"What is it?" I shouted as the thing bounded across the platform. I raised my scimitar to meet its first blow, and then to match its next – but try as I might, every blow I landed did no good. Short of actually chopping his arms and legs off, I thought in alarm, how were we going to stop him?

"Ignis! Ignis Ata!" Danu bounded beside me, and, ridiculously, he tried to swing a *punch* at the unstoppable attacker.

"No – Danu!" I managed, just as Danu's fist burst into red and golden light, and he slammed it into the thing's gut.

"Kreurk!" This time the creature really *did* seem in pain, as it swung back, flames spilling up its chest to engulf half of his face. It dropped its broken blade as it flailed awkwardly, staggering on its heels.

"Danu – what did you do?" I gasped, to see that Danu was just looking at me incredulously.

"I – I don't know? It was the first spell that came to mind…" he gasped.

From the end of the walkway came another groan, and we looked up to see more of these strange warriors stumbling and jogging towards us, raising a collection of axes, swords, and pikes. *Who were they? What* were they? I kept on thinking.

"Fire!" Gamba the lion-pelted shouted. "It's the fire that the boy used. I've read about this before – accursed and dark beings are always driven back with fire!"

"You heard her, ladies!" Once again Afar raised her bone staff, leaping to my side to level her staff at the charging group, as the other witches did the same on either side of me.

"Ignis! Ignis! Ignis!" they shouted, and this time the bolts of eldritch energy that burst from the tips of their staffs were hot and burning orange and red. They hit the first wave of our accursed attackers like shooting stars, exploding into sparks of crimson upon impact. The groans of the fighters turned into shouts and, as far as they seemed capable – screams.

"Lila?" It was Danu, at my side with his eyes wide and white with worry. "Are you okay? Are you hurt?"

"No – no, I'm fine," I said, falling back to let the five witches march forward against the strange band. One blackening figure, now a raging inferno, staggered forward, almost to the edge of the firestorm, but Afar stepped forward and calmly hit him with her staff, exploding the top half of his body into blackened and charred cinders. The inferno continued for a little longer, as the witches kept up their spells until all of those after us appeared to be still.

"Gamba – do you know what these things were?" Afar was leaning on her staff, wheezing and coughing. The power of the magic had taken a heavy toll, not just on her, but on the other four witches who also appeared exhausted.

"I don't, Afar. But in the deepest south, they sometimes tell tales of creatures like this. People who will not die, who walk after they have expired." Gamba rubbed a shaking hand over her face.

"What has Ohotto done?" Afar muttered in horror, looking at the smoking remains, as more growls and groans sounded behind the buildings, coming towards us. "There are more, and our magic is low. Quick! To the library!"

"Your magic is low?" I cried in alarm, as Danu grabbed me by the elbow and forced me ahead of him.

"Magic isn't inexhaustible, Lila," he panted beside me as we ran past huts and down walkways, dodging the roving packs of undead whatever-they-were.

Great, I thought. "You could have mentioned this before, Danu!"

"I didn't think to. It's different for me," he said, frowning. "Crux lends me his energy, and I don't get as tired when I cast spells."

Afar suddenly halted by the edge of a hut and peered out over the wider walkway beyond. We could hear more of the undead roaming the witches' town as if they were patrolling or searching for us. But where were the other witches?

"There is the library. We will have to quick," the witch said, raising her hands over our heads. *"Unsee, Unsee,*

Unsee..." she murmured, her hand shaking and her shoulders stooping as the magic sapped her strength.

Maybe that's why Chabon is so frail, I suddenly realized. Because the magic saps her vitality!

But Afar's charm appeared to work. A haze settled over us and peering through it was like looking at the rest of the village through an opaque, semi-translucent mirror.

"She's cast a concealment charm," Danu said, his voice sounding muffled and distorted like he was speaking underwater.

And then we were hurrying across the last walkway, in plain sight of the undead warriors, whose myopic white eyes looked straight beyond us – or through us.

The library hut was large, with the same white-daub walls as the others, but with no ornate windows around its walls. It appeared to be two stories high, with a peaked, complicated roof.

Afar thudded to the side of the oval-shaped wooden door, passing her hands over the heavy door handle and chains, her eyes fluttering closed as the chains clanked to the floor. With that, we slipped inside.

I was grateful when Danu thumped the door closed behind us and set one of the chairs under the handle. I remembered this place from before as a series of concentric, warren-like rooms made of bookshelves, with thin avenues between them, and small, metal and glass oil lamps hanging at intervals for the benefit of readers.

All around us the other five witches slid to the floor in exhaustion, some holding their heads or massaging their temples as if in pain.

"Are they going to be all right?" I whispered at Danu, as Helga the crow-witch passed around a phial of dark green glass. She was black-haired, and probably the youngest of Afar's band, although she still looked weary.

"They will, but they need a rest." Helga looked at me with sunken eyes, the only of the witches able to talk. "We all need a rest," she amended. "But you should know this. Those… things we just faced… I think I have seen them before."

"You have?" Danu said incredulously. "Why didn't you say?"

"No – not them as they are, but I have seen their *style* before. Their style of clothes, their pale skin." She gestured self-consciously to her own. "They appear to be very similar to the mountain tribes of the Wild Coast."

"The Wild Coast?" I shook my head, not knowing where it was she talked about.

"Past the Dragon's Spine Mountains of Torvald," Danu said quickly. "Far to the north and west of the mainland, there is an area of wildlands given over to mountains and forests and deep fjords. The histories tell us that it was almost always ungovernable," he explained. "But there have always been different tribes of people who lived and fought there, sometimes coming to make war with the Torvald or Roskilde."

"Well, it seems that Ohotto has found a way to – what –

use them? *Enchant* them?" I said uneasily. I didn't like it. Had they once been men and women, as living as I or Danu? Or had Ohotto raised them from the dead?

"The Darkness…" I heard Afar groan, raising her head with great effort to blink at Danu. "Chabon warned us of it. The Darkness… You must find out about the Darkness…"

"What is she talking about?" I asked as Danu quailed at my side.

"An old legend. A nightmare." Danu's look was troubled, but he was already turning into the library. "One from a long time ago…"

"Danu!" I hissed, as loudly as I dared. Although Afar's enchantment might have made us invisible to them for a little while – I did not know if that meant that we were still protected in here, or that the dead outside – and the other witches – could not hear us.

"What? Lila – this is our chance! We have to find what this Darkness is that Ohotto has summoned." I had never seen Danu so serious and fervent. His eyes burned with a holy determination.

"But Danu – Senga and Adair are still out there. And Crux," I said. As much as I knew that what he was saying was important – was vital, even – I couldn't leave Crux and the others out there to face this strange evil alone. Now that I knew something that would stop them – flame – then I had a chance. I had a weapon.

"Look, Danu – you've always been better at books and old

scrolls than me. You grew up here. You know what you are looking for. *I'm* going to help them fight!" It was, after all, what I did best.

"But Lila – no, out there…" Danu looked suddenly uncertain.

I gave him one of my father's reckless grins. "Don't worry, Danu – I have a plan."

CHAPTER 8
DANU, AND THE DARKENING

I've got to be quick, I thought as I moved—panicked—through the Library of the Witches. I didn't want Lila to be out there alone, facing those things – and not just the undead sailors, but Ohotto and Calla's witches, too.

She has Crux. The Phoenix dragon will come to her aid, I fretted as my feet took me further past the histories section of the scrolls, and on into prophecies. *At least, I hope that Crux will hear her...* My feet suddenly lurched as I remembered the enchantments that the witches have always had over our isle.

Enchantments to stop outside magic. Enchantments that seemed to dampen the dragon bond.

"Damn it!" I hissed, feeling torn in what I should do even as my eyes alighted on the names, carefully burnt into the wood of the nearest shelves—*Matriarch Ella, Matriarch Gorlas, Matriarch Chabon–* and my choice was made.

The prophecies of the Matriarchs, and all of those wise women whose visions had been collected and collated here. My hands strayed to the largest section of all – that of Chabon's, naturally. I had already heard the Prophecy of Roskilde, both Lila and I had read it here in this very aisle under the watchful eyes of Afar the last time we had been here.

But did it contain clues to the Darkening? Something we hadn't noticed or understood when we'd first read it?

My hands skipped over the scrolls, hunting the shelves for any clues as to my quest. They were stacked haphazardly, loosely organized by both prophecy date and subject. So, it was easy to find Roskilde under *Matriarch Chabon* and to reread the same lines that I had copied several times over the winter during my stay on Malata.

"A girl is born from the waters, rising from the north-east sea, under a dragon's angry call and upon her head is a crown made of leaping waves."

"The Sea Crown will be lost, and then it will be found once more, but the one who finds it will not come from the royal line.
A girl will rise from the sea to seize the crown, with a bloody

sword in her hand, and in her other she holds fire."

"A boy with a forked tongue accompanies this girl. They will bring with them blood and fury, and before them and behind them, there will be the dead."

"The boy and the girl with the crown will turn the islands upside down, the girl must take her rightful throne, but the crown will still fall into dark waters. Roskilde is surrounded by dangers and dark deeds, but there is a slim chance that the throne will be restored..."

Dark waters and dark deeds – but nothing about *the* Darkness, as Chabon had called it just a few hours ago. But it mentions the dead, I thought, feeling once more that shiver of unease as the words perfectly matched the events of today: *"...and behind them, there will be the dead."*

"How does she get it so exactly accurate, every time?" I thought, remembering how it had been from behind the hut, and behind Lila that the dead sailor from the northern wilds had attacked.

Maybe these prophecies were much more literal than I thought. I reread the earlier part. Rising from the waters... under a dragon's angry call...a crown of leaping waves. *Yes, right again.* That was how I had first met Lila.

"But still no Darkness…" I put the scroll carefully back and instead started to search for the subject. Darkness, Darkening, Dark….

There was surprisingly little in Chabon's prophecies about the dark, save for very vague premonitions of a coming darkness to the western islands. Nothing *specific*. But Chabon had called it *the* Darkness like it was a thing. A force.

"Hang on…" a memory tickled at my thoughts, pulled from my earliest days here on the island, and my long lessons of learning letters, copying out scrolls with the other acolytes and sisters.

Hadn't there been a Darkening long ago? I thought, walking down the line of Matriarchs, past Gorlas, Ella, and heading back to the histories section. In here there were all the amassed books and scrolls of ancient times, many of which I had never opened, for they were not the work of the witches.

Where had all these books come from? I wondered, running fingers over the spines, pulling one heavy, leather-bound book to reveal the stamp on its cover: a dragon with a long tail over a triangle of a mountain.

"Torvald." I remembered Afar telling me that many of these volumes were from the libraries of Torvald – the very ones that had been sacked and burned by the Dark King Enric.

"The *Dark* King…" I whispered. Was that a clue?

I started hunting for references to Enric, to his family name of Maddox. Within just a short time I had amassed a small collection of books, mostly histories. I frantically leafed through the contents' pages and genealogies.

Enric Maddox was a scion of the Maddox tribe, a group of warriors from over the easternmost mountains of the world, with access to strange and terrible magics. They helped the aging line of Torvald against a terrible enemy – but then seized power.

"Okay…but still doesn't help me…" I groaned, realizing that I would have to go back further still, into the prehistory of the Torvald empire if I were to find out what the Darkening really was.

I growled in the gloom with frustration. *This is taking too long!* I skipped pages, shelves, looking for lists, summaries, names.

The Torvald Empire was once but one of Three Kingdoms. The Middle Kingdom, ruled by the Torvalds. I pecked and picked bits of information. The further back I went, the more I saw that there were *always* references to "the Darkness" or sometimes "the Great Darkness." It seemed to be a constant enemy of the Middle Kingdom of Torvald – and, more specifically – the dragons of Torvald. But few of the histories talked about the Darkening itself, as though all record of it had been erased from the histories. Maybe in one of Dark Enric's purges of books, I thought with a scowl. What sort of man destroys knowledge? I grew only even more glad that Lord Bower and Lady Saffron had somehow managed to vanquish him from the land, and more resolute in my belief that Lila had to become a queen as Saffron was – noble, protecting the people and the history of the world.

"Fire versus dark," I mused. Just as the fire was the only thing able to vanquish the dead. Maybe I was looking in the wrong place. I hurried past the histories section, instead heading towards the shelves dedicated to Elements.

"Fire." I read the transcription, as the shelf opposite me read "Water." A quick scan proved that there were no shelves dedicated to "Dark" even though many of our magics could be said to be devoted to hiding.

"Well – if fire is the Darkening's enemy, maybe this will tell me more…" I thought, picking at the primers and scrolls that seemed to be the most abstract.

"Fire is warmth and light personified. Fire is pure and drives out the darkness."

All normal, usual stuff. Stuff that I knew anyway. I shook in agitation, thinking about the battle that Lila might already be having out there. *Come on, come on!* I tried to read quicker. *I can't leave Lila out there,* I thought.

"Fire eats the darkness, but it also creates it…" I skimmed the words of one philosopher-witch, before pausing.

"Hang on a minute…"

The bottom of the page had a small annotation to another volume 'The Fire of the Dragons' which I turned to hunt for. If the Darkening was the dragon's natural enemy, then this, surely, would help me understand…

The Fire of the Dragons was dusted with cobwebs, a slim,

uninteresting volume that appeared to be nothing more than a straightforward discussion of what the dragons *did*. They breathed fire. It was hot. Who would have guessed?

"The dragons sun themselves every morning, catching the heat of the sun. It is said that they give praise to every rising sun..."

That much was true, as I had seen Crux, Kim and Thiel all voice their dawn chorus at the first rays of the sun to break the horizon.

"The sun is light and warmth and hope, and the source of all life," the book read. *"The dragons, therefore, are the natural enemy of the Darkness – but they are also caught in a never-ending cycle with it, for just as light creates shadow, the power of the dragon can be used to create the darkness..."*

Now it was starting to get interesting, I thought. What did they mean? Is this where the Darkening came from?

"The dragons are magical beings, burning with the inner power of the sun. Their blood can be used to extend life. To heal injuries. To cheat death entirely."

"By the stars..." I realized. This was exactly what Sym, Crux, and the Dragon Queen Ysix had warned me about, on their sacred home island. That Ohotto had kidnapped the young newts of Sym in order to power her dark magics. I hadn't known that these dragons had meant it so literally, just as Chabon's prophecies seemed meant to be taken at face value.

"To cheat death..." I whispered. Those sailors of the

northern wilds were undoubtedly already dead, and also certainly alive in some strange, horrific fashion. They must be powered by this stolen power of the dragons.

"It is said that the dragons used to give their power freely to their chosen human friends, but clever and evil sorcerers of old found a way to steal that power, from their very flesh and bones..."

The words made me feel sick, but I read on.

"But the power thus stolen from a dragon perverts the natural order; it is always hungry, it can only grow. They say that this darkness can be powered by dragon's blood to eat souls, to swell with every snippet of life that it steals until it is a storm that will block out the sun and throw the entire world into death and damnation. This is the eternal threat of the Darkening of our world..."

The Darkening. That was it, described. My hands shook as I saw, finally, what it was that Ohotto was trying to do. She was doing just what the other evil sorcerers of the past had done – she had stolen dragon power and used it to control or summon the dead. This Darkening would only grow with every life it snuffed out until the whole world was destroyed.

"This is the same darkness that Lady Saffron and Lord Bower fought in the form of the Dark King – himself an evil sorcerer," I whispered. "The same darkness that the dragons have *always* been fighting."

I jumped to my feet, clutching the neglected and seemingly inconsequential book of philosophies to me. We had to use the dragons to destroy this power. And that would mean that we needed more dragons on our side. Not just two or three. We needed all of them.

The blood of the dragons can be used to heal injuries, I thought as I retraced my steps back to the larger, 'lobby' area where Afar and the other witches were gradually recovering.

"The gift," I burst out, looking at Afar and holding the book up for her to see. "That is what you meant, wasn't it?"

"Danu? What have you found out?" Afar looked at me carefully, standing, but leaning heavily on her staff.

"You said that there was a gift that could heal Chabon, but that she wouldn't want it, and that it wasn't ours to give. You meant dragon blood, didn't you?" I demanded. Even saying it made me feel sick.

Why is Chabon so old? I thought, as my world rocked underneath my feet. Hadn't this book here said that the power of the dragons could extend life itself? That their *blood* could? Previously, I had thought that it was just a side-effect of having magic, that there was something in what we did that also extended our life. But I was aging normally, wasn't I? I looked to be the youth of seventeen summers that I was. No more, no less.

How old is Afar?

"Afar? Witches? I need to know where your power comes from. Where *our* power comes from. And I need to know now," I said defiantly, earning heavy glances from Gamba and Helga.

"That is not the tone you use to speak to a senior sister…" Gamba started to say, but Afar silenced her.

"The boy has a point. He needs to know." She spoke heavily, and I watched as, with extreme effort, she straightened to look me direct in the eye. "Yes. You are right about one thing – that I knew the dragons could give some of their power to heal Chabon."

"But it is not a thing that Chabon ever wanted to do, or have done to her," she said. "I knew that dragon blood and crushed dragon bones could heal her. Could invigorate her, and all of us – but we have never used it or done it here on Sebol."

"But it has been done somewhere else?" I said in disgust, even though I knew I shouldn't be surprised. Everything I had read today pointed to dragons' blood and bones as the source of all dark magic.

"It has," Afar said darkly. "In Torvald, a long time ago…." A pause from the older woman. "We believe that Enric may have been performing this rite, but we have no sure evidence of it." My mentor pulled a face as if there was a sour taste in her mouth. Her reaction, at least, didn't surprise me – everything about the Dark King Enric left a sour taste in the mouth.

"But Torvald…?" I murmured. I had always grown up thinking that the Torvald of old was the place where the dragons and humans had lived in harmony. *How could it have happened there?*

"Even Torvald." Afar nodded. "Indeed, legend has it that is

where this vile practice started."

Well, that changes my view of things. A wave of despair settled on my shoulders. The Dragon Academies and the long-lost Dragon Monasteries were not the great centers of friendship and learning that I had thought them to be.

"And Chabon's age? Your age. Our magic. Where *does* it come from?" I blurted out, my voice sounding less furious, and now almost desperate as I knew what I *didn't* want her to say. Afar was my mentor and my guide, and even, perhaps, someone I had considered a friend.

"This is a secret for a senior sister," Gamba muttered from her seat.

"Or a mage," Afar countered, steadily. "He has earned it. Chabon, and I, and just about every witch that you see here *is* older than you think, young Danu. I, myself, am almost a hundred and eighty years old."

"One hundred and sixty-two," Gamba added her voice.

"Ninety-eight," Helga said in a quieter tone.

After the witches had called out their impossible ages, Afar continued. "I remember only a little of the reign of Enric Maddox. I was a lot younger then and only knew that he was a terrible ruler who held the entire world at his mercy, it seemed. I remember his terrible purges, and how many good people fled his reign, heading south and west in the islands." My mentor's eyes looked distantly, and they were troubled as she seemed to peer onto different, nightmarish times.

"They were terrible decades," she confirmed. "We thought

that the end had come. The end of the Torvald empire, certainly." A glance at the other witches at her feet. "I, myself, was born far in the south and raised in the hot deserts there. Enric's enchanted, mechanical soldiers, not needing to stop for drink or food or rest, even reached my home. I fled here, to the west, with what little powers and charms that I had."

Despite my agitation and frustration at the truth – I was rapt. Afar had never told me about her own past before, just as all of the witches here seemed to begin their life here, not elsewhere.

"Anyway, I was told of an island to the farthest west where scholars and free-thinking women were gathered, and so I made my way here over treacherous seas. I was taken in by Chabon. We were all at that time – all of us witches who trained under Chabon—certain that we had to discover the source of Enric's dark power." She gave a sad smile. "But we never found its ultimate source. We only knew that it was something to do with him capturing and holding magic to him, and allowing him to live for many hundreds of years - but beyond that…?" Afar shook her head. "It wasn't long before I started to see a connection between age and magic. When I arrived here, Chabon was herself already some two hundred and forty years old."

"Two hundred and forty!?" I quickly calculated. "And you said that you were one hundred and eighty, so…. Chabon is over four hundred years old!?" I said, aghast. *How could that not come from dark magics?*

"Yes, I believe that to be the case, although I do not know an exact figure." Afar nodded. "She trained us, she taught us how to harness our powers, and how to watch, and wait for the right time to act."

"But *where* does the magic come from?" I said in a trembling voice. "You still haven't told me *what* makes you all so able to live for far longer than normal…"

"The dragons," Afar admitted, and I could have wept. "But not as you think, young Danu. You still have much to learn. Do you know *why* it is so rare for humans and dragons to bond? *Why* dragons rarely take on human companions? *Why* they prefer their home mountains?"

I shook my head, feeling as though I were being lectured.

"It is the same answer *why* the Middle Kingdom of Torvald, with its Dragon Academy, and before that its Dragon Monastery, has always been the target of terrible men," Afar said gravely. "What it does, and has always done, is to help humans and dragons bond together in friendship. There are many in the world who believe that to be unnatural."

"Never!" I said, even though I couldn't feel my current connection to the rare Phoenix dragon thanks to Sebol's enchantments. I had always felt it like a thread of gold from my heart to his. It was a strengthening, warming connection. It did not feel like one that was evil or wrong.

"Exactly. But here are the secrets that I can only hope that you are mature enough to know, *acolyte* Danu." Afar sighed heavily. "The answer to all of those questions that I asked is the same: When a dragon takes on a human companion, what we call a dragon-friend, it shares its power with that person. That power of life, of courage. You may have found your own magic growing stronger around Crux?"

I nodded. It was also the reason why I was not exhausted, as these witches around me were. Somehow, my bond with Crux – as I am sure Lila's bond did, in their own way – made me stronger, more confident, braver.

"We do not understand the mechanism completely, but we know this: the children of dragon friends often live unnaturally long lives. That they are sometimes gifted with magical powers, able to command the elements or have true dreams."

"So…my parents…?" I said in confusion. My fisherfolk family had never appeared mysterious or mystical to me. My brief, toddler memories of them never had father or mother calling down the storm winds or raising fire from their hands.

But they had taken me to the cliffs to watch the Sea Dragons, I thought, remembering that one, shining, crystal-clear moment in my past as I was held to my brother's chest, both watching the diving smaller flashes of turquoise sea-dragon as they dove into the seas, and hearing their happy chatter in my mind. I had been too young to understand what it meant back then, of course. But now I knew that it was because I had the dragon-affinity or bond. *It was the same reason why the witches agreed to train me, because of my special gift to talk to dragons.*

"Do you mean to tell me that my parents were dragon friends?"

"Perhaps." Afar shrugged. "But more likely not. As I said – we do not understand the mechanism, but we also know that dragon friends can arise spontaneously. Just as human friends can bond over nothing more than a shared word or a chance laugh, so it is with dragon friends. There is something about *you*, Danu, about the shape of your heart, that is perfectly matched to that of a dragon's. And, I would say that the same is true for Lila."

"But she has no magic," I pointed out.

"Not that you know of, yet," Gamba said, and I felt another shock to my world. *Was Lila suddenly going to start casting fireballs in front of me? To do what I did?*

"Oh, Danu... you are still so young!" Afar cursed, her frustration rallying her energy, it seemed. "There are many types of magic. Not just the showy sort that we do (but that is what we specialize in, here on Sebol); but there is also the magic of friendship, of saying the right word at the right time; there is the magic of having a way with animals, or plants, so that they respond to you; there is the magic of reading waves, or the currents of the air, or the magic of overcoming your fears."

Or inspiring others? I thought. Lila was stubborn, but I had seen her do that. I knew that people listened to her, that they responded to her when she asked them to put their faith in her. I had thought it was that she was a natural queen – but maybe it was something else entirely.

"These are all dragon gifts, although the original dragons and their human companions might have long since died and passed from the world. These gifts spread out, mix, diffuse, strengthen, until, it is Chabon's belief that we all have a touch of something fey about us," Afar said in reverential tones. "*That* is why some of us live so long, and why Chabon has lived for so long. She knew that she was a dragon-friend, and she even had a bonded dragon here in the Western Isles."

"She did?" I was stunned. I had never known a dragon to ever visit our shores.

"Yes," Gamba said with a long face. "It is a sad tale." The southern witch looked up to Afar to tell it, as she was the closer to old Chabon.

"Chabon was a girl from these islands like Lila herself was, or Saffron. She told me that she bonded early with a great Giant White called Zenema," Afar said.

Zenema? "Where do I know that name?" I muttered.

"It is what Lady Saffron of Torvald calls herself: Saffron of Zenema," Afar said. "Because Zenema was also her dragon-mentor, as she grew up on Dragon Island."

"But Saffron never came here, did she?" I said, shaking my head.

Afar smiled sadly. "No. Things might have been different if she had – although I could not say if it was better or worse.

Chabon was Zenema's human friend before even Saffron was born. The White and the witch had many adventures through the Western islands, but eventually, even Chabon grew old, and her companion kept on growing. A human dragon friend might live for an unnatural lifespan, but it is still but a blink of an eye to the oldest of dragons. Chabon grew too old to ride, too old to fly."

"So, she retired here," Gamba said seriously. "To start this place, as the Dark King Enric Maddox secured his stranglehold over Torvald. Chabon knew that she was too old to fight him, and she could see that there were others coming in the future; Saffron, Bower, Lila, perhaps *you*, Danu," Gamba said. "Eventually, the great dragon queen Zenema fell in the wars against Enric, and it broke Chabon's heart. She grew weaker and frail, but she never stopped amassing her knowledge and her prophecies, in the hope that it would always be an aid against the darkness."

"By the sweet waters and sacred stars," I said, feeling an echoing sadness in my heart. What must it be like to lose a friend that you had spent hundreds of years with?

"So, you see, Danu – now you know our deepest mysteries. That we are a community of dragon-friends without dragons," Afar said wearily. "And that is the gift that could save Chabon – the gift that only a dragon can give, but because of her love of them, the gift that the Matriarch will not accept."

"And every day, the curses of Ohotto eat more of her mind and body away and Ohotto feeds on the dragons," Gamba hissed. "It is too sad to even contemplate."

It was. "I, I am sorry, sisters. I should never have doubted you."

"No," Gamba said sharply, to a murmuring *shush* from Afar.

"But now you know for what we fight. For the friendship of dragons. To keep the light of dragons burning in the world."

I could see it clearly now. And I could see clearly what danger Ohotto really represented. "If these old books I have found are true, then you are right that we face a terrible evil. It said that dragon blood and bones can be used to pervert the laws of life and to raise this power that was known as the Darkening in the past. The fact that Ohotto has managed to raise the dead only proves that she really is intending to harness the power of the Darkening."

"By all that is holy…" Afar shook her head and looked down at her feet. It was at that point I saw my old mentor in a different way. Had she suspected that this was the case? Had she seen how powerful Ohotto was and wondered where her vast stores of power had come from? At that moment I even felt a little bit of pity for the woman who had taught me everything, and who I had always looked up to. She had lived a long time and had seen the world change around her. I wondered if she had been desperately trying to convince herself, to hope, that she would not live to see this evil rise again?

But, I thought grimly, I knew a power that could defeat it.

CHAPTER 9
LILA, THE BATTLE FOR SEBOL

With my new-found weapons, I raced through the strange walkway streets of the witches' township, heading for the harbor.

"Crux!" I shouted as I ran, craning my neck to catch glimpses of the fight happening before us.

Pheet! Pheet! It seemed that the dead of those accursed black ships had found their weapons, as I watched small clouds of ugly little crossbow bolts shoot up towards the two dragons that harried them. Crux, the larger bull dragon, swerved through the air with great sweeps of his wings, disrupting their trajectory, and putting himself in the way of the thinner, younger Sinuous Blue, Kim.

Crux – careful! I thought, seeing a few of the darts appear

to his side and flank, and remembering how he had been attacked in the Battle for Malata.

"Skreyarch!" he bellowed fiercely, in pain, but swept out over the stone walls of the docks and the churning waters beyond, unfazed.

One of the black boats was a towering inferno, but none of them had broken from their aggressive line across the harbor. Why would they fear death? I thought, miserably. Instead, each of the three boats were firing potshots at the dragons as they swooped and attacked. How long would it take for the dragons to fire all four? *Could* they set fire to all four? I wondered. How much dragon ichor did a single dragon have?

I cursed myself as I did not already know the answers. These were things that a commander *ought* to know – and things I hadn't thought to ask Crux.

"Girl!" A horrible, croaking rasp came from behind me, and I turned to see that a group of the dead sailors had been attracted by my shout. They were rounding on the harbor, four of them bearing rusting weapons. I could see old scars and the marks of already wounded flesh on them – cuts to their heads, limbs, and bodies that would have killed breathing men and women.

But I had a plan, and it was held in my left hand.

"Hoi, fishheads!" I shouted at them, waving my scimitar in the air to attract them closer. Not that I needed to, as they were already running towards me. But I wanted them to only be thinking about me, not where any of the other witches were hiding.

"Come and get me!" I shouted, and bolted over the last section of planked walkway, leaping onto the pebble beach beyond. My pace instantly slowed, and my boots crunched with the sound of displaced pebbles. At my back were the lapping grey waters of the sea, unmarred by the burning bits of black wood from that one boat. On my left were the larger, shining boulders that broke the end of the harbor, and it was to those that I started to back towards as I hefted my knapsack in front of me.

I pulled out first one, and then another of the small oil lamps that I had stolen from the library. Each was barely bigger than my hand and smelled strongly of oil, half of which must have sloshed into my knapsack – I could only hope that there was enough left in the shaped reservoirs for what I wanted to do.

I fumbled in my pocket for my tinderbox as the first wave of the dead hit the beach. They were faster than I had thought they would be.

The small wooden box was a gift from my father – a nice bit of Roskilde workmanship, I thought ruefully—and by snapping its brass cogs that held shaped flint pieces against a steel plate, I got the first spark to fly into the lantern.

Whump! The oil lit almost immediately, and I hefted the glass lantern in an overarm throw, just as if I were throwing fishing spears.

It hit the leading dead sailor square on the chest, the glass smashing at the force of my throw and spilling the flaming oil onto the man's chest and his frizzled beard. Flames leapt up to his face and the man stopped and flailed, whirling first one way and then another to attempt to brush away the flames.

"Girl!" one of the nearby un-dead moaned. If any of them noticed the fate of their colleague at all, they did so by swerving away from the wildly waving man, and continued on in their awkward, loping run.

"Come on, strike! Strike!" I hissed at the next lantern, having to pull the cog several times to get the spark, and then again to get a stronger spark to light the next lantern.

The other lanterns were still in my bag, and I didn't have time to fish them out and light them. Instead, I scrambled up the rocks, leaping lightly from one slimy, seaweed encrusted rock to the other. I was used to this; I had been doing this my entire life, and I knew how *not* to put my full weight forward, and how to go faster than I thought I could.

Behind me, the dead were less proficient– or maybe their death had made these sailors forget, as they slipped and scrambled upon the rocks, only to slide back down onto their fellows, and begin again.

Plenty of time, I thought victoriously, taking a steadying breath.

"Girl!" the undead below croaked and shouted from rotting teeth. There were a whole lot more of them on the beach now.

I lit and threw my remaining incendiaries into the press and scramble of un-dead bodies at the base of the rocks, waiting for the satisfying moment when the flames took hold and formed a living wall of fire between me and the others.

But that fire won't last long, I thought, backing out along the rocks, farther out into the harbor. On either side of me were the lapping waters of the sea.

"Crux!" I shouted, as one by one, the burning bodies fell back– to be replaced by scrabbling, climbing, pock-marked arms.

"Skreyargh!" came a deafening shout of rage as his shadow engulfed my tiny rock peninsular, and powerful talons enclosed around me and lifted me up.

"Little sister! How brave you are!" At the mere touch of his claws, our bond was as strong and clear as if there were none of the witches' strange magic laying over the island. The wind was wild and roaring in my ears as I patted his claws to let me up. I saw a flash of slate-grey waters below as I swung out, clutching onto his scales as I clambered to his back and secured myself to the blanket and leather saddle that I used.

That feels better. I settled into position, looking out over the battle.

Kim was dive-bombing the four boats, but it seemed that, unless she used her fire, all she was managing to do was attract crossbow bolts from the un-dead crews assembled on deck.

The problem was the attack-run. which gave the crew plenty of time to fire their bolts straight at her – and Senga's, and Adair's – faces. I watched Kim pull up once more as the dead swung their crossbows to meet her.

"The bolts do not hurt so much…" Crux boasted, but I could feel through our connection the many small, stinging wounds he had earned, mostly in his chest and flanks.

"No!" I said immediately. My father had schooled me well in the arts of war – *look for a weakness, dart in, attack, get out of harm's way.* That was the Raider way, and it seemed that it might be the only way for us to defeat this strange foe. "Pull back!" I shouted, and in response Kim slapped the water with her long tail in frustration, sending a great plume of water high into the air.

That was it! I thought. "Crux – I have an idea. Can you relay my message to Kim?"

"Of course, but I will need to be closer to her, thanks to this strange isle," the Phoenix said, and we swooped upwards, joining the angered Blue and her riders.

"Are you hurt?" I shouted across to Senga and Adair when the harbor was little more than a dinner plate below us. The wind howled and whipped, and the air was cold – but my exhilaration and the heat of the dragon beneath me kept me from shivering.

"A little scraped, but nothing serious," Senga boasted,

rolling the sleeves of her tunic up to show an ugly red mark across her shoulder.

Waters, damn it! I gritted my teeth. If that bolt had been just a hands' span to the left, it would have thudded into her chest!

"It's too dangerous to attack head-on. We need to distract them, create a diversion," I shouted, imitating the dives that I wanted them to make with my hands. Adair got the plan immediately, punching the air in fierce joy. Senga, on the other hand, seemed less impressed.

"Looks like we're going to get wet then…" She rolled her eyes, fixing her short cloak tighter about her.

Yes, we were.

"Dragon Raiders – fly!" I called, hunkering down to Crux's neck as he forced us up again on powerful wing beats, hanging in the cold airs for just a moment before we started to turn, tracing an arc over the seas. My stomach jumped as Crux pointed his snout and neck towards the boats and suddenly we were diving.

"Woohooo!" It was hard not to share my enthusiasm for this feeling; racing downwards faster than thought, faster than any boat that I had been on. The boats of the dead grew larger in a heartbeat and we could see the pale dead lurching and raising crossbows towards us. The flat greys of the sea turned into white-topped wave flecks.

"Now!" I shouted, and Crux flared with his wings. We missed the first boat. Instead, Crux shoved outwards with his claws, skimming the surface of the waves to one side of the ship. Plumes of white water exploded on either side of us as we plowed across the bay, past the other boats and almost to the rock boulders where Crux rose from the waters in a low arc, spiraling higher and higher.

There was another roar of water-strike as Kim, Senga and Adair did the same maneuver behind us, sending up great gouts of water, and –

Making waves.

One of the many things that I knew about fighting on board a boat was this: that it got a *lot* harder to fight when the seas are rough. And if the seas were unnaturally calm around the island of Sebol – then we could always *make* them rough with the dragons.

I turned in my makeshift saddle to see the four boats (one of them now a towering inferno) bobbing up and down like corks. The next great water plume hit them from Kim's attack, and the second boat rocked onto its side, its aft end spinning backwards slowly.

"Again!" I called. Our dragons were fast, and so long as we kept turning at the last moment – hitting the water with maximum power – then we could avoid the crossbow bolts.

But waves died down *really* quick, and by the time Crux began his next swerving dive, the three boats were already settling again. Not in their original positions, but not in danger of tipping over.

"Wait!" I called to Senga and Adair, realizing too late they probably had no chance of hearing me.

"Wait!" Crux echoed my command to Kim, who instead circled once more as we hit the water just as we had the first time.

A torrent of water spray soaked the decks of the middle ship (not that the dead cared) but then our bow-wave crashed into the boat, as we flew off to the hiss of crossbows striking open water behind us. The boats once again rocked back and forth.

"Now!" I shouted, and Crux chirruped for Kim to start her attack run.

We had to time it just right, as Kim hit the water and sent the next wave smashing into their side. The middle boat was the worst affected, spinning and rocking side to side– almost at a forty-five-degree angle every time. But it was the boat at the back that was the first to get in serious trouble. The waves we had created pushed it out to the harbor rocks, where its prow smashed into the boulders, and the tide dragged it along the boulder wall.

"Dragons, attack!" I screamed, and Crux, sensing my intention, was already turning. The muscles all along his neck and shoulders tightened, and the flame-sacs at the base of his neck swelled before he roared his fury at the rocking boats.

The ships of the dead were in too-wild waters to fire back at us, and Crux's plume of flame hit the second boat in a clear broadside, flaring past the shields and over the decks.

Kim fired the third boat, leaving just the one on the rocks still untouched by dragon fire.

We were doing it! We were winning! I thought, as Crux concentrated his fire on our victim.

But the battle wasn't over for the Isle of Sebol, for sparks of lightning began to illuminate the area behind the huts. "The witches," I said. "They must be fighting Calla's faction!"

"Shall we help them?" Crux said, lifting off from his attack of what was now a burning pyre.

I was hesitant. A crossbow bolt in the wrong place was dangerous enough. But a witch's magic? I didn't want to endanger Crux any more than I had done already.

But Danu was out there. My loyalties towards both Crux and to Danu warred. I didn't want *either* of them to be hurt!

"Silly Lila. It is not for you to choose the danger for me!" Crux laughed in my mind, sounding arrogant and bullish as he roared, pounding his wings to force him upwards into the sky over the harbor.

"But there is still one boat to be set aflame!" I said, clutching onto Crux and pointing at the grounded boat on the harbor rocks.

"Kim is more than capable," Crux assured me, flying low over the huts towards the loudest fighting. His savage anger and elation mingled together through our bond, and, although I shared some of his feelings, I also felt apprehensive, and not for the first time since I had bonded with him, did I contem-

plate that Crux the Phoenix was not entirely like the other dragons of the Western Isles. He was fierce.

"You are right. I am." Crux laughed as we flew through a black plume of smoke, and onto a scene of skirmishing battle.

Something flashed to my right, and the eaves of one of the huts exploded in a plume of smoke. We were flying over the center of the village, where the largest hut stood, struck with many blackened scorch marks, whilst some of the smaller huts on either side were smoking. I saw flashes of movement in the walkway "streets" below, as women in robes with staffs leaned out from their hiding places to blast at each other.

"Where are they? Where are my enemies!?" Crux roared, flaring his wings and reaching out with back talons to grab the largest roof of the Main Meeting Hut, settling on it with claws digging into the wood.

He roared louder than I'd ever heard before, flashing his tail behind him to pulverize rooftops and walls, swinging his head down into the streets to search for any who would dare to fire a spell at him. The screams and shouts from below fell suddenly silent as everyone, it seemed, was cowed by his great presence.

I saw a movement between two of the smaller huts, heard the collapsing drift of wood, and Crux snapped his neck around to hiss at the empty street (making sure that any hidden watchers saw his sword-length teeth).

"Who opposes me! Who dares!" he roared, and although I

knew that none of the witches could understand him, they must have caught the drift.

Another high-pitched shriek answered Crux's as Kim's shadow flashed overhead, circling the stilled battle. Two dragons now – who living would dare oppose us?

"Crux! Lila!" I heard a shout as one of the doors of the nearby huts fell open, and Danu staggered out. His hands appeared to be smoking – or emitting a strange heat haze. He must have been fighting for his life against Ohotto's followers.

"Danu? Where's Afar? Are you okay?" I called, but before he could speak, my answers were given by Afar rising from the other side of the street, leaning heavily on her staff and waving.

"We have them now, Lila. Thank you, great Crux, and your other dragon friend," she called to us, before nodding to her side for other shapes emerged from the shadows. The five 'combat' witches who had gone to find the library were now joined by the fifteen other witches who had followed on behind. Afar turned to shout towards us – *no*, towards the Meeting Hut that we had perched on.

"Calla! It is over," Afar called to the hall. "You must know that by now. The dragons have destroyed your allies in the harbor, and now they are here, over your heads. Come out and hand yourselves over to us!"

There was silence for a moment, and then the scrape of wood and a muffled shout came from below us.

"Why? You'll only feed us to that dragon of yours!" a woman's voice snapped back.

"Of course we won't!" Afar shouted. "We do not execute people on Sebol, Calla!" She spoke in exasperation as if the other witch had been a petulant child.

"I cannot eat her?" Crux turned to look at me with grinning teeth.

"No, you can't," I said hurriedly, before adding. "Please."

"I don't like witches anyway. Too stringy." Crux lolled his large, forked tongue out over his open jaws, which gave me the unsettling question: had he eaten a witch or two before?

"I need to have your word!" the muffled voice of the rebel witch shouted from below us.

"Can't I just smash the walls and get her for you?" Crux sighed, weary of our slow human solutions to problems.

"No, you can't!" I hissed at him angrily, to earn another whistling laugh.

"You have *my* word!" I shouted, glaring at the dragon I sat on, who only blinked slowly and said nothing.

The silence stretched until finally there was another scrape of wood as if something heavy was being dragged out of the way, and a figure emerged from the hut beneath us, wearing a silvery-grey dress, under a dark, velvet-blue robe. She had straight mouse-brown hair and a black wood staff and flinched as she stepped out, turning to look up at us.

"Good afternoon, human," Crux said as he turned his head slowly towards the witch. Calla raised her staff defensively.

"Calla! Drop that, you fool – or else the dragon will eat you up faster than you can say fish!" Afar snapped, striding across the burnt and broken walkway to slap the witch's staff from her hand. "And the others? Your followers?"

I watched Calla look balefully first at Afar, and then us up above her and Kim, Senga and Adair on one of the smaller huts opposite. "Come on you lot. Come out. It's over," she called, and I tensed as, one by one or two by two the rebellious witches picked their way out of the hut beneath us.

Thank the stars that they decided to give up, I thought, as their numbers continued to swell and grow in the street. If Afar had twenty or so loyal witches here, and another twenty protecting Chabon – then Calla easily had the same total number or a few more in front of us.

But not all of them wanted to follow Calla, I thought, as some of the younger witches around the edges looked confused, distraught, and anxiously around them.

But no Ohotto, I saw.

"You're being ridiculous, you know, Afar," Calla shot at the senior witch as now Gamba had joined her. "Getting your dragon friends to come save you. The time of Chabon is over! She's a dying woman! She cannot save us from the Darkening!"

"The Darkening that *your* master is summoning herself?" Gamba hissed, nodding out to the harbor, where the burning pyres of the dead boats could clearly be seen. "What did you think was happening, when Ohotto sent word with *those*?" she spat.

"A necessary alliance. Ohotto is using the powers of darkness against itself!" Calla said.

"And you believe that, do you?" Afar scoffed.

"Yes! Havick is the only one strong enough in these isles to defeat the Darkening. And Ohotto is the only witch strong enough to join with him." Calla shook her head in impotent fury. "You place your trust in these *Sea Raiders*? They are thieves and bandits! They will flee your side as soon as they face the true Darkening – and you know it, Afar!"

"They have the true heir of Roskilde," Danu surprised me by stepping forward to shout at Calla. "Havick will topple, Roskilde will stand tall."

"That's not what the prophecy says now, is it?" Calla laughed. "And do you think that the people of Roskilde will decide to follow a girl raised as a Sea Raider? Their natural enemy?" She shook her head, laughing cruelly. "Fools!" she spat.

"Where is she? Ohotto Zanna?!" Danu snarled at Calla.

"Yes, where is she!?" Crux echoed.

"How do I know? I am not Sister Zanna's superior!" Calla laughed at my friend, making my blood boil. "But where do you *think* she could be? On Roskilde? With Havick and all of his navies and soldiers, probably. Good luck getting to her now!"

"Skrargh!" Crux suddenly shouted in agitation. I shared

his sense of frustration. Roskilde was a *large* island, with thousands of soldiers and hundreds of galleons in her defense. We could not simply fly in, defeat Ohotto, and fly out.

"Take her away," Afar commanded Gamba, watching as her staff was taken from her, and Calla, unresisting, was led away by the lion-pelted witch.

"And what of these others?" Helga nodded to the much larger numbers of dejected-looking witches.

"Sisters!" Afar called to them. "You have been seduced and fooled by Ohotto Zanna and Calla. But now it is time to realize your mistakes!" The old woman looked stern and tall, more imposing than any other time that I had seen her.

"I will offer you an opportunity, my sisters – as it was stupidity that led to your mistakes, I hope. You may either drop your staffs and submit to our will – no access to the library, not to use magic unless authorized, to work off your crimes against Chabon and the Isle of Sebol—"

A sizable number of them moaned and grumbled at these conditions. *"Drop our staffs? Sanction our magic?"* It seemed that what Afar was telling them to do was a deep insult.

"—or you may leave, and never darken our shores again. For, if you do – we *will* fight," Afar said stoically.

"What is she doing? She will let her enemies go freely?" Crux said to me in confusion, for the idea of a peaceful surrender must not have ever occurred to him, as a young bull dragon.

"There are too many rebellious witches here for her," I

whispered to the dragon. We Raiders did similar things when we had managed to take a far larger crew of a galleon. Split them up. Get them out of the way. "Afar is trying to remove their threat from Sebol before they realize that they have sizable numbers…" I muttered.

"Humans. So complicated." Cruz cocked his head and blinked inquisitively at the goings on under his claws.

"Never!" I saw a few of the older witches shout. "We will submit to your will, perhaps, but you can never deny us our magic!"

"Never!"

Afar and the twenty or so other loyalist witches tensed, and I knew that they were wondering if another battle was going to break out right now.

Crux decided to shorten the debate, by bellowing suddenly into the air, reminding everyone here that there was still a very large (and angry-sounding) dragon standing over them.

"Go," Afar said, taking the opportunity to point to the harbor. We watched as perhaps fifteen witches broke ranks from the fifty or so that were there, walking proudly and scornfully past their sisters (with their staffs) out towards the harbor.

"Helga? Take a few sisters and make sure they leave." Afar nodded, and the crow-witch did so, nodding to three other of the loyalists at her side, to escort her sisters into exile.

"Any more?" Afar shouted angrily below us, but the rest seemed too cowed by Crux to even raise their eyes.

Good, I thought, as Afar saw to the collection of all their staffs, and their division into smaller workgroups to start repairing the damage to the town that their battle had caused.

"Not even one to nibble on," Crux sighed dramatically, earning a reproachful stare from me. He only laughed.

"Lila?" It was Danu, walking up to the hall to wave up at us. He looked tired, exhausted, but also worried.

"Danu – thank the waters that you are safe," I called down, as Crux shook his wings and clambered down into the street – just barely wide enough to hold him. As soon as he did, Danu darted forward to pat the great Phoenix dragon affectionately.

"I could say the same for you both," Danu agreed. "But I have serious news. Lore that I found from the library. The witch Ohotto doesn't just seek to steal the Western Isles for her ally Havick – she seeks to raise an ancient evil that threatens us all!"

"This Darkening that Calla and Afar mentioned?" I asked in alarm and listened as Danu explained, in rushed terms, what he had discovered about fire, and dragon's bones, and the perverse curse that could be summoned from misusing that power.

"That is why she steals our young!" Crux snapped and hissed, lashing his tail to demolish another of the huts behind. Oops, I thought.

"We will get to her, Crux, I promise," I said, hoping to calm him down.

"I think those dead sailors are only the start of it," Danu

warned. "We need to raise the dragons again – it is only dragon fire that will defeat the darkness."

"Will they fight for us?" I said in alarm.

"They will fight to save their young." Crux was certain.

Another dark thought suddenly occurred to me. If Ohotto and Havick were now using these undead sailors to do their bidding – then wouldn't they seek to bring their vengeance down on the Free Islands of the Western Archipelago?

On Malata?

"We fly home," I said, as Senga and Adair joined us. "As soon as we have provisions, and the dragons' wounds are treated, we return to Malata to warn them of the dead fleet, and then we will have to fly northward to raise the dragons against them."

Why did I suddenly feel like I had spent too long on Sebol already?

PART II
The Dead Fleet

CHAPTER 10
DANU AND THE FULA

Our flight from Sebol and Batash was full of foreboding and worry, and even the skies appeared grey and overcast every day that we flew.

"There is something bad in the waters of the world," Crux said cryptically on the morning of the second day out as he emerged from the waters of a small islet that was barely bigger than a spire of rock with a few trees. We had stopped to rest and to eat – although Lila clearly wanted to keep on going.

"Crux? What do you mean?" I asked, to only hear the equivalent of a dragon-grunt.

"Bad magic."

"Lila?" I turned to Lila, standing impatiently on the small ledge of rock, already packed and suited in her leathers.

Maybe because she shared his mind, she would know more of what the drake had sensed. Behind my friend, Adair and Senga still ate the last of their meal – dried fruits and cured meats given to us by Afar and the witches.

Lila cocked her head to one side as Crux clambered up the rocks (Kim was on the other side of the rocks, preening her scales). I felt that surge of electric *heaviness* in the air between them that happened every time that they shared thoughts, but after a moment Lila just made a frustrated growl.

"He doesn't know. Or can't tell me exactly. Just that…he can sense a change in the waters. A scent, maybe." Lila adjusted her belt once more, patting her scimitar at her side. "Which is all the more reason that we should get going."

"Aww! Really? We only just stopped!" Adair groaned, massaging his aching legs. I knew the feeling, as riding a dragon non-stop for two days straight wasn't the most comfortable of experiences.

"The dead won't stop," Lila said grimly, bringing reality crashing down around us. *The Dead. That was who – what – we faced.* It was a thought that turned my stomach, made me feel nauseous. *How could Ohotto do such a thing?* How could her heart have strayed so far from the witches' path?

"She's right," I said, stuffing the last of my rations into my own pack. It looked like Adair and Senga might argue some more, but any negotiation of resting a bit longer was quickly quashed when Crux shook out his scales with a noise like clattering tree branches in the dead of winter.

"Agh!"

"Ugh – Come on!" the pair shouted as they were sprayed with seawater from the dragon. Crux opened his mouth in a wide, tongue-lolling grin that I had come to recognize was his way of laughing – it made me smile, but when I looked over at Lila, her eyes were fixed on a point far to the south-eastern horizon – the point where Malata would be.

※

Whatever it was that Crux had sensed earlier, we didn't need dragon senses to detect something wrong when the dark shapes of the Free Islands started swimming into view ahead of us.

"Look – what is that!" I shouted, pointing not at the islands, but a nearer shape on the seas. It was too small and low to the waters to be a galleon or a boat – but it nonetheless was floating on the grey waters.

"It looks like some sort of platform," Lila hissed through gritted teeth. "Take us down, Crux – I want a closer look…"

"That's not a platform – that's a flotilla," I said as Crux's wings took us closer. What we were looking at was a collection of what looked like barges or yachts, cobbled together with board planks strung out across them to form a larger flat surface. Sail cloth had been haphazardly strung from poles to provide shade, I guessed, and underneath it sat a huddled collection of people.

"*No! Get away!*" they screeched and shouted as soon we drew closer – no surprise, considering that we were flying on a gigantic fire-breathing lizard.

"We mean you no harm!" Lila shouted, waving her open hands over her head. They didn't look as though they believed us.

"Okay, Crux – take us in slowly. But *slow*. Try not to scare them…" Lila said as Kim above us started circling in wide circles, cawing loudly.

Crux leaned back and flared his wings as his splayed-out feet hit the water. It wasn't as violent a water landing as I had seen him do before – but it still caused a ripple of screams and shouts from the floating people. I even saw one man – thin, sun-tanned— seize up a large oar defiantly, then look at it, look back at the dragon, and sit back down again. *Yeah, I guess there is nothing a person could do if a dragon wanted to eat you...* This close, I could see how disheveled and even injured some of them were. They wore dirt-smeared and torn rags, and several people lay unmoving under the sailcloth awnings.

"We mean you no harm!" Lila called again.

Still, the people we circled didn't look as though they believed us.

"What happened? Where are you from?" I called to them, earning only a sign against evil.

"We have nothing, you know! No money, no food, no gold!" one of them shouted – the same man who had almost picked up the oar in defense.

"Then we will try to find you food, at least!" Lila shouted back, standing up on Crux's back as he paddled, circling the platform. Its decks were wider than most of the boats we see on the waters, but it rode the sea awkwardly, and I could see different sections pulling and lowering. It wouldn't be long before it broke up.

"Why would you do that?" the man shouted back. "I know you. You're the Raider girl. The one who talks with dragons!" The man had heavy dark eyebrows that made his scowl only all the fiercer.

"Sckrrr…" Crux issued a warning grumble from the back of his throat at the man's aggressive tone of voice, but Lila soothed him by stooping to pat him affectionately on the neck. She didn't take what he had said as an insult at all, I saw – even if he had said it in alarm.

"Because it's the law of the sea!" Lila shouted. "Even Raiders obey the law of the sea – unless you're our enemy, any target that's rudderless, stranded, or scuttled, needs to be offered aid by any other that passes. It's what all of us in the Free Islands believe – and that is where you are from, right?" she said a little exasperatedly.

"Fula." The man nodded. "We came from the Island of Fula, about a day north-east from here."

Lila nodded. "I know of it. Good, strong people on Fula. What on earth happened?" We circled around them one more time, as the man conversed with some of the other people on his makeshift raft in harsh whispers. It seemed that they were arguing whether or not to trust us, but, after a heated exchange, the talking man lost, as he turned back to tell us.

"Something came to our shores not two nights ago. Overpowered our guards, attacked our villages." His tone was heavy. "It was all that we could do to try and escape on our boats – until they pursued us."

"Who were they?" Lila said, but both she and I had a sinking sensation that we already knew what it would be.

"At first we didn't know. We fought them with bows and spears, just like we always have, but – they didn't die." The man's voice shook. *"They wouldn't die."*

"And their ships – were they black? Nothing you had seen before?" Lila asked, earning a nod.

"The people of Fula are strong, as you say, but we couldn't all outrun them. Their black fleet smashed through our small armada, leaving most of us dead or drowned. By the time that the dead had their fill of slaughter and moved on, there was only us left. We don't even know if any survived on the island."

"By the airs and the waters!" Lila visibly paled beside me. "This is it?" She nodded to their craft, containing perhaps twenty or thirty people. "You are all that's left of Fula?"

The man nodded, tears running down his face.

Lila was too shocked to speak for a moment, but she regained her composure just as quickly. Once again, I marked how smoothly she took control of the situation, even without thinking of it. "You are right that we are Raiders, and we're on our way back to Malata. You are welcome to join us there; our community has always been open to new members..."

The man shrugged as if one island wouldn't be any different from any other, but, after some more shared words with what was left of his community, he nodded.

"We will gladly accept your kind offer," he said humbly. "But I do not know what good even a dragon can do against the army of the dead."

"Just you wait and see," Lila said determinedly, looking at me. I nodded, knowing what she was thinking. We had to stop Havick and Ohotto.

It slowed our progress down considerably, but by the time that the midday sun was above us, we were making good time once again. We had just enough ropes between all of us and the Fula refugees to secure lines leading from Crux – still in the water – to the edge of the platform, while Kim, carrying Senga and Adair flew high above as a lookout. Crux swam along the surface in his leg-kicking paddle, powering the platform along the waves faster than it could ever hope to go by the use of oars and wind alone.

"Hold on!" Lila shouted, sitting on Crux, and around me, the refugees grabbed what bits of wooden edges and boat scraps that they could as we bounced once more on choppy waters. It was something that I would almost have enjoyed, had I not at the moment been trying to tend to the injured on the platform.

"Easy now…" I said, as the groaning man shook and rolled in the swell and fall of the water. I didn't have half the supplies as I would have liked, but Afar and the witches had provided me with some extra supplies of healing unguents, bandages, and tonics. I could only hope that we wouldn't meet many more such refugees on our journey, as it took up most of what meager supplies I had on the burns, scrapes, and broken bones that I encountered here.

The worst problem was, of course, dehydration and hunger. They had been able to fish for food – but there hadn't been any rainfall over the last few days that the Fulanians had been on the water, so we gladly gave them all that we had in our own water pouches, knowing that we could always get some more on Malata.

But a dragon swimming is never going to be as fast as a dragon flying, and it was getting towards late afternoon when the skies were split by a *"Skreyar!"* from the skies above.

"Kim?" I murmured, looking up to see the young Sinuous Blue splitting the sky, racing towards us.

"What is it?" I shouted, wobbling to my feet on the platform.

"Skree-ip! Sckrch!" Kim shared the whistles and shrieks of her dragon-tongue with Crux below, who immediately became agitated in the water.

"Lila!" I shouted. "Lila – what is it?"

Her face looked back to me in shock. "It's Malata. It's burning."

CHAPTER 11
LILA, HOME?

Come on, come on, come on! I twitched and jittered with frustration at the sight of the approaching ship. Luckily, perhaps, Kim, Senga and Adair's news weren't only that they had seen dark clouds over our home – it was also that they had spotted the *Ariel* out in the seas beyond the reef.

Not wasting any time, I had asked her to get a message to the *Ariel* to get over here, as fast as they could – changing course wasn't something that my father would like to do if he was captaining the boat, but I also knew my father. He was a pragmatic man. *Something that I've learnt from him,* I thought. A dragon would be better in a fight than a boat – and if he came here to pick up the refugees from Fula, then it would free Crux, me and Danu all the quicker to help where we could.

But still – waiting for my father's ship to loom larger on the horizon and finally speed towards us was possibly the longest wait that I have ever had in my life.

"Father!? Is my father on board?" I shouted as the *Ariel* sheered towards us. I could see the frantic and worried faces of my Raider friends from the decks – a skeleton crew, with only wiry little Sulin up in the rigging, and only a few other Raiders racing to throw down rope bridges for those people behind us.

"No!" shouted the large, dark-skinned Sailing Master Elash. It was a surprise seeing him taking charge of the *Ariel,* and instantly my heart sunk in my chest.

"He's back on the island, isn't he?"

"He wouldn't leave Pela. She said that she had to be the last off the island." Elash said, his bald head gleaming in the sun. "Get those people up here, double quick and turn us around!" he was barking at the *Ariel* crewmates.

As we helped transport the Fula refugees to their new floating home, I explained as quickly as I could that they had been attacked by the Dead Ships – a new type of enemy on the waters and one that was masterminded by Havick.

"We know what they are – that's what's been attacking us for the past night and day!" Elash barked. "Appeared out of the fog last night, attacked our fishing fleet. We tried shooting them, boarding them – but every time we send Raiders on their decks, they don't come back. They have Malata blocked in and are picking us off, boat by boat!"

"They must be holding Malata in check until Havick arrives with the rest of his armada," I said to Danu, who was looking at me seriously.

"What do we do?" he asked.

"We fight," I said, severing the rope that held Crux to the platform – and, echoing my own rage, the Phoenix dragon let out a sky-shattering roar of anger and frustration. We barely had time to scramble to our places before Crux was beating his wings and paddling faster.

"We'll get there as soon as we can!" Captain Elash was shouting from behind us, but we were already too far away for me to shout anything useful back to him. The powerful muscles of the dragon contracted and punched outwards everywhere beneath me, and I heard the thunderclaps of his feet as he started clawing through the water. With a sensation like being hit by an unexpected storm wind, he leapt upwards – and instantly all tension, force and fury disappeared as the air took us and held us, and we were flying.

Flying home, I thought, and flying towards disaster.

The skies were black over Malata, and we saw the pall of the fires long before we saw the island that had been my home all of my memory. It was heading towards dusk, and the skies were still overcast, making the glowing lights of the orange flames leap out all the brighter from the dark waters.

"Look – the fog," Danu said, pointing to the shifting greys that sat off of the northern Bone Reefs like it was tethered there.

"It's like the same fog that was around Sebol," I thought, and wondered if the two had to be connected somehow.

"Witches can summon sea fogs," Danu advised me. "It has always been one of the ways that the West Witches protect themselves, and then there was Ohotto's magical fog that day of the battle…"

I nodded. He was right. Lord Havick and his witch had only managed to escape our dragon fury because she had somehow summoned up some unearthly fog that hid them from our view. Not even the keen dragon senses could penetrate it.

"It must be Ohotto. She must be in there, directing *them*," Danu said, and I saw his nose crinkling as he even thought about what it was we were facing. The dead.

Black ships dotted here and there all around the waters of the Bone Reef.

Pha-thoom! A plume of fire spit from one of the black galleon's sides, and then a cloud of smoke and fire erupted from the dark hills and buildings nearest. The dead ships were using explosive shot, it appeared.

"Well – two can play with fire," I growled. "Crux? Pull us in low and hard. I want to go in under their firing arc."

"Attack their unprotected bellies. Attack fast and strong – yes, I like this idea," Crux agreed.

There were two of the Dead Ships between us and the ship bombarding the island. I held my breath as Crux suddenly flicked his wings, and we rolled in the air to one side of them – and then crossed to swoop past the other like an acrobatic hawk. I heard the hiss of things in the wind around us, and the clatter as bolts scattered along Crux's flank.

"Rakh!" Crux grunted in pain. *Oh no! What had I done?* But there was even less time to wonder how hurt he was as he skidded just a meter over the water and the stationary dead ship rose above us.

"Now, Crux! Now!" I shouted.

"Hold tight to me, humans," came the whisper of Crux's mind inside mine, and then we were flipping over with the sea as our ceiling as Crux raised his wings—

"SKREYAR!" I felt the thump of heart and organs as Crux roared his dragon flame out at the sides of the Dead Ship, and then he was flipping back over and we were once again upright, with the spikes and spires of the Bone Reef just below Crux's belly and legs. He swung out wide and climbed, now over the calmer waters of Malata's little inner bay, and now rising over the cliffs that had once been his home and the dark hills of our island itself.

Pha-thoom! I heard another boom from behind us, close enough to make my ears whine and suddenly, the ground exploded to our right. *The ship we'd attacked was still firing!*

"I got it!" Danu hissed, and I turned to see him holding out a hand in the direction of the flaming ship.

The Dead Ship stood in the same position where it had anchored itself just off of the Bone Reef, and one side was now licked by Crux's dragon fire, racing up the rounded curve of its hill to the leap hungrily to the rope.

"*E Nama Ulomo – Ulomo-Vitis...*" Danu said, and a sudden chill raced down my spine, and even shivered through the great reptilian body beneath me.

"Danu – what are you doing!" I shouted. I had seen him perform his strange witch magic before, of course, but it wasn't often. It wasn't like the magical darts of energy that the witches could summon with their staffs. This was something different, something that felt *too powerful*, like the time I had decided that I could pilot a skiff in roaring storm winds.

"*Ulomo-Vitis...*" I heard him beg, hiss, and wheedle at the Dead Ship as Crux flew – and then, to my surprise, the entire galleon of the dead began to shake and tremor.

It was rocking where it sat; not because of any wave or wind, but merely as if its blackened beams themselves didn't want to be a boat anymore, but rather wanted to be flotsam and ruin.

The entire Dead Ship wobbled backwards, shaking wildly and turning on its path.

Pha-thoom! There was another, almost petulant burst from one of the ship's side cannons, but the boat was now far wide of its original position, and I watched as the shot smashed into the reefs to the south of the island. Under Danu's will, the ship turned again, pushing toward the nearest of the other Dead

Ships and I saw his intention – drive them together, make them crash – but suddenly his powers failed him.

"No, no!" He was crying, shivering with the effort. I twisted to reach out a hand to steady him.

"It's alright, Danu, you did what you could. That was amazing!" His body was oddly clammy and cold in my arms, and he shivered as if of a fever. I remembered the witches of Sebol when we had managed to make our way into their library – they had collapsed with all of the effort of their recent magic. I didn't want that to happen to Danu.

"No, it's not all right," Danu was saying angrily. "Ohotto is out there somewhere, and if I cannot even counter her magic…"

"This magic is old and strong, little mage. Too strong for Ohotto even," Crux's wise words swum up into both of us, as the dark land swam underneath us.

Crux had flown us up the small ridge of hills and highlands that protected the southern edge of Malata, flying us away from the reach of the cannons before he turned back down the small wooded vales to the township – and into the smoke.

Somehow, the ships of the dead had managed to set fire to parts of the village itself, although I couldn't see how as there were no Dead Ships in our secluded harbor. Instead, I saw that weaving through the smokes and around the fires there were smaller forms. Raiders and others, men in dark armor – and they were fighting.

Screams swept up towards us, and I spurred Crux on, while I yet tried to steady Danu as we flew like a shot arrow over the houses. We flashed through the smoke, to see that there were Roskildean soldiers fighting my father's men – in our very streets! Quickly, I pulled one of the leather straps of dragon saddle that we had made, looping it around Danu's middle so that I could free my hands for the fight. Danu slumped forward, but he wasn't going to fall.

"How could they get on the island undetected?" I called, as I quickly took my bow from my back, selected an arrow and took aim.

"The fog." Danu shivered behind me, and I knew that what he said was true. It was that strange, unmoving fog that lay off of our north side. "Ohotto must have used the Dead Ships as a distraction – when really she was landing an invasion force of Roskildean soldiers!"

"But the Dead Ships will be firing on their own men – don't they care?" Danu said as I released my arrow.

"*Urk!*" My shot found its mark – that unprotected place between head and collarbone that few soldiers bother to cover up. The Roskildean somersaulted backwards and fell to the floor.

"I don't think Havick cares about anything." I selected another target, fired.

In the blink of an eye, we were racing out over the harbor again, towards the blockade of Dead Ships that held my people trapped. *Just like they had planned to do at Sebol*, I thought. Blockade their enemies, and then either force them to surrender or slaughter them. Clearly, Havick had chosen to do the latter.

"Scratch their bellies again?" Crux urged me, already swooping low on the waters towards the first of the Dead Ships.

"Do it," I snarled, even firing my bow up at the ranks of the dead on its decks – although the man I hit didn't even stop from picking up his crossbow and firing it after us.

Crux roared another explosion of dragon fire – but it wasn't enough to engulf the entire vessel. It clung to the front end of the ship and we were out, zigzagging low across the waters to avoid being shot. *Where were Kim and the other dragons – the ones that had stayed behind to train with their Raider partners?*

"Up ahead!" Danu shouted, and I raised my eyes to see, just in time, that we weren't alone out here on the waters. I could have sworn that there were only three or four of the Dead Ships attacking Malata – but now I saw that the seas around the Bone Reefs were scattered with more of the dark-hulled monsters.

"Five. Ten. Fifteen…?" I hastily tried to count as my father had taught me to – and then Crux was roaring and turning, angling his wings first one way to make us dive to the right, narrowly missing one of the ships of death, and then angling his wings down to the left to avoid the one that was close behind it. We crisscrossed in front and in between these boats like a crab scuttling between rocks. There were too many of them!

"Skrargh!" A roar of flame shot out as the other dragons attacked the fleet. There were Kim and Thiel, Lucalia and Retax. In the distance over the mainland, the shapes of the other four Raider dragons wheeled in a returning attack vector.

Thoom! A blast of super-heated water sprayed across me for a minute, making me cough, before I realized that the Dead Ships were firing their cannons– apparently not much caring if they were endangering each other in their attempt to shoot us!

Pheet! And then, a storm of crossbow bolts hailed upon us. A moment ago, I had felt like a vengeful deity, falling upon my enemy with all the speed that a striking dragon can offer – now I felt like a fish, caught in the killing runs of a much larger predator.

"Crux – out! Out!" I shouted, and he appeared only too happy to agree – with a single flap of his wings we shot up and over the next Dead Ship and kept on climbing and swerving as their shot followed us into the night sky.

A shriek, and something dagger-shaped and lightning-fast exploded out of the sky over our shoulder. It was Kim, with Adair and Senga on her back, and she was swooping low over the masts and sails of the Dead Ships, drawing their fire away from us. *Thank you,* I prayed silently after them, as we ascended to a higher and wider circle over the battle. This gave us a small moment to look back and down, and that was when I saw it.

The Malata township was half-burned, and now twenty or more ships of the dead had effectively crippled our fleet. There were soldiers fighting in the streets, and the undying waiting to pick us off. No matter what impressive tricks that Crux, Kim, Thiel and the other dragons and us riders might be able to pull off – we would never be able to defeat all of them with so few numbers.

"This is like the Battle for Malata all over again," I breathed in horror at Danu, remembering how at the end of last autumn, just before the winter storms had closed off the seas for the season, Havick had sent his entire armada after us. "We had only managed to fight them off because we had advance warning, and the dragons came to save us," I whispered.

"The dragons?" Danu said. "Could Crux call the dragons again?"

"Would they come? They want Ohotto, don't they?" I said.

"The fog!" Danu pointed, and I could hear his frustration with me clear in his voice. "That's an act of magic, and I bet that's Ohotto behind it! That's proof enough that she must be here?"

"I'll call," Crux growled, and he altered his approach over the island, not back to the battle in the streets, but towards the fogbank on our northern borders. His anger welled up through his body and his mind against mine. He meant to kill. And so did I.

CHAPTER 12
DANU, MAGE OF MALATA

Crux raised his head in the smoke-filled airs and *sang*. I could feel the pulse of yearning and the beat of despair in that song, and his emotions bled into mine to perfectly match my tormented heart. His song was long and ululating; not like the clicks, whistles and whirrs with which he used to communicate with the other dragons nearby – this one was more like an echoing call of an owl perhaps, or a keen of a wolf.

Below us, the dark landscape of Malata was flashing past in a blur of speed. I heard screams and shouts caught on the airs of battle, and now the roar of the other dragons – *not* the dragons from the rest of the archipelago, sadly, but the dragons that had adopted a trusted few of the Raiders.

"There's Kim! Thiel! Porax and Retax, Holstag and

Grithor, Ixyl, Viricalia and Lucalia!" Lila was shouting, pointing as the assorted motley of (mostly) young dragons rose on the smoke-filled airs. They had been harrying the Dead fleet it seems – or trying to, anyway – when Crux's call had summoned them from their efforts to join us in the attack against the magical fog – and whatever was beyond it.

"Will the other dragons come?" I called, knowing that Crux would be able to hear my words even amongst this howling wind.

'I cannot say. It is a long way, and by the time they get here – we may already have won!'

Dragons are nothing if not enthusiastic, I thought. 'Failure' didn't seem to be a word that even existed in their language.

Ahead of us, the northern part of the island was blanketed in this thick, static fog that seemed to glue itself to the hills, trees, and rocks and hang low over the waters like a blanket.

"Fly higher, my friend – I want to look down into it, let us see what we are facing!" Lila suggested, and Crux roared in agreement, powering his wings to rise up and over the fog as the other four dragons followed in our wake.

Four dragons. That would be enough to take down Ohotto, wouldn't it? Surely! I thought, but there was a sliver of doubt in the back of my mind. They were young, a few summers younger than Crux maybe – and I worried they hadn't bonded as deeply with their pirate riders as Lila and I had done with Crux. In fact, looking over my shoulder it was only Kil and

Lucalia that had their humans with them; Retax and Thiel had still not had a chance to pick up theirs.

Would that matter? Could they fight as a unit without them? I knew from the descriptions contained in the scrolls of the library that the Dragon Riders of Torvald always had two riders per dragon – is that what we needed too? Or would the young dragons follow us into battle anyway? I didn't know the answer – and now, I realized, there was only one way to find out!

"Dammit!" Lila swore as I shook my head against the headache from the magic I had so recently cast and followed her gaze to what caused her outburst.

It was the fog. It was thick and churning in the middle of the mass, dark with greys and blacks, and impossible to see into. "Crux?" I shouted. "Can you sense anything at all in there?"

The dragon twittered and whistled in unease, before snorting a little gout of soot and smoke from its nostrils. *"Nothing. The fog clouds my mind. Makes everything confusing."* Even his mental voice had lost some of the crisp-edged anger that had filled it so recently. How deeply was this fog of confusion affecting the dragons? I thought in alarm and shared a worried look with Lila, who only made a quick turn of her chin, cutting off any anxious questions that I might have.

"We have to do this. Malata is at stake. No matter what foul magics they can summon."

She was right, so I closed my eyes and tried to remember

the charm for summoning the harsh north winds, which might disperse this magical fog.

"There's people coming out of it…" I heard Lila say and tried to listen even as I tried to clear my mind at the same time.

Borealis. That was it. Borealis is the name of the north wind….

"They're wearing armor. They're not the dead…." Lila said, from somewhere far away.

Borealis Ignitis? No, I don't think that's the one. I tried to picture the scroll that Afar had me study so many years ago. The four winds that blew into the world from the four corners. North Borealis. Eastern Cumulus. The Southern Vesper…

There. The simple of the north wind – I could see it clear in my mind, and as soon as I could see it, my magic uncoiled inside of me like a leaf waking from winter.

"*Ia Boreal!*" The words ripped from my throat, but it was like it wasn't even me saying them at all. I could hear myself shouting them, chanting them over and over, but I was also not-me, looking down at myself from outside, seeing the strange, stocky young man holding a hand out to the north and screaming into the wind for it to obey him.

"Danu…?" I heard Lila's worried voice, but my eyes were still fixated on the far northern horizon. I could feel the power in me, reaching out, like lightning, jumping from my heart and down my arms to the tips of my fingers.

There was a sudden flash, and a clap of thunder from

ahead, and an answering screech from Crux below me. It was night now, so the skies were already dark, but directly to the north came a pool of black clouds that whipped the waters ahead of them.

"It worked! It actually worked!" I shouted in glee, pulling my hand down into a fist, straight at the magical fog beneath us. In response, the storm picked up speed, bearing down on the island of Malata as if it were possessed. Which I guessed that it was, in a way. By me.

"Danu – is that you?" Lila asked. She looked at me with wide eyes. She was worried. *Why was she worried?* "I am a mage!" I heard myself cry out. "Do not worry, Lila!"

Again, I felt that odd, slightly disconnected feeling of seeing myself from the outside as I shouted in joy. Was this an effect of magic? Why now? I ignored it – maybe as I grew older and my powers grew stronger, then so too did my trance-states that accompanied it. *Whatever.* All I really needed to be worried about was dispersing this enchantment of Ohotto's…

The storm swirled and howled about us, and now I could feel it plucking at my hair and my clothes. Its howl was in my ears – only now it was no longer plucking, it was raging like a torrent of air – and still, I didn't care.

"Danu – it's too strong!" I heard Lila say, but I ignored her. *What did she know of such things?* I needed strong magic to counter other magic, didn't I?

"*Danu!*"

I brought my hand down in a fist to the witch's magical

defenses below me, and the storm broke over the fog with multiple flashes of blue-white lightning.

But nothing happened.

What?

The storm was black and raging, tearing itself apart as it swept over the fog bank – but perversely, in a vision that defied all sense and reason, the fog bank stayed exactly where it was. It was like those strange experiments that I had seen Afar do with different potions and oils, where a layer of oil of a different color could sit atop water, or, if she was really careful, where different bands of colored liquid could sit one on top of the other without mixing – completely impossible to the eye, and yet there all the same. That was how the storm raged over the fog bank – without mixing.

"What's wrong!? What did I say wrong?" My anger flared. I could still feel the flush of power leaping from my heart to my fist, and so I called again, my voice harsh and breaking this time.

"Ia Borealis!" I smashed my fist down.

There was another scatter-flash of bracket lightning, and suddenly my cheeks were stung by sharp needles of hail as the storm broke its full power all around us.

"Danu – stop this!" Lila cried, but no, I couldn't. I had to defeat Ohotto. *I had to be the one to defeat Ohotto*. I was a mage, and this would be my test…

"Ssssss…" There was a rising sound on the airs, though, a hiss that came and went with the wind, but some trick of the storm meant that I could hear it clearly now. A low, hissing chant, like the sound of voices heard in another room – and it was coming from below us. As I looked in fury at how they defied me down there, I saw changes in the churning greys of the fog bank in between the biting storm winds. Its surface was boiling and bubbling, changing hue and texture like water boiling over.

With a sudden *snap!* the fog started rising *into* the storm that I had created. Wisps of its tendrils scattered away instantly, and I felt vindicated by that – but the larger bulk of the grey mass kept on rising – and then a strange thing happened to my storm. The winds died down, the lightning grew less and less frequent, and the dark thunderheads that I had summoned slowly sank – and mixed with the fog bank.

"You're making it grow, you idiot!" Lila shouted as I looked in horror at what was happening below me.

"By the Sacred Airs…" I whispered. She was right. The northern storm that I summoned had somehow added to the fog bank's bulk, making this large, boiling mess of cloud that obscured everything underneath it – and it was now spreading across half of the island of Malata, and the Bone Reef outside.

"*Sanctis!*" I called, summoning on every cantrip and trick that I knew to dispel my own magic. *"Begone, in the name of the Sacred Elements!"* I shouted, but it was no good – whatever magic I managed to invoke, all it did was feed the dark magic below.

CHAPTER 13
LILA AND CRUX, FIGHTING

"Lila – I'm sorry, but there's nothing I can do!" Danu wavered behind me as I half-turned to try and shake some sense into him. I wanted to slap him out of it – but I didn't. In fact, I didn't even shake him, because he was as white as a sheet, and even his lips had taken on an ugly bluish hue, his stare wide and raving. He looked sick to my eyes, as sick as that strange fever that had started this year for us.

"He is sick, but he doesn't know it. The magic is too strong for him," Crux snarled into my mind, and he sounded annoyed. Not as annoyed as I was, I thought grimly.

"You idiot! What did you do?" I shouted at Danu, to see him blink and his hands starting to tremor. Oh great. Now he was going to have one of his seizures, as well, I thought critically – before instantly feeling bad for thinking that about my friend.

Danu was my friend, of course – but sometimes I wished that I could give him a good solid slap.

But he doesn't know how strong his magic is, I reminded myself. He's as much a victim in this as we are. I tried to be sensible – which was damn near miraculous, given that we were a few hundred meters up on a dragon who was only barely managing to stay airborne in the midst of an evil, magical storm summoned by a powerful witch.

Right. Plan B.

"Take us down!" I called to Crux. "If we can't get into it from above, we'll see what good we can do on the ground." On home soil. My territory, I snarled at the storm below me.

But where were the other dragons? I looked around in anger and alarm. I could see the shapes of Kim and Retax, but I couldn't find Lucalia or Thiel. Had they been blown off course by the magical storm?

"I cannot hear them. All of this fish gut magic!" Crux snapped into the air, as he turned just slightly, and suddenly the winds were hurtling us through the air. We were in danger of overshooting the island entirely, but I could feel the mighty strength in Crux's wings as he fought to hold them steady as he sliced and turned through the gales, approaching the land.

"Danu – brace," I called, clinging onto Crux's tines as I always did. He came in low and hard to the scrubby fields and orchards that sat behind the township and my parents' mansion house. I felt the jolt as he clawed at rocks, trees, and earth, before skipping over a small paddock containing a terrified donkey and stumbling through a small orchard that had once grown some very excellent pippin apples.

I was thrown and bounced and jostled before we came to a stop at the far end of the orchard. The winds were still howling all around us, and Crux was daintily taking his front claw out of a centuries-old hedge and swishing his tail back and forth like an angry cat. There goes the last of the pippins, I thought, at the sound of splintering and breaking.

"Halt in the name of the king!" someone bellowed, and I saw that there were already soldiers scrambling down the sides of the low rise and into the path of destruction left by Crux's awkward landing. They had the small, rounded metal helmets favored by the Roskildeans, as well as breastplates and greaves. In their hands, they carried long tridents with wickedly sharp points. It looked as though Havick had been doing his own preparations over winter, I thought, as their captain hastily ordered his men and women to fan out into a wide semi-circle and approach as one might an angered boar.

"You think you know how to take down a dragon? Who wants to die first?" I jeered at them, hoping to at least give them some pause as I turned to check on Danu.

He was still attached to the dragon, thank the waters, but he wouldn't be for much longer. He was twitching and groaning and had slumped between two tines of the dragon's spine nubs. "Danu?" I hissed, this time *actually* shaking his shoulder. "Danu – wake up!" But it was no good, he was groaning and shivering in pain or illness, just as he did every time that he tried to control his magic.

"Easy men – no heroes. On my command…" the Roskildean captain said, as they crunched through the destroyed orchard, their tridents lowered.

"Skrrrrr…" Crux lowered his head on his long serpentine neck and growled at them. I could feel the murderous rage inside of him, I knew it because I felt it too.

But I couldn't fight with Danu like this. And the skies above us were howling with black storm winds. Would we even get airborne again if we decided to flee?

"I am not fleeing this time. I came for blood. And blood I shall have!" Crux burst into my mind, shocking me with the force of his rage.

Time's up, Lila, I told myself, as I knew that I would rather not argue with a vengeful dragon. There was only one thing that I could do with Danu if I didn't want him either to get spiked with a trident or thrown off in the melee. Grabbing him by the scruff of his cloak, I yanked him off of the dragon's back and threw him into the still thick part of the hedge below.

"Just don't step on him!" I called desperately to Crux.

"I have never trodden on anything that I didn't intend to squash," Crux snarled back.

"You're not filling me with confidence here, big guy," I muttered.

"Never mind confidence – fight!" Crux lunged forward

suddenly, his muscles exploding forward like the time that I had seen one of the wildcats of the northern islands take down a mouse. It was all I could do to hang on as his snout grabbed three of the tridents that were facing him, and quickly jerked his head up. One of the trident's metal shafts bent and the warrior fell back to the ground with a garbled yell, whilst the other two were stupid enough to hang on and were thrown some five meters in the air and over the heads of their fellows.

But the captain was a wily one, it seemed. As soon as Crux had raised his head to fling the attacking warriors, the captain had darted in with the trident, thrusting it forward.

"No-!" I tried to swing myself out with my scimitar – but it all happened so fast, and I was already too far away to catch the tines before they punched into Crux's scales.

The Phoenix dragon recoiled suddenly, raising up on his hind legs.

"Now! In for the belly!" the captain shouted at his fellows. *How had he known that was what Crux would do?* I had a split second of clarity when I realized that he must have known that an injured dragon would rear up – but how could he?

"Crux!" I screamed, but it appeared that the vicious Phoenix dragon already had his own plan to deal with the Roskildean soldiers. His shoulders flexed, and he spewed a jet of flame straight at them. It was like the difference between walking in the cold night outside to suddenly walking into a room with a roaring fire. The heat of the dragon's breath hit me like a wave – but not as badly as it hit the soldiers in front of us! They were thrown back by the blast, and their screams turned into wails as Crux kept moving his flame over them – completely destroying them *and* the orchard which once had its fine pippins.

I couldn't watch. Even though these foul men had tried to hurt my most beloved dragon, it was still a terrible way to die, Suddenly, all of my murderous rage evaporated in an instant. I just wanted this battle to be over, and I wanted these people off of my island.

"It is done. They are gone." Crux dropped back down onto his front paws, his chest moving in and out like a bellow. He hadn't killed them all, of course, but he had decimated their numbers and there were several running for their lives out of the orchard. Crux did not appear eager to chase them, even though I still felt his anger burning strong within him.

"You cannot even eat them," Crux moaned, before adding in a way of explanation. *"Too much metal."*

"Danu? Danu – you have to wake up!" I shook him again, earning only a pained groaning sound from the acolyte of the witches for my efforts.

I had him laid out on the small bit of un-trammeled sward left and tried to do my best to examine him. It was no good, of course – it was a magical illness that I was sure that he was suffering from. I had seen it earlier with the West Witches of the Haunted Isle, and now, in Danu.

Above us, the winds still howled, and the fog was still slowly moving over my home, completely cutting off all sight of what lay beyond it. I could see its tendrils reaching the top of the rise of hills and trees that lay just above us. Any moment now, it would be upon us – and then we would all be lost. I could hear screams and the clash of blades from the township behind. I had no idea how the battle to save the island was going, but I did not expect it to be going well.

"C'mon, Danu. I need you!" I said in exasperation. As much as I had been annoyed at him for summoning that storm, he hadn't known that the magic of the evil witches would be stronger. He had only been trying to help…

And I need all of the help that I can get right now.

The ground shook as Crux bounded back to our side, raising his head gingerly and holding it slightly cocked in an awkward gesture. I could see thick gobbets of green blood running down the side of his scales where the captain had spiked him.

"The enemy is near, but they dare not approach." Crux informed me, looking first one way, and then another to screech and snarl at the distant shadows.

"The enemy is everywhere," I grumbled, trying one more time to shake Danu to wakefulness – but it was no good. "Great. We're going to have to carry him."

"Why didn't you say?" Crux deftly leaned in – despite the

fact that he was hurt and picked up the young mage with one of his front paws and held him carefully close to his chest, as you might hold an egg.

"But you won't be able to fight!" I said.

"A dragon can always fight." Crux peeled back his scaled lips to reveal his rows of wickedly sharp teeth, his canines each almost a meter long.

I'm sure you can, I thought, nodding. "Okay then. Let's see what's happening out there." I drew my sword and led the way out of the orchard, into the practice courtyard where my mother had taught me to fight. I could clearly see the Town House where I had grown up just a little way above us. There were sparks and glints of metal in its grounds, and I heard distant screams and shouts.

"Defend the perimeter! On our northern side!" A rough shout met my ears from up ahead.

It seems that the enemy had even managed to attack there as well, and, seeing no better alternative – I pointed towards my old home. "There," I said, and set off at a run, with the bounding, now on three-legs dragon crashing behind me.

"Crux!" I shrieked just in time and felt the wave of heat pass over my head at the knot of Roskildean soldiers that had been charging down through my mother's practice yard.

Their screams were quick and futile as the fireball incinerated them, and we were turning and running again.

The grounds of the old Town House had once been formal gardens, back when the old Kings of Torvald had outposts and governors out here. But that was a long time ago now, and since my mother and father had taken over Malata, they had either left the wisteria, lavenders and laburnums to grow ragged and wild, or they had turned the wide precinct of land into training yards and practice areas. My mother Pela was, of course, the rightful architect and champion of all of this – as she was the best duelist on the island, and it is through these courts that we ran, me dodging or jumping over the wooden sties that separated one 'court' from another, and the dragon just crashing through them behind.

There. The old willow trees, whose branches scratched at my window on the second floor. It stood at the end of the courts and right beside the little cobbled area where mother hauled out the washing every day and drew water from the well. There was a knot of Raiders congregating there, clearly re-grouping from the attack.

"Thank the waters – it's one of the dragons!" One of the Raiders hailed Crux as we ran up. It was Costa, one of my father's trusted quartermasters with his eyepatch and his short dark salt and pepper hair.

"It's me, Lila, as well," I gasped, clasping them in a quick Raider's embrace. There were barely ten assorted men and women here, no one seriously wounded, but all bearing the signs of a night already spent fighting for their lives. Crux set Danu down carefully at the foot of the old willow, and he groaned in discomfort as I took off my cloak and rucked it under his head.

"Are we pleased to see you." Costa nodded, flicking his eyes up to where Crux was rubbing the side of his wounded neck against the willow. "And don't get me wrong, but we are *really* glad to see that dragon of yours."

"Well, that's what we're here for," I said, nodding to the house. "My mother? Father?"

"Your mother is in the house, treating people with the healers, your father…" Costa frowned, his brow glistening with sweat as he nodded in the other direction, towards the town.

"What, Costa?"

"He was down there, trying to fight to keep the harbor so that we could launch what was left of our galleons."

"Useless," I said with a sharp shake of my head. "The Dead Ships have blockaded the Bone Reefs. As soon as he gets a ship out of there, it'll be blown to smithereens."

"He won't give up his home harbor, Lila," Costa said urgently. "He's given everything for it. He told us to retreat here, to save what people we could and defend your mother."

"I'm sure my mother can defend herself," I said, although I was also thankful that this team of tough men and women were guarding her back. My mind was already decided. I knew where I had to go. In fact, of either of them, it was Mother whom I was *the least* worried about – she had always been better at fighting and strategy than Father, who was a pirate through and through. *He's run off to defend the harbor, hasn't he? Thinking that a sword and a strong arm can solve everything.*

"I'm sorry, but I cannot stay to help you here – I need to find my father," I said.

Costa grimaced in dislike of my decision, but it seemed as though he could see why I had come to it. "Well, with that dragon of yours, you should be able to get down there," he said.

"No. Crux is staying here, with you," I said. I knew that Crux would only draw the fire of the Dead Ships once we had got to the harbor.

"No! Anywhere my human-sister goes, Crux must go!" Crux suddenly snarled.

"Crux, please…" I turned to him, moving quickly to his side. His neck was still glistening with green, but the flow of his blood had at least slowed considerably. "You are already injured, and I need the *very best* to defend my mother and Danu, too. Who better than a brave, fierce Phoenix dragon to do that?" I said because what little I had learnt of the ways of dragons is that they liked to be praised.

"Well, you do have a point. But I still don't like it." Crux lowered his snout to me and let me throw my arms around it in our traditional gesture.

"I don't like it either," I confided in him. "But sometimes we only have bad choices left."

He made a sound like a huff, but I didn't know if he was agreeing or rebuking me. Either way, he did not try to follow as I stepped backwards, and instead, he went gingerly to stand over Danu down at the foot of the old willow tree.

"Don't die, wave-rider." His words swam into my thoughts. *"I will be here,"* I heard him say, and I knew, in his strange dragon way, that he meant that he would be here where he had agreed to be by the tree, as well as *here* in my mind with me at all times. For some reason, I found tears pooling into my eyes.

"I will return," I promised, and turned to race into the storm-filled, magic-stricken night.

CHAPTER 14
LILA AND THE CHIEF

The streets of my hometown were as I had never seen them before. Smoke swirled above the roofs of the wooden houses – those that were still standing, that is – but most were only flames and blackened rubble. And our boats were currently scuttled and sinking in the harbor, their wreckage below making me grit my teeth. *No. This cannot be. This shouldn't be!*

Why had hardly any of the Raider ships gotten out of the bay? We had around-the-clock watches. We had fast boats usually out in the seas around Malata.

Was it the fog? A wave of sickness washed through me. *Had the witch obscured her attack with that accursed sea fog?*

The ships sat in the harbor like broken teeth. It would be hard to describe what this feeling was to anyone who wasn't a

Raider. Our ships were as important to us as our houses—more important, probably. I had as many childhood memories aboard the *Fang,* the *Ariel,* and the *Claw* as I had in my mother's practice courts.

Where were we going to go? How could we raid?

There was Skua's Cove, on the far eastern end of the island: a place where we always kept a few fat-bellied boats in case of such an emergency. But they weren't fighting boats, and we had never thought that we would need them.

Thoom! There was another blast and the ground shook underfoot. The Dead fleet were still shelling the harbor from the entrance at the Bone Reefs. Looking up, past the smoke and blackened timbers I could see winged shapes swooping down amidst the uncanny ships. Thiel—I recognized his blue and striking shape – and the other green? That must be Lucalia. They had decided to try and fend off the fleet. *Fall back!* I flung the thought desperately at them, unsure whether it was wise for them to draw the ships' fire or plain suicide.

Ten young dragons, five hundred or so warriors, I thought in dismay. If we could just get everyone onto the boats, then we might have a chance to escape. Except there were no ships. The pier was empty, and the harbor too. Or, not exactly empty, I realized. But there was no way to get anyone aboard our boats.

No. This can't be happening. Malata was my home! It was the only home that I knew, and despite the revelations of last year – that I was born to the line of Roskilde, that I had *another* family of peoples to the north of the Western Archipelago, *this* place was still the only home that I could feel any kinship for.

There, I saw the ruins of the grand old tavern of the *Drunken Sailor*, already a half-ruined, baroque pleasure boat permanently docked at the side of the warehouses, when my father's father first claimed this place and had since become the unofficial after-raiding party for many of the Raiders here. I had learned the complicated steps of the Captain's Jig inside that building; I had laughed at Finibar, our resident minstrel (well, the best singer and lutist that we had, anyway) many times; I had fallen asleep curled up beside its wide stone hearth. Now it was just another half-building. It's three stories must have made it an easy target for the Dead fleet.

Where will we go? I thought, and the image of the Fulani refugees that we had picked up on our travels came to me, and how their haunted eyes had met us from their ramshackle floating platform. *Would the Raiders share the same fate?* I wondered as my steps slowed and I cataloged the devastation around me. There wasn't a street that was untouched by fire or bloodshed. It would take years to rebuild all of this to what it had been – and years that we Raiders didn't have. We had always lived a frugal existence, harsh sea-salt lives that were punctuated by the influx of a rich raiding success. We might have gold and coin and supplies a few times a year – but never enough to expand, to build, to become something other than what we were: a small island nation, clinging onto the edges of much greater world powers.

This is it, isn't it? I paused, the fires of the town cleaning my vision to see what it was that was happening. *It is over.* I was witnessing the demise of Malata, and the demise of the Free Raiders of the Western Isles.

Selfishly, I bit back my voice to prevent a sob of remorse – and, I had to admit – a good deal of guilt and self-loathing. *Why hadn't I been strong enough to save this place? Why hadn't my dreams of the Dragon Raiders helped save us?*

That was what my dreams had been about, for years – to befriend the dragons as the wild Queen Saffron had done, and then to turn the Sea Raiders into a force that could shake the Western Islands forever.

Looking at the ruins of my hometown, I was sure that all I had achieved was to plunge Malata into disaster.

"Lila! Psst!" A voice from one of the sides of a blackened building, and I looked to see that it was Shep, one of the hands of the *Fang*. What was he doing out here? Why wasn't he on the *Fang*? I thought, before realizing that I was being stupid – as the *Fang* itself was clearly visible, its prow sticking high in the air over our small pier as its aft had been scuttled.

"Shep – where are the others?" I hissed, running over to him.

"No time!" He looked worried, eyes wide, sparing a glance behind him in the alley. "They're everywhere."

"They? Which ones? The Roskildeans?" I said, readjusting my grip on my scimitar.

Shep looked, if anything, haunted as he turned to me. "Yeah them – and the other ones."

The dead. The dead must have come ashore. I remembered the way that they had taken arrow shot and sword blow on the witches' Haunted Isle and had kept on loping forward on legs that had long since wasted to sinew and bone. As my stomach turned to ice, I found a curious sort of determined calm settle in its place. *This man here is scared. He doesn't know what is happening to his home, and he doesn't know where his captain is.* We Raiders might be a disagreeable, argumentative bunch – but unlike much popular belief, we had a great deal of respect for the chain of command. If our captain was strong, then we could jump over gunwales and into raging storm waters for them. If they were weak…

"Listen to me, Shep," I said, finding that same sharp tone of command that my father had mastered so well. "You can kill them. The dead. But you need to do so with fire. Dragon fire is the best, but normal fire will do if you throw enough of it at them."

Shep looked at me seriously, as if trying to memorize my every word.

"They can die, Shep. They can die." I reassured him, and I saw him mumble the words to himself, repeating them as he nodded.

"Fine." He nodded, brushing the sweat off of his brow.

"Now listen to me – where is my father? Where are the first mates and the captains?" I barked at him quickly, not giving him time to think and to despair.

He stared at me blankly, as if he couldn't process what I'd asked.

"Shep—think! Where did you last see them?" I commanded him.

"Down by the docks, sir," he replied instinctively. "Your father was getting Captain Lasarn off the *Fang*. He was trying to protect the village, to save time for…"

"For Pela up at the Town House," I cut in. *That made sense why there were guards up there.* "Good man, Shep. Good man. Now – I want you to grab a torch – a burning timber will do, and make your way up to the Town House, you hear me?" I said.

The man nodded, licking his lips.

"Tell them that my orders are to fall back to Skua's Cove, prepare any boats that you can," I said sharply.

"Aye, Lila, but – doesn't that mean…?" Shep said awkwardly, and I wondered whether it would be sensible just to shout at him. *But no, this time the man deserves an explanation.* He knew as well as any Raider what my orders would mean. Skua's Cove was little more than a stream outlet on the furthest eastern side of the island. We barely used it for anything other than storing a few boats, and we always had a provisional plan that, should everything go terribly, then we could escape to Skua's Cove, load up where and what we could, and leave the island.

That was what I was advising. The evacuation of Malata.

"Yes, Shep. You heard me. Get to Skua's Cove. Load up. We do what we Raiders have always done – we sail fast and hard out of trouble, regroup, and decide where to attack next."

"Aye-aye, sir," Shep said, and it must have been the tone in my voice and my sharp glare that made him turn so quickly and race back up towards the Town House at the top of the village. *'When the storm is high and blood is falling,'* I heard the old advice of my father to me, whom he wanted to be his first mate and eventually, Captain of the *Ariel* after him, *'... then it doesn't matter how great your plan is, or how clever you are – you are fighting a war with the fear in every man and woman's heart who serves under you. You have to win THAT battle first, and then you can win THE battle.'* That was what he had advised. Give your crew something to be inspired by, give them a plan to believe in – even if it was a terrible one.

And so far, my plan for the rescue of Malata was to abandon it – how much more terrible could that be?

"If your prey is faster, stronger, and quicker than you – then it is stupid to keep on hunting." Crux suddenly breathed his soot-laded thoughts into my mind. I could feel his approval of my decision to abandon the island.

"You think?" I whispered, taking a ragged breath as I

chose the best route down to the harbor that would keep me out of sight.

"I do. We dragons are taught when young to never die needlessly. The sky wants us to sing within it, the sun wants us to welcome it. Why throw your life away if you cannot win?" he said.

"Well, I guess you have a point…" I thought, before suddenly wondering if he was talking about me, and what I was doing here and now. I would have asked him if he thought my mission to save my father was suicide – but before I had a chance to formulate my thoughts, there was a clank of armor and the stamp of feet.

"Hide, wave-rider!" Crux informed me, and I slid my back down the wall, until I was crouching in the soot and slurry of the floor.

"This way!" I heard a man growl, his voice guttural and clearly out-of-breath. "Bloody fiends – why don't they stop firing?" his' voice muttered, just as a group of men in the breastplates and helmets of the Roskildean soldiers ran down the avenue towards the harbor. In their hands they held long swords and shields.

I decided to follow them.

I knew these streets better than they did, and, even though their route was simple, I knew which alleys would take me around which warehouses and keep me out of sight even as I rejoined their path. It meant racing down narrow spaces between the broken-open and smoking buildings, pausing, turning and racing back, but I was just in time to catch snatches of the soldiers' arguments.

"…almost there…"

"Quick – that accursed witch's mist is almost on us…"

At that phrase, I pulled back into the shadows, looked around to see that the man was indeed right. The thick blanket of fog was starting to spill down into the township itself, flowing slowly through the streets and entirely swallowing the buildings in its grey, lifeless embrace. It gave me the creeps.

"If I have to spend another minute on this island…"

"Shut it, Venner!"

"No – these 'new fighters' give me the creeps!" I saw one of the soldiers at the back argue. There must be only five or so in total of these soldiers. But that was still too many for me to kill alone.

"I will come." Crux leapt into my mind joyfully.

Thooom! Another whistling cannon blast sounded in the streets around me, and a plume of rock and timber dust flew high into the air.

"No!" I hissed into the night. "You are hurt. I need you looking after Danu – please!"

I could feel Crux's resentment, and I knew that he *almost* disobeyed my wishes then and there, but he didn't. *"As you wish, wave-rider."* He was sulking, but I didn't care. Better a sulking dragon than a dead one.

"We got 'em! That big brute and his gang!" One of the Roskildean soldiers said from up ahead as I turned to run back down the alley, climb through the broken window of one of the already half-demolished dock warehouses and clambered over the debris of torn sailcloth and ropework until I could see out onto the large harbor area just outside.

And I could see my father outside, kneeling on the floor of the stone docks.

My father was a large man. Not tall, but large in that all-round stocky way that had made him jokingly referred to as "the Barrel" when the crew thought that he wasn't listening. Of course, he always knew, but he encouraged their jokes, knowing that it was another sign of their affection for him. At the moment, his large shape dominated the collection of other Raider prisoners that the Roskildeans had gathered at the front of the harbor.

I saw on one side of him the much older and a little smaller Captain Lasarn – he had an eyepatch and one leg, and it looked as though he was holding his side where a large blood stain was. I could see the sailing masters there, too, as well as three first mates from various of our boats, and a handful of other senior hands. They all were sitting, collapsed on the floor or kneeling as my father was in rough circle, as a team of Roskildean soldiers had their lowered steel tridents encircling them.

Oh, Father – no! I almost cried out but bit my tongue to stop myself from doing so. *You don't help anyone by getting killed* – that was another piece of my father's favorite wisdom. *And hadn't Crux told me the same thing just now?*

The soldiers surrounding them probably outnumbered the Raiders two-to-one, and most of the Raiders appeared wounded or crushed in some more spiritual sense. But still, if I could get weapons to them then they might just be able to fight their way clear. We were a tough bunch – even when wounded. It must be this fierce reputation that we Raiders had that was inspiring the soldiers to treat their hostages as if they were dangerous animals. They had already kicked all of their weapons into a pile behind them, and they maintained a two-meter trident-length distance between my people and themselves.

Cowards, I thought. *Why not face us in battle, like real men?*

I felt useless, and out-of-place. I should be in there, next to my father, even if it meant that I would also have to be a captive.

"Where are we taking them?" one of the guarding soldiers was saying to the newly arrived ones. I saw that one of them – a man with a peaked and rimmed helmet as opposed to the rounded ones of his fellow waved his hand for silence.

"We're not taking them anywhere yet. My orders are to hold these prisoners and wait."

"Wait for what?" the previous 'Venner' who had been arguing said, earning a shove by one of his fellows.

"Wait?" one of the guarding trident-soldiers said in alarm. "The bloody undead are shelling the harbor!"

"But have they hit any of you? *No,*" their pointed-headed captain said. "No. Because maybe their aim behind a gun is better than the lot of you! We *wait.*" The captain spared another look at the ominous gathering of black-hulled ships just a few hundred feet out. His wary glance told me that he shared his men's fears, despite his command.

"And anyway – if *you* want to be the one to go explain to those hags that you've got a better plan, then, by all means, go and do it…"

Hags… Does he mean there's more than one witch we have to worry about? I thought there was only Ohotto.

Whomever he had meant, the trident-bearing soldier did not seem to be in any hurry whatsoever to take up his suggestion. So instead, they waited as the battle continued out over the troubled waters.

"Skreeykh!" I heard the cries of the dragons and saw a sudden jet of crimson from the Green – *Lucalia* – and hit one of the boats. Thiel, too, turned to add his own flames to hers.

"That's it!" I whispered into the dark. It was clear from several smoking vessels that they had already tried to set fire to the boats, but the blackened hulls seemed to be oddly resistant to flame. I wondered if this was more of the witch's strange protections or just some quality of the undead fleet. I might never know – but that didn't matter as I saw that their concentrated fire was enough to take a hold, burning up the sails and the masts of their chosen taken and causing the masts to fall back onto their boats.

Maybe that was the answer, I thought. We have to attack them one at a time? Using dragons? But that would take forever, wouldn't it, with the few dragons that we had at our disposal?

Where were the others? I thought reaching for Crux inside my mind to ask him.

Where are your kin, dragon-brother? Why are they taking so long? I thought at the dragon-shaped space in my mind, the place where *his* mind began.

Nothing.

What?

I reached for it again, only for the sensation of dragoness, the feeling of reptilian charm and ever-hot, almost boiling heat – but I couldn't find it. I could only pull up a childish picture of dragons colored in ink and wax that I had made as a child, or the memories of his great shining eyes as he looked at me.

Something was wrong. This wasn't right, was it? Usually, as soon as I pushed towards him in my mind, I would be able to feel that essential dragon nature in just the same way when you walk out of doors on a sunny summer's day you *know* that it is summer. The sensation and the thought of it were the same. But now? I couldn't feel him, his living, fiery mind against mind. All I could find were *my* memories and impressions of him.

"Crux?" I whispered. "What's wrong…?" I was already halfway up from my crouch behind a big coil of rope when I froze. What did I know about dragons, really? And – *what did Danu call it? A dragon bond, that was it* - what did I know of dragon bonds, really? Maybe when a dragon is injured it draws back from your mind, and Crux was injured, wasn't he? There were loads of times when I couldn't hear him inside of my thoughts – what if this is just one of those times?

No. My heart knew, instinctively. Even in those times that Crux, either because of his short-temper, stubbornness, or maybe just because of the fact that he wanted to be alone, pulled back from my thoughts – I could still *feel* his dragoness at my side there.

But now…? It was like I had never found a friend in him, nor bonded as I had. It was as if I was alone.

"Good." A voice broke my worry, and it was the sort of voice that made me freeze to the spot. It was cold and full of sighs, and it made my bones ache as if I had spent three days in the freezing waters of the far north.

"You have them," the voice repeated, and I saw that the soldiers in front of me were pulling back, some stumbling, clearly as stricken numb by fear as I was.

Who is that? I almost screamed. *What is that?*

I managed to force my knees back down into the shadows

once more, despite every muscle and bone in my body not wanting to move at all. I could hear my heart hammering in my chest with fear – but why? It was only a voice, wasn't it?

I looked to see that in my moment of agitation over Crux and my connection, I hadn't seen that the witch's fog had almost inundated the town. It was thick at the edges of the stone docks – creeping closer to the ruined door of my own warehouse, and, when I spared a look back through my hiding place to the window at the far end, then yes, I could see that it was thick with grey-white fog out there too.

For some reason, I didn't want to step into that fog at all – and yet I knew that I had to. *And I have to do it with the others out there...* I turned back toward the horrible events outside.

The fog was shredding over the waters and the pier, and flooding out from between the buildings, forming a natural sort of clearing amongst the ruins. The Roskildeans were falling back from it, reaching the clearer airs in barely-contained shock and panic, as, from the densest fog walls, and nearest to me stepped a group of figures.

They were the dead.

They were like the dead that we had encountered on Sebol, the fog clinging and wisping around their cold and pale forms. But they were solid enough, I thought, hearing the large, calf-length leather boot of the nearest one stamp on the harbor stones as he trod forward.

These ones were much more graceful than the others, though, I could see. The other dead that we had encountered had been quick enough – but a little awkward, as if their dead flesh wouldn't quite obey their wills, or they were still unused to it. These dead were also in better condition than the others that we had fought, too. Their pale skin, such as it was, was desiccated and drawn back, but they had no ugly tears or dried-up wounds across their bodies. Their clothes, although strange, did not bear the hallmarks of having been rotting in some grave-pit or at the bottom of the sea for however long.

These ones are chiefs or captains of their kind, I thought. Who would have thought that the dead have their own captains and leaders?

Instead of the usual rags and massacred fare, these ones wore strange garb indeed. Their boots were made of a rough sort of tan brown calf skin, thick with straps securing it to their legs. Their breeches and shirts were of a rough linen, not like the finer cottons that we traded for heavily in these islands – and they each had cloaks. *No, fur pelts,* I thought, *that is what those things are called.* I could see two that were a mottled color, another that was grey and brindle, and the final was heavy and white, with long hairs. I didn't even know what the name was for half of those animals – but I knew they did not originate from the islands.

The one who had spoken was blond, with a pale, squarish face and piercing blue eyes. Not milky-white with death. These eyes were steady and as cold as the sea could be, and his wiry fair beard was thick and long. "You will halt, there."

This one whispered, but his voice carried easily to the living Roskildean soldiers.

The soldiers seemed to need no other invitation to go no nearer to their allies that they obviously feared, and they turned their heads to avoid even looking at them, leaving my father and my people at the mercy of these strange dead.

The Dead fleet had stopped firing, I suddenly noticed. When did that happen? It felt as though it must have happened at the very same time these undead chieftains had emerged out of the murk. Could they send orders to their fleet without raising their voices? I thought and then realized – if *these* were the captains of the dead, then I might have a chance to kill them.

No. Ridiculous, my fear said to me. There were four of them and only one of me. How could I do it? The dead don't die easily.

But they can die, I remembered my words to Shep. I needed fire. I looked around me – but there was nothing, and already this leader of the dead was stalking closer to where my father stared at him with malice and proud determination.

"You are their chief?" the dead man whispered.

Lasarn and the other prisoners flinched, looking toward the Roskildean soldiers, who still had their tridents lowered at them. I knew the old man so well that I could almost voice his thoughts: were the soldiers so scared of their own allies that they could be overwhelmed by unarmed, defenseless pirates?

"Who are you, and what are you doing on Malata?" my

father spat back at him, and I felt the fire of pride. My foster-father wasn't even going to give them the courtesy of answering their questions, but instead, demand his own.

This answer seemed to please the dead man, as he laughed in small, breathy jerks. "You have so much spirit. So much fire, I like that." He breathed once more. "I used to be like you, once. I used to think that if only I shouted loud enough, then the whole world would listen."

My father glared at him, managing to somehow appear bored.

Fire! I thought, casting around again. Was there anything? *Anything* in here? But this warehouse had been a place for storing rope and sail – not an ammunitions cache, and not even the painting shed, with its turpentines and spirits. I couldn't immediately see anything, and every second I looked took me away from what was happening to my father.

"Maybe you are not the chief, maybe this one is…" The dead man cocked his head towards Chief Lasarn. It was an easy assumption to make; Lasarn was the eldest of the group. He was still well-muscled, with gold teeth and gold rings on his hands. His eyes were also defiant and full of hate.

The dead man moved suddenly as fast as a striking shark. *Pow!* He had stepped forward and one of his hands was clamped over Lasarn's face. One of his cold, white hands. I could see the old leather of the man's shirt, and an ancient silver torque with some strange designs on it glint from the distant light of burning buildings. And then Lasarn screamed.

"*Aiiii!*" Lasarn shrieked and coughed, but it was quick, and whatever the dead man was doing to him it was all over in an instant.

"Get off him!" my father snarled, jumping up from his kneeling position – but before he could get into position one of the other dead – the one wearing the long, grey and brindle furred pelt had seized him by the wrists and held him fast. This other one had gloves on, or perhaps they didn't have the same powers as their strange chief, and so my father did not suffer the same fate as Captain Lasarn.

Father! I opened and closed my mouth but didn't make a sound. *I need fire, dammit! Fire!* I crabbed backwards into the warehouse, determined to find something that would cause a spark, something that would work against these foul beings, and that I could use to rescue my people.

There was a crumpling thump from outside, and the prisoners were wailing and shouting.

"What did you do to him?"

"Lasarn's dead!"

"He looks dried out – like he sucked the life right out of him!"

"Monsters!"

The shouts were rising until the dead chief snarled a sudden shout. It was like listening to an iceberg if it could scream.

"Silence! I am Jarl Lars Oldhorn, the Bloodhammer of Berrusk," the man stated proudly, and it echoed strangely in the fog. "I have fought men and I have fought dragons. I have fought creatures in the far north of this world that have yet to be named, and I have died, and yet am alive once more!"

I froze in my search. Something in his words made me want to curl up and cry, to pretend that this was all a bad dream – but it wasn't.

Move, Lila – move! I forced my hands to start pushing aside sailcloth for the equipment cabinets underneath. *Please, if only there was a flint in there…* I prayed as the litany of the dead 'Jarl' continued behind me.

"Know this, people of the sea: When I ruled the far mountains to the north of here, I had heard of these islands. *Fierce,* this place was called. *Too dangerous,* the other Jarls claimed. So in that, you may take some pride at least – if you like boasting of scare stories!"

I ransacked the first cabinet only finding old rope-splicing tools.

"My people have been brought here, and I find that the people of the islands are not fierce and dangerous. They are weak! They run and hide! I thought that the Raiders, at least, the ones I had heard so much about in my second life under the stars would be worthy opponents – but look at you! You have allied yourself with dragons!" I could hear the disgust in his voice, even back here in the warehouse.

"It is such a shame…" Jarl Lars Oldhorn's voice was heavy with disappointment. "Maybe in your next life, you too will understand what I mean…"

I heard a gasp, and then a gargled shout – not just from my father, but from all of the captured men. There was the sound of coughing and shouting—the same sounds as had come from Lasarn and yet different for mingled within them was the deep tenor I recognized as my father's voice. This time I did cry out.

"Father – no!" Seizing my scimitar up, I ran for the other end of the warehouse, uncaring if I could hurt the dead with it or not—

The scene that met my eyes made me stumble, freeze in dismay. My father lay on the floor, his face turned away from me, but his large barrel-like size was gone now, strangely. He looked shrunken and smaller – and standing over him was this undead Jarl Lars pulling on a leather glove over pale hands. The other dead chiefs stood over the bodies of the others – the first mates, the other captains, the sailing masters and senior hands. Each and every one of them had suffered the same fate as if their life had been sucked from their bodies.

"*NO!*" I screamed, brandishing my sword.

Lars' cold blue eyes flickered upwards to pierce mine –

And that was when a dragon took the roof from my building.

"*SKREYACH!*" the Phoenix roared, flames bursting over the harbor as I had a split-second image of his gigantic claws reaching for me, curling around me in the same way that a fishing eagle snatches its prey from the surface of the water –

It was like being thumped in the chest and the back at the

same time by a team of horses, (I imagine, as I had never ridden a horse – but my father had, my dead father…) and all of sudden my ears were ringing and my stomach was turning over as timbers exploded past us, and Crux rose into the air, his great wings a blur far above me, filling my vision and blocking out the storm winds and the smokes.

I had been saved, but I had failed to save my father.

CHAPTER 15
DANU, ADVICE FROM A DRAGON

I awoke to a pounding headache and the sensation of floating. *Was I flying?* I thought immediately – maybe because that was what my dreams had been about; flying on the back of Crux, but a much larger, impossibly large Crux whose wings stretched from one end of the horizon to the other.

But no, I wasn't flying, sadly. But I was floating – my headache was pulsing in time with the rise and fall of my body. I blinked, seeing the orange-pink blush of the dawn, and the deep blue of night already giving way to the lighter cerulean of a new day. If only I wasn't in so much pain, then maybe I could appreciate it a bit more.

Lila! My heart hammered as I remembered the events of last night. The second battle for Malata, the Dead fleet that was blocking the island, the vision of the township in burning ruins.

The storm.

What did I do? A wave of guilt washed over me as heavy as a storm surge. I knew with an absolute certainty that, somehow, I had made whatever Ohotto's magics were, worse. She had used my own powers against us – she had found a way to draw on the powers that I had summoned to only enhance her own.

Was I the cause of Malata's downfall?

"Lila…?" I said, sitting up and massaging my aching head. "Where are we?"

"He's awake," a voice said, a voice I recognized: Pela, Lila's foster-mother, and now that my eyes were finally able to focus through the pain I could see the stocky woman sitting just a few feet away from me, her long braid unraveling and her face pale and smeared with soot. Her voice sounded as weary and as broken as the woman looked as she turned to me. "You can stand? Walk?" All mercy had been drained out of that voice – but she wasn't angry, and she didn't sound accusative; just soul and bone weary.

"I, I think," I managed, struggling to my feet. We were on a boat, rather unsurprisingly – but it wasn't one of the usual pirates' galleons the Raiders used. This boat was broad and, I could feel through my feet, with a shallower rather than steep hull. Good for navigating the shorter stretches between islands of the Western Archipelago, and good for carrying lots of cargo. Not a raiding vessel.

The ship was filled with other Raiders, both men and women, fighters with bows at the ready as well as the old and the young. There were large barrels of water on the deck from which some were filling pouches, and, stacked on another side were crates of dried fruits and bread. This was, I realized, a boat of refugees.

"We've lost, haven't we?" I said in a quiet voice. Pela didn't even raise her head this time, but she sounded crushed.

"Aye, lad. The proud Sea Raiders are no more." She picked at a splinter on the deck idly, as if there was nothing better to do. I wondered if, for a fierce Raider, accustomed to being the scourge of the sea and inspiring nightmares in the other islanders, a certain dis-spiritedness was only to be expected.

"But where's—?" I started to say, just as dragon shriek cut off my question. Looking up, past the fat and full sails I saw the flash of sun on scales as, from high up, there was a dragon. I could tell it was Crux even before he flew out of the sun's glare. For a moment I wondered at that – had I recognized his voice, so draconian and like the others? Or was there some other sort of bond that we shared?

"Of course, we share a bond, Danu. I have already chosen you as my rider, as I have chosen Lila on my back." His voice was as strong as if I were sitting up there with her, and I felt with it a flush of gratitude. With so much loss and resignation

down here, I was only too happy to share my thoughts with my brave and courageous friend once again.

"You have Lila?" I murmured under my breath, picking my way past the idle Raiders on the deck and leaning out to the side.

"Of course! Where else would she be?" was the almost sarcastic reply.

"They're back," Pela said, sounding a tad lighter, if only for her face to instantly become clouded. She wasn't (just) talking about the dragon and her daughter I saw, but she was looking out to where the *Ariel* was scything through the water towards us, taller and with a sharper-prow than our vessel as she gained on us and quickly pulled alongside.

"Hoy!" came the brusque tones of the Sailing Master Elash, the same man who had captained the *Ariel* when we had rendezvoused with her before the battle. He looked just as tired and uptight as he had before, which was understandable, I thought, considering the circumstances. There were different faces at the rigging and working on the railings as well, faces that I recognized not from the streets of Malata, but instead from the refugee platform of the Fula. It seems that they had decided to join the crew.

"Any news?" Pela shouted over to Elash, but the older woman's eyes were wrong somehow. They were cold, hopeless. *She has already given up,* I thought. *But why? She has her life? She has her family – where was her husband, Chief*

Kasian? And then it hit me. Why wasn't he the one to take charge of his favored flagship, the *Ariel*?

Oh no.

"We're not more than a couple days out, by my reckoning," Elash hollered across the water. "The *Ariel* could make it by tomorrow morning, but we'd be leaving you alone in unfriendly territory…"

What were they talking about? I thought, looking from one to the other. They seemed to be discussing something *very* important indeed.

Pela just shrugged as if it was no matter. "We have the dragons, in fact." A weary glance up above. "We should get Lila here. She needs to be helping on this decision, now."

Why now? I thought.

"Because Lila is now first daughter," Crux informed me. It was a term I had never heard before – not amongst the Raiders, anyway.

"What do you mean?" I whispered.

"It's a dragon saying, and I think one Pela understands, even if she doesn't think she does. Dragons obey their mothers. Once in a while, we have a Bull King, but bulls – like me – are usually just the consorts of the mothers, and the mothers are under the Brood Queen."

"Oh." I nodded. It was like what I had read about the prides of gargantuan desert cats, far to the south. They were ruled by a matriarch, who called on the entire colony to help raise the young. *A bit like the West Witches have our Matriarch Chabon, too,* I thought.

"The Brood Queen has a first daughter. The first to come of age, the first to fly off to start a new den, maybe herself become queen after the old one dies. Lila is first daughter to the Raiders now their Bull King has died."

"Kasian is dead?" I murmured in shock. Part of me must have guessed it as soon as I had looked into Pela's eyes – but now Crux had confirmed the full, terrible facts.

"Yes." Pela looked back over her shoulder at me, where she stood calling out to Elash. "My husband is dead." Her words weren't angry, she didn't cry. Her voice sounded curiously flat.

"I'm sorry…" I said quickly, feeling stupid and ashamed. I had never known Chief Kasian well, of course, and he had been one of the most suspicious of me, 'the witch-boy,' to start with. But I could see that he also had an open heart, as the witches say. He had warmed to me when he realized that I actually had a bit of skill at sailing. And I knew that Lila admired no one more. She would not be the same without him, I feared. She might be even more reluctant to leave her people and step into the role she was born for.

"I wish I had gotten to know him better," I said awkwardly.

"Hm." Pela just nodded and turned back to Elash. "Lila has to help us decide," I heard her say.

I nodded as I understood the dragon's words now, feeling the gravity of the stricken. Of course, Lila had *always* been this 'first daughter' to the Raiders in some way, but in the past, that position as child of the chiefs had never been paid much importance. And though she was allowed to travel to the far Dragon Isle according to her dreams, her father had always been trying to recruit her as his first mate. *As if he knew that this day was coming.*

But now that Kasian, and most of the other leading Raiders and captains appeared to be lost or dead? That made Lila's word much more important.

"That's what I said!" Crux swooped down onto an empty patch of open sea, his claws spraying water everywhere before he settled into his curiously swan-like paddle. *"She is first daughter. Lila wave-rider, air-rider, first daughter to the islands."*

As I looked over to my dark-haired friend, seeing how she was already raising a hand in greeting at us all, and saw the dawn light catch her face – she seemed like a figure out of a different time, a different age even. A princess who belonged in the legends of the heroes, riding dragons and fighting monsters, clear-eyed and beautiful.

First daughter indeed. I surprised myself by blushing.

"Lila! We would have your counsel," her mother called, and Crux languorously paddled in our direction. When he arrived, he raised his head to sniff delicately at me on the side of the boat, and I returned his gesture with a pat on the nose.

"Hello, my friend," I whispered to him.

"Danu! You're awake at last." Lila looked visibly relieved, standing just behind his neck.

"I am. How long was I out?" I said, immediately feeling a wave both of embarrassment and shame. *Was I the one who had caused the fall of Malata?* I found it difficult to look her in the eyes.

"A day," Lila said, her eyes finding mine out anyway. "Danu, tell me – how are you feeling?"

"Fine," I waved her off, earning a derisive snort of sooty air from Crux. "Your mother and Elash have something that they need to talk with you about."

"And you, mage," Pela said heavily, steering me to the side of the railings. We stood there, the two boats slowly bobbing in the waves forming two sides of a triangle, and the dragon Crux as the third.

"We have to decide if we want to land as a group, or explore first," Elash shouted across.

"Land where?" I asked, earning a slight frown from the sailing master.

"The mainland," Lila explained. "We're only a few days away from it now, and there will be shelter, food, and water there…"

"And our enemies!" Elash countered. "Everyone knows that the mainlanders have never liked us islanders!"

"That's not true," I said. "Well, not really…"

"What?" Elash glared at me, and I once again felt stupid and worthless. *This was all my fault that they were here, in this position. If I had just listened to Lila and stopped my magic, then maybe the fog wouldn't have come, maybe...*

"Danu? What do you mean?" Lila was asking me, as I tried to shake the dark thoughts from my mind.

"The mainland, ah, they trade with the Western Archipelago. Always have. There are records at Sebol dating back hundreds of years to prove it."

"Sebol." Elash shook his head contemptuously. "The *Haunted* Isle, you mean."

Haunted Isle. I kept forgetting what the rest of the archipelago called us. It seemed that not all of the Raiders had broken their suspicions of me, despite the time that I had spent with them over the last year. And they were right, too, I thought dismally. Maybe this was why Afar and the others had always been hesitant to train me to be a full mage. Why they have never trained men before – because the histories of mages have always proved them to be too dangerous?

"Well, *witch*," Elash continued harshly. "Maybe the mainland has always been good to you – but not to us Raiders! We've fought their patrol boats more often than not, and I'm guessing we won't get any better reception when we land!"

"Well – what would you have us do?" Lila retorted back at him. "Do you know of any other island near here that will take us? That will harbor the enemies of Lord Havick?"

"We don't need allies. We need boats!" Elash said proudly. "Let me go raiding again. I'll be able to pick off some small patrol ship, I'm sure. Then we'll fill her with Raider fighters, we'll use it to get another boat, then another…"

"Madness," Lila said with a snort of disgust. "You want to take the *Ariel* to raid, one on one, hoping to capture a guard boat of all things? What are you going to do with the crew – make them walk the plank?"

"Well…" Elash shrugged.

"No." Lila was adamant. "We may be fierce – but we're not murderers. You want to throw your life away then, by all means, do it on a rowboat – but you're not taking our last galleon—my *father's* galleon!"

Elash muttered an angered sound, turning to Pela, who only appeared to be looking disconsolately in the waters between the boats. She had been destroyed by the loss of Kasian, I saw now.

"Pela?" He barked at her.

"Huh? No. You heard my daughter." Pela roused herself. "We have to make landfall. And all the islands are under the yoke of Havick now, I guess…"

Leaving only the mainland as refuge. I saw their dilemma.

"We scout it out. Send the dragons to look, and, if we find that the coast is clear -quite literally – then we'll guide the boats in," Lila said resolutely. "But the *Ariel* stays with the *Orchard*." She nodded to the wide cargo boat that I was standing on. "We need it to keep our people safe," she underlined for Elash, due to his grumbling look.

There was silence for a moment, before Crux raised his

own great head, dripping from the water to look between the two boats. His head was the size of one of the smaller longboats, and it was clear that anyone currently riding a dragon probably had a great advantage in winning the argument.

"Fine." Elash slapped the wooden railing. "You go off and light the fires for us. At least the dragons will be good for that, I presume…"

"Sckrekh!"

Everyone, apart from Lila, it seemed. jumped at the sudden snort of flame from Crux's mouth.

"Dragons don't take to being insulted, sailing master," Lila said coldly.

Elash had jumped back and I could see him lick his lips in nervousness. "Well, yes." He endeavored to recover some of his dignity. "But all I meant was, if we had *more* dragons, then maybe we wouldn't have lost Malata."

"Perhaps," Lila said, cold, hard hatred still in her voice. Elash must have also heard a little of the same tone as well, for he quickly saluted. "As you wish, ladies. The *Ariel* will accompany the *Orchard* to the mainland, *sacred waters help us,*" his mutterings carried clearly but then the man was gone, barking orders for his men to adjust the sails and fall in time with the *Orchard* that I and Pela were standing on.

Why hadn't the dragons come? One of the last things I remembered was hearing Crux's long and ululating call echoing out into the night above Malata. What had happened?

What possibly *could* have happened that meant that the rest of the dragons hadn't arrived?

Didn't they want a chance to fight Ohotto? For revenge?

"Mother?" It was Lila, her voice much closer now as she scrambled along the broad neck of Crux to leap lightly to the decks. I looked up, suddenly able to see the terrible cost that the last few days had on Lila as well as her mother. Her harsh composure in front of Elash crumpled in front of my eyes, and Lila the princess transformed back into Lila the young woman. Her eyes were wide and filling with tears, and her lower lip wobbled as she ran into her mothers' arms.

"Oh my child, I know…I know…" Pela whispered. "Your father loved you," Pela said. "He was so, so proud of you…" At that moment I suddenly knew I should not be a party to their private misery.

"Then come, Danu dragon-friend. You have spent too long lying down already." Crux's snout gingerly brushed against me, making me stagger a little backwards.

"I don't know, Crux, maybe I should stay here…" I thought, feeling stupid and ashamed. This was all my fault. Maybe I was the reason that Kasian was dead. Maybe I deserved to witness their grief.

"Danu! We need to fly. We need to hunt to bring back food for the brood! We need to keep our senses sharp and look far for the good of our family!" Crux said, suddenly angrily, surprising me by baring his long fangs at me. Having a dragon

flash its teeth at you suddenly can be a *very* unsettling thing indeed. *"And you need to come with me. Now!"*

There was no arguing with him, and I did not know how someone even began to argue with an irate dragon. So, I nodded, reaching up to catch a hold of his sweeping-back horns on the top of his head, before making my way, carefully between his neck ridge of spines, to the spot at the base of his neck where Lila usually sat, and where she had left her rope and leather seat.

"I know what you are doing, dragon," I groaned, feeling sorry for myself. "You are trying to keep me busy so that I don't fall into a despair," *like Pela has,* I thought.

"I am trying to keep you useful, young human!" Crux shook his head in agitation. *"Dragons know sadness. We have very large hearts, after all – but dragons do not despair. It is useless to borrow from tomorrow or even yesterday when the food that will fill your belly comes only from today's hunt. Lila is first daughter now, and she needs time with her mother, you do not. You need to hunt."*

How do you know that? I thought – but, considering I had already managed to make Crux a little annoyed with me, I decided not to push it. "Okay. What are we doing again?" I sighed.

"Danu?" Lila turned around in her mother's arms, looking at me with worried, tear-filled eyes. "Are you well enough to go flying yet?"

"Crux will look after me. I need to catch up on lost time,

do my share of patrolling," I said. And I also needed to do a lot of thinking. Like about why the dragons hadn't answered our call.

"Right." Lila was nodding, raising her hand in farewell. My heart almost broke to see her so upset. But how could it not?

"She will heal, Danu dragon-friend. The best you can do is to be strong. Now," Crux growled.

Yes. I took a deep breath and raised my hand to wave as Crux turned and powered his legs on his charge out of the ocean and into the open skies.

CHAPTER 16
DANU AND THE OTHERS

The wind was in my hair, the skies above were pale blue, and my body was aching again – but it was that good sort of ache, of muscles that had been worked and used. The dragon had been right, I *had* been lying down for way too long. It was good to be up in the air, and it was good to be flying once again.

"When have I not been right?" Crux read my mind with apparent ease. Our mental bond was stronger when we were in actual physical contact, I knew. Added to that was my own innate ability to hear the speech of dragons—should they wish to share it with me, that is—and I wondered if this was how it also was for Lila too.

Lila, who was now mourning her father. The thought hit me like a thunderbolt. Again. I was worried for which way she could go now – would she despair and grow quiet like her mother? Or would her temper flare, and make her heedless?

"Lila will not despair!" Crux informed me savagely, coughing a small cloud of smoke and flame into the skies, but I wondered if I detected a small worry behind the dragon's assertions. *"We will kill those who have hurt us! We will have our revenge!"*

"But taking rash action can also be just as unwise," I counseled him.

"Rash? What do you mean?" Crux's mind lapped against mine in puzzlement. Oh yeah, I guess when you are the largest, fiercest thing in the world then there really isn't any decision that you could take which would be deemed 'rash,' right?

"Just that we have to be careful about what we do next," I explained. Crux had tried his best to inform me of what he had seen at the second battle for Malata – in his own dragon-way of course, but I would also have to get Lila's more human description of events. I understood this much, at least – that the magical fog swept over the island (*my fault, my fault, my fault,* the words reverberated underneath my thoughts) as the Dead fleet had pounded the township with their cannons. Our young dragons had tried their best to keep the Dead Ships at bay, but there were too many of them and not nearly enough dragons.

Why hadn't Queen Ysix and her den come to our aid? That

was another mystery that had yet to be solved, I thought glumly.

Anyway. Our own dragons – who were now acting as scouts for the Raider flotilla – had found that the Dead fleet were resistant to their fire, at least, until they concentrated their attacks on a single target. Meanwhile, the fog had masked the arrival of hundreds of Roskildean soldiers as well as what Crux called the 'Dead Chiefs' from whom he had rescued Lila.

"They were like the soulless ones, but they were brighter in my eyes and mind," Crux said cryptically.

What did that mean? I could have cried out in frustration.

"A dragon sees things not as they appear to be, but as they are in the world, what they do. You are sitting, and scared, but you have a great inner strength in you. All of that is what you ARE, Danu," Crux informed me.

"I am? I mean – I do?" I said, unsure of whether to feel patronized or complimented.

"And these soulless ones who killed Lila's father were bright in my mind, bright as you humans burn – but more so. It wasn't healthy, giving fire, though – but a cold one. They were wrong. An insult to nature."

This wasn't the first time that I had heard that the dragons thought of themselves as somehow 'guardians' of the natural order. There was still so much we didn't know about dragon lore and history, I sighed.

"That is only more reason why we have to be careful. If

Ohotto has managed to summon the Dead"—*the Darkening,* I remembered the scrolls from Sebol— "then the whole world could be in danger…" Which was why only the rest of the dragons could help…

I was about to ask Crux again, what he thought had happened – but a sudden shift in the dragon's attention swept through him and into me, pulling my gaze in the direction that he was looking. It was a tall cliff face, made of a ruddy-orange rock.

"We're here. The mainland," I whispered. I had very few memories of this place – I had only been a child when I had left, and I didn't even recall what the name of my village was. *Would we pass over it? Would I see the people who had been my parents?* No – we were too far south, weren't we?

"We are in the southern airs. The hot lands are beyond those mountains," Crux informed me.

"What mountains?" I asked, but however great I peered, I still couldn't see them. Instead, the cliffs rose in our view, and the Phoenix dragon beneath me rose accordingly, revealing a landscape of scrubby browns and ochres, dotted with greens behind it. There were low hills and rising land – and then, to the south-eastern edge beyond that, I could see a dark line of peaks.

"Over those mountains, the land grows hot and scorched for many, many days," Crux said.

I wondered how he could know so much about world geography. "Can you really see that far?" I said in wonder.

"No. I come from a mountain far beyond even that desert, but I traveled over the hotlands, and fought many times with the Orange drakes who lived there."

"You did? It was a long way to come," I said. "Why come all of this way to the other side of the world?"

"Because my bond was here," Crux informed me simply, as if that explained everything. His unquestioning loyalty – to a person and a place that he didn't even know, humbled me. I would have to do better. I will not despair, I told myself. I will be a better friend to Lila. And I will see her wearing the Sea Crown of the Western Isles, I thought in determination.

"Not there." I shook my head again as we had pulled back to scout the cliffs. At the base of several, there were shingle beaches, but I feared that they would be inundated at high tide, or else that the Raiders following a day behind would be stranded here. No, we needed to find a bay or a sheltered inlet, one where they could hide…

"Let's try a little further north of here," I said, and, in response Crux turned his wings to slice through the air at my suggestion. I could see a trio of gulls exploding from the cliffs beneath us, and the white surge of the surf on the beach. If I hadn't been here because of tragedy, I would have enjoyed this flight a lot more.

We rounded the headland cliffs to see that the coast was

much more broken up here. There were chimneys of rocks and even small atolls – and beyond that, I could see inlets. One of these would have to do, I thought. It would be a perfect place to hide – the choppy water around the rocky outcrops would keep away pursuers – but that same protection would also make it difficult to navigate.

But the Sea Raiders would be able to do it, I knew, as we flew in between one and then another column of rock.

"Others," Crux snorted, flaring his wings as he snorted up to the coastal highlands.

"Who? Where?" I scanned, wondering what it was that he had seen. A flash of orange and green, I think, against the ochre tones up there. *Was that a flag? A person?*

"Best take us up and take a closer look," I said. "But please, Crux – don't scare them. This might be our only chance to make friends."

"As if I would scare anyone!" Crux sounded offended, although he had opened his mouth and was panting in that laughing way that I recognized.

With just a few flicks of his wings, we had floated on the rising thermals to the headland and were scudding across the skies. I saw that the land was a little greener here and deeply rutted with small streams.

"Where have they gone? Can you smell them?" I asked, but the dragon was already ahead of me. He flared just the tips of his wings and immediately turned in a direction that followed a stream, straight towards where a dense thicket covered both banks of the stream and evolving into a full-blown wood. Scanning the horizon, I saw that the wood was only eventually broken by the heads of the foothills before the peaks. There were no smokes of cooking fires, however, and I could see no settlements.

"Where are they?" I asked. I wished that there was some way to signal to them that we didn't mean them any harm. Some sort of universal call or a flag or something…

"In there, I think." Crux slowly turned on the wing, much like a hunting hawk.

"You think?" I said. I'd never known a dragon to be wrong about what it could sense.

"There are lots of smells in there. Lots of smells and lots of movement," Crux informed me. *"Trees, boar, deer, squirrels, voles…. Streams and rock pools…"*

"Okay, I get it," I said. "There's too much going on down there to make them out. But what was it? Human?"

"Yes. Just one. Riding a horse."

"Great," I thought. "We've probably alerted the locals then…" I considered heading further south until I realized that 'the locals' probably weren't *that* local at all. I couldn't make out any sign of flags or cities near here. That person might have been a scout or a wanderer themselves.

"Come on, we still need to find the right spot," I thought, and Crux turned to shoot back over the broken hills and over the waters.

In the end, it didn't take us as long as I had feared, as just a few bays on, I found what I considered to be the perfect spot: a deep inlet with a wide, sheltered cove, with rising rocky hills on either side. There was an easy ascent up to the headland beyond when the Raiders wanted to explore (or had to escape) and it was sheltered from the sea by more chimneys and atolls of rock against any sea pursuit.

"This is it!" I said gladly, and Crux turned to a large rock that jutted over the bay and reached down to scratch at it with a swipe of his claw as we passed.

"The dragons will find this place again," he said.

"Then I guess we'd better get back to them," I sighed. I felt bad for leaving Lila for so long. "We won't get back before midnight now, anyway…"

"Sckreeech!" Suddenly, the sky was split by a vicious shriek of indignation. It was dragon sound, and it didn't come from us.

"Crux!?" I said, turning my head.

"Beware!" Crux snarled into my mind, folding his wings to plummet out of the sky, and away from the out-reaching claws of the dragon that swept towards us.

Where had it come from? Why hadn't we seen it flying? I thought, clinging on for dear life as the wind tore at me. Sparing a glance over my shoulder, I saw that the dragon that followed was smaller, but it had a longer tail than Crux's was. It was a deep sandy orange, deepening to an almost ochre color, or highlighting to a sunny brightness. It had a smaller snout like that of a falcon compared to an eagle, and it *roared* at us.

Fhwump! Crux opened out his wings just before the water, and we scudded along the surging inlet like a skipping stone. But the smaller orange dragon was fast, and on our tail and just above us.

"Orange drakes," I heard Crux snarl, as he bobbed and weaved to try and throw the pursuer off. We were nearing the outlet into the sea. *"They must have smelt my scent and remembered me crossing their territory."*

"So, you didn't make many friends when you were last here?" I gasped, as suddenly the air grew colder and we were flying out over the open sea, and the cries of the Orange drake were turning back. It didn't like the water, it appeared.

"Orange drakes are very territorial. But they are also very small." Crux was turning in a wide arc back towards the inlet. I could feel his hurt pride and savage anger burning brighter inside of him.

"Maybe we should just find another cove. If this one is home to that angry little thing…" I started to say.

"No. You don't understand. The Orange drakes think that the entire south is their territory." Crux snarled as he beat his wings and soared higher over the rocks. I couldn't see our smaller tormentor ahead of us, but I assumed that it must know that we were coming.

I saw Crux's shadow on the waters and the rocks below. We looked big, even to me.

"*Now that this one knows that I am here, it will not stop until it has driven me away. Wherever I land in the south.*" Crux was starting to cough smoke and gobbets of flame, and I could feel his neck muscles swell. "*I must defeat it,*" he snarled.

"Uh…" I wasn't quite sure how I felt about that. *What was the first, last, and only law of magic?* I remembered Afar and Chabon's wise words. *'Do what you have to do when you have no other choice.'* I knew that little rule was one of the core reasons why the Western Witches of Sebol had previously stayed out of politics and didn't advocate violence, either. If they fought a war, or killed or cursed an opponent, then they would have to live with the consequences.

But did Crux – the much larger, fiercer Phoenix dragon really have to kill the smaller Orange drake? I thought in horror. For some reason, it seemed like a terrible omen to start the Raiders' new home.

"*I see you!*" Crux snapped, and I followed his jerky head movements to see a much smaller shape flitting from one rock to another. The Orange drake looked fantastically smaller compared to us.

"Crux-?" I began, but the Phoenix was already tilting downward, screaming through the air at his smaller foe.

The Orange drake gave an angered shriek and turned this way and that as it desperately sought to escape. We had flashed past the cove where we had wanted to bring the Raiders, and now the Orange drake was following the river up into the mainland, following the curves as fast as a darting hummingbird. It was quicker than us in this confined space, and there was barely the space for Crux to fully unfurl his wings.

"I will not play to your call, little dragon," Crux crowed, and, with a powerful downbeat he soared up and out of the cut in the hills that formed the river, and we were able to see the landscape around and follow the actions of the little drake below.

And see the other dragons converging on us.

"It was a trap!" I said in alarm.

Crux bellowed his indignation.

There were easily two or three of these Orange drakes on each side of us, with more rising from the rocks behind. How many did that make? Eight? Twelve? Too many for Crux to fight off all at once.

"It's no good, Crux – we have to…" I was about to say 'retreat' but the smaller dragons chose that moment to attack. They had given us no choice.

With a high-pitched shrieking, they darted low towards Crux's head, forcing him to flap and turn awkwardly in the sky. I screamed as I saw another set of orange-colored claws reaching for me, but Crux belly-rolled just in time.

The Orange drakes were probably each a little less than a quarter a size of Crux, making them roughly the size of a cart or a wagon. They were still large and strong compared to me.

Magic. There must be some magic that I know that will save us... I thought.

"*No!*" Crux suddenly batted at me with his anger, even as he turned and rolled and twisted in the air. I was stunned (if I had enough time to feel anything, that was). Why didn't he want me to use my magic?

More screeches, more whistles, and then a sudden roar from Crux as he let out a mighty gout of dragon flame. The smaller and quicker Orange drakes scattered just in time, only to converge like the mobs of diving seagulls once more over our heads.

They were driving us down towards the ground, I saw. We were not only ten or so meters from the earth. *They're trying to ground us.*

In fact, I saw that they weren't even trying to *strike* at us, not really. I had the luxury of noticing this, I think, as Crux was too busy moving and snarling and snapping at them. *Did that mean that they only really attack when their prey is grounded? Or that they weren't trying to kill us?*

"Wait! Stop!" I called out to them, holding out a hand in warning as I did so.

"*What are you doing! We must fight them!*" Crux was snarling, and I jolted as his claws scraped along the ground. Five meters.

"I have an idea," I shouted, turning my heart and intention towards the clouds of screeching, shrieking drakes. I tried to find that place in my mind that connected to Crux, that affinity and ability that I had to hear the other dragons' thoughts. From there, I opened my mouth and spoke to them.

"Wait! Sons and daughters of fire!" I called at them. "We are not your enemies! We mean you no harm!"

"Idiot. The Orange drakes do not speak as we do!" Crux snarled, once again snatching at one of them, only for it to avoid his grasp.

A hiss and a screech came from the nearest flaring forms of our enemies.

"Children of the sun! We are your friends!" I shouted at them, willing them to hear me.

There was a confused shrieking as the Orange drakes suddenly veered away from us, giving Crux just a little bit of room to skim the ground.

"I don't like this..." Crux snarled, expanding his neck, making ready to bellow fire at them.

"No wait, please, Crux–something is happening," I said quickly, once again lifting my hand up. "I am a friend to dragons. And I would be a friend to you!" I shouted.

"Pheep-ip?" The whistles and cries of our adversaries were changing. They were turning into the whistles and questioning clicks of a creature that was interested, confused – not just angry and territorial.

It's working! I thought. *If I can communicate with dragons, then I must be able to talk to them...* I tried again. "We mean no threat to you and your nests!" I shouted. "We honor you, children of the skies!"

More whistles greeted me, and I saw that, one by one, the smaller Orange drakes were pulling back just a little – but still flying in a close murmur all around us.

"Set us down, Crux – I think, I think that it's going to be all right," I said to him and felt his resistance to the idea, but still he was carefully lowering himself to the scrubby ground below. We touched the dirt with a jolt, and I could feel the tense worry in his limbs as he stalked in a wide circle, the Orange drakes settling all around us.

"Well, if they decide to tear us scale from bone now, it will be all your fault," Crux said, keeping his throat and chest inflated so that he could spew his fire should he need to.

"They won't," I said, easing myself from his shoulder and thumping to the ground. *I hope.*

"Pheep-ip?" The nearest, and apparently bravest one said, cocking his head to look at me. It reminded me of the way that a seabird might look at a particularly interesting rock. *Or something that it was about to eat,* I tried not to think.

"Er, hello?" I said in my more normal voice, reaching out my gloved hand.

"Skrawr!" the Orange drake suddenly shrieked, flared its wings and jumped backward (even though it was much larger than me). I felt the ripple of alarm spread through the surrounding flock of the dragons.

Oh no. Instead, I straightened myself up and once again reached out with the dragon ability as I spoke to them.

"Little friends. We are mighty hunters from the sea. We

will nest for only a little while. We will bring fish for you to eat." At that offer, there were more excited whistles and clicks. Crux had said that they didn't travel over the sea. Maybe they were scared of it? That also meant they probably had never eaten fish – and everyone knows that dragons just love fish.

"Food." The word appeared in my mind, and I could tell that it came from the nearest, larger of the drakes.

"You can speak!" I said, amazed. I had thought that they were like Messenger dragons, unable to speak with their minds at all.

"They're not as good as us larger dragons though..." Crux snorted indignantly.

"But they can speak – and if they can speak, then we can communicate!" I said, eagerly turning around.

"Food," the Orange drake returned, and then worryingly, a very different word. *"Rival."* As the word hit my mind, I could feel some of the bright, fast-moving dragon mind behind it. It was filled with images of large, monstrous forms of dragons raining fire down on them from above.

"Rival... You mean Crux?" I shook my head. "No, no..." I started to use my dragon ability whenever I spoke to them now. "This one is like your big brother. He is no rival. He will not hurt you. He will share his food with you."

"Share?" The word was repeated back, this time with a perfect picture of mental confusion and bewilderment.

"Oh. You guys aren't so much into that then?" I

murmured. "Bring you food. For you," I said instead, earning a sort of dragon equivalent of happiness.

"We will come back, and there will be more of us. People, like me." I put a hand to my chest. "And large dragons, like Crux here," I said, wondering what reaction that would provoke.

The answer was absolutely none it seemed, as they just turned back to chittering, chattering, whistling and shrieking at each other instead.

"Well – that wasn't too bad, was it?" I turned to whisper to Crux, slowly stepping between one and the other of the Orange drakes until I had reached his side. Very gingerly, I reached up to his shoulder tines and pulled myself up. The Orange drakes couldn't have paid me any less attention if they had been asleep. "I think we're good to go," I said to Crux, who was fuming, quite literally, as there were wisps of smoke rising from his mouth.

"It is your voice. The voice of a dragon-friend. They recognize in it that you are a friend to dragons," he grumbled.

"Thank the lucky stars!" I nodded, as Crux padded carefully away from the crowd of the Orange drakes and then loped faster and faster still before leaping into the air. We were on our way back to the Raiders, having found a safe place to for them to moor.

Things were still terrible, with Kasian's death and the loss of Malata – but at least we might have made some new allies, I tried to convince myself.

CHAPTER 17
LILA, PROTECTOR OF THE FREE ISLANDS

"What do you mean, we have to split our forces?" I said angrily to Senga and Adair. Maybe I shouldn't have been angry with them directly, but right now I couldn't stop it from spilling out. Here we were, leagues from what had once been our home, in open shipping routes, with not enough warriors, with no home to go to – and now Senga and Adair were telling me that we would have to divide up!

"There's a battle coming our way," Senga said seriously, jutting out her chin to meet my eye defiantly. "We saw it on Kim's back, and it'll be here before nightfall."

In desperation, I wished Danu and Crux were here! We were standing on the decks of the *Orchard,* with the twin's dragon Kim paddling alongside in the water. It's not that I had to ask Danu for his wisdom – it was just that I would feel so much better with him at my side. *And Crux.* There is nothing like having a dragon on the other side of your mind to bring you a boost of confidence.

"How many?" I said.

"Five boats all in all. Three are islanders, and two Roskildean."

"Three Free Islanders? Well then – we have plenty in our favor…"

"They were merchant's vessels, Lila," Adair informed me. "They're fat and low and have no proper defenses. One of them is listing as she moves as well. And the two Havick ships are the large guard caravels."

"Guard ships. Outstanding," I spat. "Okay. *No* Dead Ships in sight?" I asked worriedly. If there were those, then we really *would be* in trouble.

'I have died, and yet am alive once more!' The sudden memory of the Dead Captain, or 'Jarl' as he called himself, assaulted me. The way that he had casually taken my father's and the others' lives; and not just by killing them, but by seemingly *draining* the life right out of them. I shivered.

"Lila?" Senga was looking at me, her determination mollified by a look of worry. "Three ships in trouble, one of them won't make it, against two of the Roskildean fleet. What do you say?"

"Ah," I shook the dark thoughts from my mind. "And we have ten dragons, the *Orchard* – which will never be able to fight, and the *Ariel*, which will." I totted up the odds. They were good, I thought. *Ten dragons against two regular guard boats?* Those were the sorts of odds that I had liked, before.

But what if one of the dragons gets injured? I thought, my mind again returning to the pile of bodies that the dead sea captain Lars and his other lieutenants had dropped to the earth. How could I allow any of those under my care to be injured, ever again? My mother Pela kept telling me there was nothing I could have done – that the dead are just too powerful... but what if that wasn't the case? What if I *could* have saved them, but I didn't? What if I had made a mistake, and now my father and the others were dead? This married horribly in my thoughts with a terrible fear that I might make a horrible mistake again – that I might cost Senga, or Adair, or any of the others, their life...

"Lila – the odds are good!" Senga was saying. "And there are three boats out there that are going to sink if we don't do anything."

I didn't know if Senga meant for us to help the merchant islanders just so that we could have their boats, or whether she had thought that we should now seek to protect the other once-Free Islanders, but I noticed that this was exactly what Afar and Danu had been saying to me over the last few weeks. *That I had to stop being just a Raiders' daughter, and now become a princess. A protector of all of the Free Islands.*

But how could I? I didn't feel up to the challenge. Not in the midst of my grief. Not with the guilt I carried.

Senga was about to say something else, but I cut her off.

"Okay. Fine. Signal the *Ariel*. I'll take her command – not that Elash is going to like that one bit, I can tell you," I muttered.

"Well, Elash will just have to lump it." Senga slapped me on the shoulder. "I'd rather have you up in the air with us, but…"

"I know. Crux and Danu are still out scouting." I nodded, feeling a surge of worry for them. I knew nothing about the mainland, only what little came in the way of stories and tales from the odd trader. Saffron, my hero and island girl, had gone off to the mainland and there overthrown the evil Dark King many years ago – but that had been in the north, the Empire of Torvald. The closest landmass to us were the southern realms, the trading city of Vala and the Southern Princes of the deserts. We got spices and silks from them, and their boats always made for good plunder, if they strayed too far off the established shipping lanes.

"Danu will be okay," Adair said confidently. "You now, he's fairly tough for a witch's kid."

"Yeah." I nodded, feeling an odd fluttering in my stomach that could have been nerves or panic or both. "Yes, he is." I knew that he was. I had seen him fighting on Sebol, I had flown with him. He knew how to pilot a boat and ride a dragon, and he didn't hesitate to try and save me or Crux when he thought that he could.

"Okay, then," Adair coughed loudly, breaking my chain of thought. "What now, oh Commander Lila?"

Jerk, I thought. Adair was always making fun of me. "We

split the flotilla. The *Orchard* under Chief Pela pulls back and immediately changes course south to keep away from the action. I, on the *Ariel,* and the Dragon Raiders, on their beasts, take to the seas and sky to see if we can chase off Havick's guard boats," I said, feeling a certain clarity now that we were in motion.

"Aye, aye – captain." Adair raced off to give the orders.

Leaving me to wonder if what I was doing was the right thing at all.

PART III
The Invasion

CHAPTER 18
LILA, AND THE BATTLE

"Hard to starboard!" I shouted, leaning out on the ropes that ran from the bowsprit up to the foremast of the *Ariel*. Underneath me, the boat responded as Elash spun the giant ship's wheel, and the lines pulled taut on the sails above me. We were heading straight into the teeth of the fight, and for a brief moment I forgot my sorrow and grinned into the rushing wind.

This is what my father would have been proud of, I thought as I eyed the two Roskildean guard caravels. They were larger than the *Ariel*, with fatter sails and the sun glinted off the metal shielding placed along the guardrails.

But we would be the quicker. It wouldn't be hard given that we probably had half the crew weight on board as any one of those boats! If only Crux were here. Crouching on the extreme front of a boat going at full speed was a *little* similar to flying on a dragon– there was the wind in my hair, the sensation of speed—but it was nothing that was the same as flying, feeling the drake underneath you surge forward, a thunderbolt of power contained in its form.

"Straight down the middle, boys!" I called, as we flashed past first one of the fat merchant vessels, and then the other two on the left-hand side. I heard a snatch of victorious shouts and saw the pale and dark faces of the Free Islanders raised hopefully towards us. It made my stomach feel giddy somehow; a feeling of pride and embarrassment at the same time, and one that I wasn't used to. Us Raiders were usually visions of fright or caution for most other islanders – even the Free Islanders that we occasionally traded with. *Are they going to raid us?* I could always remember their eyes saying.

Not this time. The Western Archipelago had changed, and that meant that us Raiders had to change along with it.

We were in open water again and the two guard caravels were coming straight for us.

"Broadside?" Elash called, meaning that we would turn and present the gun ports of one of our sides to our enemy so that we could fire a full volley.

"No!" I shouted. "Raiders to all guns!"

"All!?" the argumentative Elash said in alarm. "We need those sailors up on deck!"

"That's a command, Raider!" I roared at them and felt an

echo of fierce, fiery agreement in my mind. *Crux?* Was it my friend? Had he returned?

"I am coming, Lila. I am coming to spill the blood of our enemies with you!" I heard his voice like a distant snarl of soot and flame – but it was so distant that it was almost hard to make out. Like a whisper against my thoughts. How far away was he?

No time to think about it, as the Roskildeans started to turn to either side around us – just as I had known that they would.

"Which way, Lila?" Elash's tone rose to a pitch of alarm.

"Hold your course. Hold, damn it!" I swore at him, as the *Ariel*, at full speed, swept straight towards the gap of open water between the two vessels.

"They'll have clear guns on us!" Elash howled in frustration.

"Not if they don't want to risk sinking each other," I called back, before looking up to the skies. *Please hear me,* I begged, before shouting into the wind. "Now, Senga! Now, Adair! Now, Dragon Raiders!"

"Skreych!" There was an answering roar, and shapes fell from the sky like hunting birds. The nine dragons and their riders dive-bombed the two guard caravels, like the way that gulls did when they were attacking a school of fish – but these dragons pulled up at the very last moment to scream low across the wave tops.

Kim was the first to strike, her claws sweeping across the Crow's Nest of one of the vessels, making it explode in a shower of wood and rope. Then came Thiel, attacking the other boat from the other direction, shooting a jet of flame that hit the boat's aft before flashing past his sister in the air. Lucalia next, flying in low in front of the boats and smacking her tail just above the water line of one, and Retax attacked last – a different direction again, and opening his mouth to pour dragon flame in an attempt to get both boats. He failed, but he managed to add to the flames of the boat that Thiel had hit.

Don't get hit, don't get hit... I watched the dragons in alarm as the Roskildeans fired their cannons after them. *Thoom. Thoom Thoom!* Had Lucalia suddenly twisted away, as if she had been struck?

"Fire at will!" I shouted, just as we entered the maelstrom, and prayed that my plan had worked.

The *Ariel* flashed through the middle waters between the two guard boats, and there were Raiders on either side of the boat at her gun ports, lighting the fuses and pulling back as the small, pot-bellies iron guns rocked back to plumes of smoke. The boat underneath me shuddered in her course, as the power of our own guns rocked us.

Thoom! Some of the Roskildeans gun ports answered us, and I felt the terrible, seismic tremor as one of them hit home, accompanied by shouts from behind me.

No!

But most of the Roskildean guns *didn't* fire at us, I was at least a little glad to see. These guard boats weren't used to fighting dragons, it seemed – they had expended most of their shot on trying to bring down the much faster and more agile creatures, leaving us to have a clear full-volley of our own.

"Reload!" I shouted. "Damage!"

We sliced through the clouds of gun and dragon smoke and out into clear water behind the guard ships. I could already tell that we weren't moving as fast as we should, or as smoothly. *Don't be taking on water, please, for all that is holy...* I prayed.

"Lila! Wait – I am almost there," Crux said, louder this time against my mind.

"I can't wait," I whispered, before hollering louder, "Turn us around, sailing master – skirmish conditions!"

It was the order that Elash had been waiting for me to give. Skirmish meant that we were now in the thick of it, and the battle was too fast-moving to be able to conduct times and precise maneuvers like I had just done a moment ago. Now, the sailing master had to decide which was the best attack course (as he was the one on the wheel, after all), and the firing crew had freedom to shoot their cannons at will. That also gave me the chance to turn and run down the deck, searching for the damage that we had taken.

It was visible almost immediately, however; the *Ariel* was listing to one side, and there was smoke coming up from one of the trapdoors.

Damn! It had hit below the top deck. I could only hope that it hadn't hit below the water line as well – otherwise, we really would be a sinking ship, quite literally.

Without thinking, I slid along the deck, seizing the lip of the trapdoor and swung myself below, to be confronted with the sound of wailing and coughing. "Who's hurt? Report!" I barked even before my feet hit the deck of the main hold.

What should have been a large and open space of the main hold, lit by storm lanterns, was instead a world of choking smoke. Some of the lanterns were still up, so I could see that the pale faces of some of the gunner crews as they looked up.

"Borald's hurt, Lila," I heard one of them say, and I rushed to his side. "The shot took out one of the guns, and Borald's foot," the Raider said, pointing to where there was a hole in the side of the *Ariel* where I could see the rushing waves beyond, and a man huddled in a nest of broken wood and mangled metal.

What are the chances of a cannon hitting one of our own guns! I hissed, moving to the side of Borald to help him up.

"*Arrgh!*" he screamed, the end of one leg looking a ragged mess – but even that wasn't the worst news for me down here; behind where poor Borald had been laying was a splintered hole where the Roskildean shot had punched through the main hold and into the bilge.

I swore. "Get him in my quarters – quick!" I called, pulling one of the other Raiders closer to pick him up. "Another two of you, grab a lantern and come with me!" I turned, my hands still bloody, and ran for the trapdoor that led down into the lower-most part of the *Ariel,* the dark and dank lower-hold known as the bilge. As soon as my feet hit the floor below, I felt the cold and heard the splash of water – and the smell.

Bilge water is undeniably gross: it's stagnant water that always seeps and collects at the bottom of any boat from the wild weather and cramped life – but right now, I just hoped that was the *only* source of the water in the boat. My foot crunched on the layer of gravel that every boat had at the bottom of the bilge as ballast.

"Lila? Captain?" The other two Raiders splashed behind me, retching at the stench.

"I know, but we need to make sure. We need to find that shot," I said, and clapped a hand back over my mouth as I moved forward into the dark. There was a shaft of light coming from the hole in the main hold above, so I knew whereabouts the cannonball must have hit. But then I saw the waters below it, and worse, I *heard* them. A sound like a dragon's warning growl. When I stopped to concentrate, I could feel the tremor running through the timbers of the boat itself.

"No, no – no!" I said, rushing over to have my worst fears confirmed. There was a wildness of water under where the cannon shot must have punctured through the hold above. There was a surge of pressure over my feet, but I wasn't knocked to the ground, so I reasoned that it wasn't a *large* hole into the dark seas beyond. B*ut still, any hole in a boat where you don't need it is a bad thing, right?* It could mean that a seam had been bust, or that a timber had cracked. Taking a deep breath, I plunged my hands into the water that was only a foot or so high, but was still freezing all the same, and felt around in the dark until I found it.

The cannonball was heavy, and I could barely move it – but there was an undeniable surge of water coming from the join between two hull slats underneath it, and the wood felt awkward and out of shape.

"We got a leak?" one of the Raiders said.

"Yeah – she's not too bad at the moment." I half lied to them. It was kind of true – we weren't sinking yet, right? "But she'll blow the hull if we let her. I need wood, nails, and pitch."

Much to their credit, the sailors took this news in stride. "Right you are, cap'n." They rushed off to get the supplies as I tried to work out the best way to fix it.

We'll continue taking on water until the strength of the water inside pops that entire beam, I calculated. *And then we really would be scuppered.* Water would pour in, and the force of it would tear more beams apart, throwing us over onto our side – and if we were lucky then there would be enough air trapped in the hold to keep us floating. If not…?

"We'd have less than a watch before the *Ariel* goes down," I muttered. How long would it take for the *Orchard* to get here? Could I use the dragons to ferry people off?

"Lila! What is wrong? You are in danger?" Crux was sounding closer.

Thoom! Thoom! The sound of more cannon shot came from up above. *Were they ours? Or were they from the*

Roskildeans? I could feel the boat moving and leaning from one side to another as Elash fought the two caravels. I felt bad leaving the dragons and their Raiders up there, having to work out how to fight on their own – but I knew that at least Senga and Adair would be fine. They would have to lead the other Dragon Raiders by example...

"Lila?" The two sailors splashed back into the bilge, this time carrying lengths of wood and pouches of the thick, treacly pitch that we used to caulk the entire boat and make it waterproof. It was dark down here as we worked, hammering a rudimentary reinforcement between the two nearest beams, sliding the edges of each other and nailing them in place to form a seal. *Would it hold?* Every Sea Raider had a fair bit of skill at boat repairs and maintenance, but I was no gifted carpenter. I wished that my father was here. He would know precisely what to do, and how to do it.

But he's not here, is he? I remembered. There was only me, and these people were relying on me.

"Okay, heat the pitch," I said, indicating that the sailors bring over the small stove that was made out of an upturned metal helmet with legs welded onto a bottom dish. The Raider filled the bottom dish with charcoal, sprinkled some of the black powder from the guns over it and lit the coals with a flint. The flames took with a whoosh! and into the helmet, he poured the pitch, before hanging the whole contraption from one of the ceiling hooks.

Instantly, the bilge started to fill with the acrid smell of the black treacly substance, acrid enough to make me cough and my eyes water. I kept on working on the wooden reinforcement as we waited for the pitch to slowly start to warm, and then steam, and then finally plop with fat bubbles.

"Okay, she's good," I said and helped the sailor to pour the hot substance all over the section that we had built. The heat would force the tar to seep into the wood and between the seams, and hopefully glue the whole construction together. On top of that, we nailed some more overlapping planks across in the other direction, hoping that would sandwich the water-resistant gunk inside.

"Will she hold, cap'n?" One of the Raiders whispered fearfully.

"Take heart, man!" I imitated one of the loud barks of laughter that my father used to use all the time. "We've been through much worse than this! Come down and check every quarter-watch, and if it looks like she's starting to break, then come and give me a holler." I clapped him on the shoulder and forced myself to turn away.

Don't let them see just how terrified you are, I thought as I ran back up to the main hold, my lungs burning, my feet stinking, and my hands sticky with tar.

※

"How are we faring?" I called loudly as I climbed up onto the deck – more for the benefit of the crew to hear me than to gain any information. I could see for myself that we weren't faring well – but we also weren't doing terribly, either.

One of the Roskildean boats was now a burning wreckage, sinking lower in the waters and casting thick plumes of black smoke across the sea-tops. Through this fog there swung just us and the final guard boat – but we were the worse off. The extra water that we had taken on was throwing us off course. We were wallowing, but still able to turn. Our rival was quicker than us, despite the dents that pocked and shattered metal shields from our shot.

"She's got more firepower than us," Elash snarled as I joined him at the wheel. "It's all I can do to keep us out of range."

"And the dragons?" I looked up, blinking through a sudden gust of smoke.

Kim and Retax were circling our surviving enemy ship, awaiting their next strafing run, but I couldn't see Lucalia and Thiel.

"One of 'em is hurt. The big green one had to pull back, and the skinnier green one went with her," Elash snarled.

Oh no. That was Lucalia and Thiel, I knew. I had seen the big green Lucalia get hit by something – I prayed that it wasn't bad.

"Skreyach!" Kim snarled, sweeping low across the water, through a black pillar of smoke, and swipe at the side of the Roskildean vessel. There was the sound of wood splintering, and more of the upper railings came apart, and I saw a tiny, windmilling figure of a guard fall overboard.

Good. No one hurts a dragon like you did Lucalia.

"Okay then, sailing master, then let's play this by the numbers. We've got two dragons and a boat. We outnumber them three to one." I nodded. "Distract and strike."

"If you think that's wise, Lila," Elash grunted with a terrible frown.

"That's captain to you," I snapped back.

"Cowards! Curs! Despoilers!" Crux's shriek was so loud that I clamped my soiled hands to my ears – even though it did no good. I had no idea that he was so close, as I had been caught up in the terror of a leaking ship – but now his shadow flashed over us, and we all heard his roar as he opened his mouth and out came fire.

Crux flew straight at the remaining Roskildean ship – which might have looked suicidal but was actually a very wise plan. Any ship has more guns on its side than on its front, and when it fired, Crux was already shifting his weight to avoid the shot. His flames hit the ship head on, and I heard screams and shouts.

"What's that?" Elash gasped, and then I heard an altogether different sound, like the angered shriek of cliff birds and another cloud of shapes passed by overhead.

"More dragons," I said in awe at the sight, as a flock of diminutive dragons swarmed the Roskildean ship. Most of them were only the size of a sheep or a hunting dog, with a few that were the size of a pony, and they were a bright, ruddy orange in color.

They didn't have flame it seemed, but they were fast. The swarm hit the Roskildean vessel, darting over the decks and under the burning sail, plucking at the guards and slashing at them with their tails or dropping them into the sea. I heard screams and shouts – and then it was all over.

"Crux? Danu!" I called, running the length of the *Ariel* to the bowsprit.

"My wave-rider," I heard Crux's proud voice as he swooped low over the water, turning back to the *Ariel* to splash home beside us, and to raise his long neck and head to my side.

"Oh Crux, I am so glad you're here," I said truthfully, leaning against his still-warm snout.

"And I am glad to see that you have all of your limbs in the right place still." Crux playfully knocked me back with a nudge of his head.

"Er, hi, Lila?" Danu said, already clambering down Crux's back to jump onto the deck.

"Danu!" I folded him into a warm embrace. I didn't realize just how much I had been worried about him until he had returned.

"Oh, uh..." he said awkwardly, separating suddenly as he looked at his hands. "Well, uh, we found a safe harbor, and made some new friends, I think?"

"Right – these dragons! Who are they?"

"Orange drakes." Crux looked over to where they were still awkwardly flocking over the Roskildean vessel. *"Vicious little dragons, but they seem to love fish just as much as I do."*

"What?" I shook my head, laughing.

"Crux hunted them some fish. They had been afraid of the open sea before, but well – between Crux and the food and my dragon ability"—Danu shrugged—"they seem to like following Crux around now."

"They like following the dragon-friend around," Crux corrected him sourly. He didn't seem to like the little Orange drakes all that much.

"Well, I am glad that at least one of us has got some good news…" I said as the *Ariel* listed to one side once again. "How far is this safe harbor of yours? Because we need to do some serious repairs."

"Not far – I'll guide you in," Danu said.

"No," I reached up to seize one of Crux's tines and swung myself up onto his neck. "*We'll* guide the boats in," I said, before calling out orders for Kim and Senga to be sent out to rendezvous with the *Orchard* and offer the three vessels that we saved any necessary aid as well, while we headed for the coast – and hopefully, a chance to rest and work out what we were going to do next.

CHAPTER 19
LILA, SAFE HARBOR?

Well, it wasn't as bad as it could be. I looked down on the small bay and the sandy beach by the side of the headland. The bay was on one side of a larger estuary, with cliffs across the water-course from us, and blocking our view to the sea. This was good, as it meant that we were also hidden out of sight from any passing Roskildean patrol boats that might be searching for us.

Down in the bay we had the *Ariel* (still listing to one side a bit) as well as the *Orchard,* the *Dagger, Aidan's Pride,* and the *Happy King* – the last three being the fat-bellied boats that we had saved from the Roskildeans. They were staffed with Free Islanders and were originally merchant's vessels but had spent the last ten years or so trading hands and loyalties from one island to another. Now, in their latest incarnation, they were refugee boats.

Just like ours, I thought with a sigh. "We're going to need somewhere secluded to repair the *Ariel*," I said with a sigh to Danu beside me, where we sat on the headland overlooking the bay. It was evening, and I could make out the scatter of bonfires that the Raiders and Islanders had started down there on the beach, as well as the makeshift huts and tents that Pela had been helping to build further back on higher ground.

"And to get some decent rations, too," Danu said glumly.

I made an agreeing noise. It was only so long that our combined ships' rations and hunting for fish would sustain us. We had, what, almost five or six hundred hungry mouths down there?

"There's a settlement further inland – I spent ages trying to talk to the Orange drakes, but all they could say is that stone huts were nearer the mountains." Danu winced and said, "The drakes haven't got a lot of language," and then he explained about the flash of a rider on a horse he and Crux had seen when they found this place.

"We can send scouts out at first light, I guess," I said, lying back with a thump as I looked up at the stars. It was still the same sky. Still the same constellations – wasn't that something that my father had always said? *'Just so long as you can see the pole star and the evening star, then you'll always be able to find your way home…'*

Well, what was home now? I thought. Was it Malata? Now

a burning, haunted wreck overrun with Havick's troops, miles and miles away?

What would you do, Father? I thought of big Chief Kasian, the man who had adopted me as a babe and had taught me not only how to read the stars but how to sail, to hunt and to swim.

"Lila?" Danu said, his tone serious and low. "You can't give up now. Not when we know what is at stake."

"I'm not giving up, it's just…" I blinked back something that definitely wasn't tears in my eyes. "It's just that it is so hard." I took a shuddering breath and thought about how haggard my foster-mother Pela looked now. Even though she still struggled to keep the Raiders warm and fed and safe, she was just going through the motions. She had lost her old fire.

"I saw them, you know…" I murmured, thinking about that night that my father had died.

"Saw who?" Danu said.

"The captains of the dead. That's what happened on Malata, why we lost." At my words Danu flinched as if I had poked him. Weird. "They came out of the fog, four of them, just like the other dead sailors in the Dead fleets, except these ones weren't so slow and stupid. They were *clever, powerful.*" I replayed the nightmare vision of them in my mind and wondered how I could have done nothing. How I could have just watched as they murdered my father and all the rest of them.

"They had my father and Lasarn and the other first mates'

captive on the docks, and," I coughed, trying to force the words out, "they stole their life somehow. Right from their hearts."

"*What?*" Danu said, his eyes wide.

"They stole their lives. Snuffed them out, and they seemed to be drinking on their vitality and power…" I said, at last speaking the words that I hadn't even let myself think. All of a sudden, a terrible shaking ran through me.

"Lila…" It was Danu's gentle hand on my shoulder, and, as I cleared my eyes I saw that his large eyes were troubled as he loomed over me. But his hand was strong, and from it flowed warmth and courage. "You are here, safe now."

"*She is not safe!*" A sudden thud as Crux landed on the headland behind us, clearly drawn by the strength of my misery. He quickly settled himself around the pair of us, until we were in a cocoon of warmth. "*We are not safe here. We are not safe anywhere – but you do not have to feel safe, Lila dragon-sister. You just have to feel strong.*"

I was about to argue that I wasn't sure I could do that if I wasn't safe – but then Crux turned his head, his eyes flashing as he spoke to both of us. "*These things you speak. Of the dead captain who still walks.*"

"Lars." I remembered his name. "He called himself Jarl Lars Old Horn."

"*It is the cruelest of magics, the stealing of life – and it can only be attempted by the theft of other life and blood…*"

"A dragon's?" Danu said, pulling a face.

"Yes. That witch who has done this has called them to life with the dragon blood – but we dragons are an old race. We know many things forgotten to the world, and that is that the life-force of the Darkening cannot be sustained unless there are magical items holding them here."

"Magical items, like…magical books? Swords?" I said. The crown, I thought with a jolt, suddenly remembering the words that I had overheard on Malata harbor. "I think I know what it is that is holding the Dead here – the Sea Crown of Roskilde." I told them the story of what the soldier had said, about his friend the palace guard who had seen Ohotto summon the dead by using it.

"The crown that should be yours, Lila." Danu's tone was serious. "So that's what this has all been about, hasn't it?" he said, speaking not to the dragon or me, but interrogating his own thoughts. "The Sea Crown of Roskilde, the legendary item that is said to be able to unite the islands of the Western Archipelago?" He looked at Crux. "How old is the Sea Crown, Crux? Have you heard of it before?"

"It is one of the Treasures of the World, of which there are many including the Dragon Stone Eggs, the Sword of Dardan, the Ring of the Gypsies, the Accursed Staff of Abbot Ansall, the…"

"Okay, I get the idea… the Sea Crown is one of the ancient treasures of the world, and Ohotto is perverting its natural power to summon this Darkening. What do you think we should do?" Danu was looking at me.

He was right. It had to be it. This had to be how Ohotto and Havick were controlling the Dead.

"I think we have to get that crown," I said.

༺❀༻

We left just after dawn, amidst the flurry of early-camp activity and arguments.

"I don't like it." My mother looked tired as she moved baskets of provisions from the longboats onto the shore. Around her there was already the hustle of activity: a line of people passing what little cargo we had, and others already working on rudimentary shelters, mostly just tents and huts made from upturned boats. And of course, everywhere the smaller Orange drakes. They had perched themselves on the rocky walls of the cliffs, lazing or watching intently at the activity of the Raiders and refugees below.

I'm not sure all of them like that attention, I thought as I saw more than one of the larger, burlier Raiders looking up apprehensively at the crags above. But it seemed that having our small cadre of Dragon Raiders fighting and working alongside them on Malata and the high seas had helped the Raiders accept the fact that we needed the dragons, at least.

How strange it is, I wondered for a moment, this was the way in which my dream – that the Raiders would live and work alongside the Dragons of the Western Archipelago—had come to pass. But at what cost?

Everything, I thought as I looked into my mother's eyes. They were still dull, despite the flash of annoyance. We had both lost so much and so quickly – but I had to make her see that this was the only way we could save what little we had left.

"We need to do this," I said to her gravely, as Pela set the latest basket down at the feet of the Raider Shep behind her, who picked it up and moved to take over her spot on the line. "You know what we face, Mother. The Dead. And I know what is keeping them here."

"Aye, the Sea Crown. You said." My mother brushed away some errant hair from her head. She hadn't bothered this morning to make the tight braid that she had always worn. That little fact made my heart break. "But the truth is, Lila–we don't know if you will succeed in this crazy mission to steal the Sea Crown. We don't know if that will even stop the Dead. You're basing all of this on the overheard words of some Roskildean bilge!"

"The Roskildeans are misguided," Danu said at my side, his brows knitting. "We need to save *them* from Havick and Ohotto as much as we save the Free Islanders…"

"The day that I break my fast with a Roskildean will be the day that I'm no longer a Raider!" Mother spat, earning an alarmed look from Danu. I hushed him with a gesture of my hands.

She was right. I am asking them to throw away their old Raider way of life, to become an army and fight for the archipelago itself. And, if I am successful, I will be asking them to throw away their old Raider way of hating Roskilde. I could be wrong. But I felt a flare of anger then at my mother. Not that I didn't know why she believed this. "Mother, I believe this information. I need to try to steal that crown, otherwise, we'll never be able to stop Havick. Don't you want to do that?"

"A Raider believes in revenge, Lila, not justice," My mother said defiantly.

At least she was getting angry now. Anything was better than that dead stare and that hopelessness.

But it still hurt, hearing my own mother challenge me like that. Did she think this was all too much? Too different from being a Raider? Did she think that *I* was trying to be something that I wasn't? That realization scared me more than even the hordes of the Dead.

"I have to try," I finished lamely, almost a plea to her.

She held her angry stare for a moment before her face collapsed into a resigned look. "I know that you do, Lila," she said quietly, taking a deep breath. "I made you a promise before your foster-father died that I would support you no matter what. I could see that you needed to follow your dreams of dragon riding, and there was nothing that I could do to stop you, and..." she kicked at the sand. "It made you happy."

"It does." I nodded. "And using dragons is the only way that we are going to be able to defeat Havick and Ohotto."

"I know that, Lila," My mother said wearily. "I just wish that it wasn't."

"So, I have your blessing to go?" I said.

"When have I ever been able to stop you from doing anything?" Pela said sadly. "You don't need my blessing, Lila. You're a leader of your people now."

"First daughter," Crux said in the back of my mind, but I had no idea what he was talking about. My mother held her arms out to me. I hugged her fiercely before she patted me on the back and it was done. I nodded back up the shoreline to where Crux was waiting, and I could feel the eyes of some of the other Raiders on me – and not all of them were entirely friendly.

"I'm sorry about that," Danu whispered. "That your mother didn't agree with you…"

For a moment his intrusion onto my thoughts just made me annoyed. *This is private!* I wanted to stamp my feet on the sand – but I didn't. Maybe I was growing up, or maybe a larger part of me was just too concerned with getting this over and done with. "It's fine. Us Raiders argue. It's how we do things," I said, which was true.

But my mother's words still stung– I wanted to part on better terms. It was even more worrying if I were to think about what I was doing would mean for the Raiders like Elash who outright hated me for my plan.

"They have to change," I explained to Danu. "Especially seeing where we are…" We paused in front of Crux, sipping our water as our eyes swept over the haphazard community. There were Raiders and there were the Fulani, and now there were other refugees from Khad, Mabol, and other islands. We were pretty evenly split, I think, between Raiders and non-Raiders – and at the moment it was our tight-knit, loyal Raiders whom everyone looked to for leadership – but what would happen in a few days? A week? Would the refugees continue to respect the Raiders – or would they split back into their old groups? Then it really would be over. The Raiders were now too small a force to protect themselves. We needed the refugees as much as they needed us. We needed to stand together, as Free Islanders.

"Lila! Danu!" It was Senga, running over the sand towards me, carrying her bow and quiver in one hand, and her curving scimitar (like mine) in the other. "Wait – we're coming." She gasped as she reached us.

"What?" I said in alarm.

"I heard about the mission. To steal the Sea Crown." Her eyes were bright. "How could I *not* want to be a part of that – it'll be the biggest raid we've ever pulled off!"

"It's not a raid, Senga," I said flatly. *This was serious,* I thought.

"Well, actually, she's right – it is," Danu corrected me.

"Ugh. No, I mean that this is serious. This is not just the Raiders' lives at stake—it's everyone's. And it's dangerous. I can't have you and the other Dragon Raiders coming with us," I said.

"Why ever not?" Senga halted, looking shocked.

"Because..." I searched for the words. *Because I don't want to get hurt. Because I can't afford to lose any more friends.* "Because I need you here," I said at last. Which was true. "I need the larger island dragons here to keep an eye on the Orange drakes, and I need as many trained riders and fighters here to protect our people."

"Oh," Senga said, her hurt expression changing to at least one of interest. "Us? Me and Adair, you mean?"

"Yes, Senga, you and Adair," I repeated. "I haven't gone through all of this in my head yet – but there aren't many fighters left, and then of *those,* there aren't that many who have managed to make friends with dragons," I explained. "I want you and Adair, and the others to be sorts of captains, only you're not on any boats, you're on Kim, and Thiel, Porax, Holstag and Grithor, Ixyl and Viricalia, Retax and Lucalia – how is she, by the way?" I asked pointedly.

"Better. The cannon shot hit her in the leg, and we think that she has a fracture, but she seems to know what she's doing."

"She will heal, given time," Crux said, and I nodded. Everyone had heard about the near miraculous abilities that the dragons had to heal – and Crux certainly was able to close up wounds and appear unaffected within days of receiving them. "Well, I just hope that she heals well," I said with a nod. "But until then, it makes more sense to have you and your brother here, looking after everyone."

"And keeping an eye on Elash, you mean?" Senga said under her breath.

"Yeah, well, him too. Just make sure that he knows that there are different views apart from his own," I said.

"You can trust me, Lila," Senga said, stuffing her scimitar back into her belt. "I guess that I don't need this then, right?"

"I think all of us are going to need to keep our swords close," I said, looking up at the makeshift settlement. Who knew what was out there in the wilds as well as on the waters? The shelters were springing up on the mainland –and there were already smaller work teams making their way to the nearest thickets for building timber and firewood. *But how long will this place last until someone else discovers it?*

"We're going to have to send people to Vala," I thought, taking another sip of the stream water we had discovered last night. I had seen the Trading City of Vala on the maps, but I had never been there myself, of course. "I wonder how they are going to take to these newcomers to their shores." I sighed. *Ugh. So much to do.*

"Well, probably a lot better than they will take to the Dead fleet," Danu muttered.

"You're right," I said, thumping him on the shoulder. "Come on, then, let's start a war."

❦

It almost felt good – if I managed to stop thinking about

precisely what we would be facing— because it *felt* like a raid, of sorts.

"*Hunting,*" Crux confirmed. "*This is what dragons are born to do.*"

"I thought that was to eat fish?" I teased him, feeling the wind in my hair.

"*That too. But we have to hunt the fish first,*" Crux argued in his dragon-like simplicity. It was hard to agree with such cast-iron reasoning.

But yes, this was what I was supposed to do, wasn't it? I thought as we flew high over the sea, flying fast and furious to the north-west. The mainland had long since disappeared behind us, leaving nothing but the line of clouds that hugged its hills on the horizon. Far below I could see the wavetops sparkling silver below us as we moved, and I even fancied that I saw a school of flying fish.

Raiding. Flying over the waves faster than the speed of the wind, to my destination of fury and adventure! I had to admit that the thought brought with it a sense of excitement. Wasn't this the exact same sort of thing that I had been raised to do, all of my life?

"Lila?" I heard Danu's worried voice and when I turned to look at him I could tell what he was about to say. "We're not going for revenge against Havick, not yet," he said.

"Why not? If I see the chance…" I said. *Maybe I could do it. Maybe I could strike down Havick and take the Sea Crown, and then all of this will be over, right?*

"Because Havick will be surrounded by guards, and renegade witches. No – we need to wait until there is a distraction and seize the crown from his throne room," Danu said.

"We can *make* a distraction," I pointed out. "We have a dragon, right? And you have your magic?" I said, thinking of the age-old Raider's tactic. "We allow ourselves to be spotted somewhere, and then fly away, faster than they can follow as they come out to investigate."

"Yes. That could work," Danu said, but that serious look was still in his eyes. "But I mean it, Lila – we are doing this for all of the people of the Western Archipelago, not just for the Sea Raiders."

"Of course," I said, but in my heart, I was thinking about revenge and blood. Havick had my real parents killed, and now he'd had my foster-father killed as well. He had destroyed Malata and he had taken the light from my mother's eyes.

If I got even the smallest opportunity to kill him, I would take it.

CHAPTER 20
DANU, UNCERTAIN

I was worried about Lila, even as we sped through the sky towards a far greater threat. But still, my thoughts kept returning to her words. Did she realize that we had to win the Sea Crown in order to unite the archipelago, just as the prophecy foretold? This, of course, triggered off all of the worries and doubts that I had about the Raiders: Would they be able to stop raiding and unite with other Free Islanders when the time came to fight Havick? Did Lila just want her revenge, heedless of whether she threw her life away in the process? Or the chance of peace?

That was the real reason, wasn't it? *The chance of peace.* The chance of a unified, united archipelago, just as King Bower and Queen Saffron had managed to finally unite

Torvald and the Three Kingdoms. *Could we do the same here, in the Western Isles?*

We islanders needed this. We needed a chance at peace, and we needed to stop fighting each other in the same way that we had for centuries!

"Why are you so worried about this?" Crux needled his way into my thoughts. *"The hunt is before us, and that is all we should be thinking about."*

"I, uh..." I looked up, but Lila was lost in her stare at the darkening horizon, as underneath us flashed another dark landmass of an island. She hadn't heard Crux's thought — and that meant the dragon had intended his words only for me.

"I guess that it's just..." I whispered into the winds, knowing that Crux would hear it with his super-sensitive ears. Or he would just read my mind, I suppose. "It's the Darkening. All the legends speak of it like an evil so terrible that it almost completely wiped out humanity and dragon kind more than once!" I closed my eyes. "I cannot believe that Ohotto has it under control and is using it to summon the dead. I am scared that if we divide our chances at all — then we will have doomed the whole world."

A snort of fire and soot from the dragon's nose ahead of us, which I guessed was his way of saying 'hmm.'

"You cannot know what will happen. Even your eyesight isn't that good, mage," Crux said to me, but his voice didn't sound as confident or as strong as it had before. Had I struck a

nerve? Was the mighty Crux himself worried about this as well?

"A dragon does not worry about anything. A dragon 'considers.'" Crux beat his wings a little faster.

That sounded an awful lot like worrying to me – but I wasn't going to be the one to correct him. "Okay, Crux. Just – we need that crown, okay? We need to get it and then work out how to lift the wicked enchantment that Ohotto must have laid on it."

"Magics." Another snort from the dragon beneath me, and I could feel his dismissal. *"Why do humans have to be so obsessed with magic, that they create crowns and spells and things that endanger us all? Magic is nothing special – just as I can fly, some people have powers, like you yourself do, Danu."*

"What was that?" Lila looked up. "I heard Crux talking."

"Oh, he was telling me his view on magic," I said. "He doesn't think that it's any good, I think."

"I didn't say that! I meant that I don't understand why you humans go mad whenever you have a touch of power! This Ohotto and her power, this Sea Crown..." he snarled.

"Well, I can't say that I don't agree with you," Lila said glumly. "Look – I see ships." She pointed to the south-west of our position, and I followed her gesture to where there was a small group of boats navigating around an island. They were tall-masted like the Roskildean galleons, and they were moving in two packs of three.

"A patrol," Lila said. "But what are they looking for – I can't see any other boat on the water?"

"Maybe they are looking for those two guard caravels we sunk," I said, the fear spreading through me. It would make sense. The Roskildean navy seemed to completely dominate the islands everywhere else. We could still see the plumes of black smoke rising on the horizon from where other islands had somehow displeased their new ruler. The burning pyres reminded me, of course, about Malata–but luckily the Raiders' island was out of sight, much farther to the south-west than we currently were.

"Well, we'd better get hidden," Lila said. "Crux?"

"Yes." At her request, the dragon pulled us upward into the mist and haze of the clouds above, until the air grew cold and the Western Archipelago had become little more than a child's picture of islands. My teeth chattered, and my fingers went numb despite their gloves and the warmth emanating from the dragon beneath us.

"Here," I said, fumbling to unwrap the blanket that was tied in front of me, and pushing it awkwardly over Lila's huddled form.

"No, it's fine – you take it…" she started to say.

"No, I'll be okay." My teeth chattered. "I'm not the rightful heir of the Western Isles, okay?"

"Oh." My friend frowned but nodded all the same. "Thank you. We won't be up here for long. Just until we see a safe place to land."

"O-Okay..." I said through chattering teeth and tried to remember the charms for warmth. After a few failed attempts, I managed to get a zone of slightly warmer than cold air to settle over us on Crux's shoulders.

"Ah. Well maybe magic does have some uses," the dragon purred appreciatively.

Ha!

We spent the night at a small islet halfway to Roskilde, as far north as either of us had ever been.

"If we draw a line due east, we'll hit the wildlands, and then the mountains, and then Torvald itself!" I said, after examining the stars here.

"Really?" Lila looked longingly in that direction. "That was where Saffron the island girl went and became a queen." I heard an echo of that old wistfulness in her words, an echo of her voice from the very first few days I had known her. Did she still want to be like her hero Queen Saffron? I was surprised, given the fact that she was a princess here in the Western Isles, and was now one of the accepted leaders of the Raiders.

"One day, we should visit," I said.

"What?" She looked at me like I had just suggested that she eat fish heads.

"Visit Torvald. When all of this is over," I pointed out.

"*Yeah,* sure," she said in a tone as if she wasn't expecting that at all, unrolling her blankets and curling up beside the fire. I wanted to reassure her that we would survive, but she had already turned away from me, leaving me to my thoughts and the dying embers of the fire. It was only as I myself was falling to sleep that I suddenly realized why she seemed so unenthused by that idea: she thought that she was going to die.

The next morning, we awoke with stiff and aching limbs and Lila forced me to go through some practice sparring matches with her. I was so exhausted that I didn't have time to question her about her comments last night. She didn't *seem* depressed or resigned at all – in fact, she seemed, if anything, determined and excited about what we were attempting to do.

The only real chance we had to talk was over the breakfast of campfire grilled fish (of course) and the few dried provisions that Pela had packed for us.

"We have two options," she said as I watched her draw a rough curve in the sand. At one end of the semi-circular curve we were, and at the top end, she poked with a stick. "That is where Roskilde is. It's a huge island, as you know."

The stick moved to the far point of the curve. "We're here. It would be quicker to go straight across." She drew a line from one end of the curve to another. "But we'll probably be seen. So, what I suggest that we're going to do is…"

The stick skipped across the water, but before it got to its destination it hopped back to the curve of imaginary islands again. "We can head north and curl back south again so that we're attacking the palace not from the sea, but from their own mainland."

"We're not attacking the palace, Lila." I frowned. "We're sneaking in."

"I know that." She flickered a sharp look at me. "But that is where the other half of my plan comes in to play."

"Which is?" I said, still unsettled by her talking of 'attack.' We were only two people on one dragon. Havick had castles and galleons and armies.

"The distraction. We need something to draw the fleet *away,* right?" She reached down and tapped the sea to the 'south' of the dirt-island Roskilde. "We should head straight for Roskilde, let them see us, and then we pull back." Lila's eyes were considering. "You know, it might even be better if we could be in two places at the same time. Like, you and Crux are seen and draw them away while I sneak in?"

I narrowed my eyes. "It's too dangerous. We can't split up – we should fly all together to the mainland."

"If they spot Crux, they'll fire at him," Lila said stubbornly.

"They won't hit me – I am too quick!" Crux raised his head from the rocks where he had been sitting, looking down into the sea at the gleaming bodies of the fish that darted past.

"I can't risk that…" Lila started to shake her head.

"And I cannot risk you against a castle of enemies." Crux stared hard at her. "I know what it is you plan, Lila wave-rider, and out of respect, I haven't mentioned it to Danu."

"What?" I said in alarm, looking between them. I knew there was something funny about Lila, ever since we started going on this mission!

"Nothing. Crux has just got the wrong impression…" Lila said.

"No. I haven't, Lila!" There was a loud thud as Crux turned entirely and laid one of his massive paws on the ground near us. It shook the nearby trees. He stared at Lila and then turned his head towards me. "Lila has been thinking that she wants to leave you, Danu dragon-friend, and me, to cause the distraction while she hunts down this Havick and kills him."

"What? Lila – no!" I said.

"And while I agree with the sentiment, Lila wave-rider," Crux said as he swung his head back towards his friend. "I cannot agree to you throwing your life away so readily!"

"What makes you think I would be throwing my life away?" Lila said defiantly. "I can fight. I am a *good* fighter!"

"But you are a better fighter with a mage and a dragon at your side. Not without," Crux said in his undeniable logic.

"This has to be about the Sea Crown, not revenge!" I said. *How could Lila be planning this? How could she risk throwing all that we have done away?* I got my answer the very next second.

"He took *everything* away from me, Danu – don't you see

that?" she said, and I felt my heart break for her. What must it be like, to know that you were a foster child and that your parents were killed for no reason, and that your entire life has been one of danger and threat? But at the same time, some small part of me stung. Weren't Crux and I *something* to her? "He won't stop until I'm dead, either. You know that," Lila continued.

"And I won't stop until you are on the throne of the Western Archipelago," I said back, glaring. "I know you want revenge, Lila, and maybe you have a right to – but you are not just a fighter or a Raider. You are more than that. You are a princess. You are a leader to your people – and now to the Free Islanders as well!" I tried to make her see herself as I saw her. "You have no idea how people respond to you, do you? They are drawn to you. To your confidence, to your bravery. *That* is what these islands will need against the Darkening. Not the story of a brave but dead girl, and maybe a bunch of your relics!"

Maybe I said the last part a bit too savagely, because Lila's eyes filled with tears and she turned her face away from me quickly. "I don't think that if you knew me, you would think that I'm brave," she said, her words thick with emotion.

"What? Of course you are. Of course I know you," I said. I had flown beside her for almost a year, and not once had I seen her retreat from a fight.

"You remember I told you about that night when I saw my father, sorry, my *foster*-father die?" She turned back to look at me with sharp eyes. "I did nothing. I tried, but I was too scared. I tried to find a light, a torch, a lamp, but I couldn't – and then when I should have run out there with my sword to stop them? I didn't, and they died. Their deaths are my fault!" She ended on a shout.

"Oh, Lila…" I said, reaching out to her. *How could she think that?* "It wasn't your fault. What good would a blade do against the dead? You must have done everything that you could…"

Lila recoiled from my touch as I settled at her side, and Crux carefully stepped around to curl around both of us.

"It is okay to be scared, Lila wave-rider," he said, and I could hear it soft and wittering in my ears as well as understandable in my mind. Crux was being considerate and gentle. I had never even thought the Phoenix dragon was capable of such sensitivity. *"I think like you,"* the dragon said carefully, and it was clear that these thoughts were awkward for him to share. Maybe they were too human, or too painful. *"That I must be fierce, and stronger than all the rest, just to be me. But dragons don't care if you are brave or afraid. Dragons know that we will be all of these things at least once in our lives. What matters is what you do, despite how you feel."*

I was stunned by the wisdom that I heard in him then. It was a wisdom that I hadn't managed to gather in all of my long years of studying at the most learned place in the islands. I knew then that was what I should have been telling Lila – not that she was bloodthirsty and wrong and didn't have a right to her emotions – but that it was okay to feel angry, and upset, and scared.

"He's right." I hung my head. "I am sorry, Lila, I have been a bad friend to you. I am sorry for your father."

Lila looked at me for a long moment, and I couldn't read her eyes, but then, quickly, she ducked in and kissed me on the cheek. It was barely a kiss at all, more just a quick brush of her face to mine, but as she pulled away it left me feeling giddy and uncertain.

That means that she's forgiven me, right?

What does it mean?

Why do I suddenly feel nervous?

What do I do in return? Are you supposed to do anything?

What...?

But Lila was already standing up and pressing herself against Crux's snout, where he purred at her with his deep throat-rattle of pleasure. If they spoke to each other, then I couldn't hear Lila, and Crux didn't share the words with me. I stood up awkwardly and looked around. Right. Pack up the camp. Yes. Check the provisions.

CHAPTER 21
LILA AND THE PALACE

Our plan was set, despite my misgivings. I still felt angry and worried when I thought about it – but I threw myself into scanning the horizon for our enemies instead. A part of me still believed that it would be safer just for me to sneak into Havick's stronghold alone – but Danu and Crux would have none of it. Every time that I turned my head, I would see Danu looking at me with his stern, serious gaze as if he expected me to suddenly jump off the dragon's back and *swim* to Roskilde!

But he was sweet, too, I remembered. But thinking about that only made me feel fluttery and nervous. *Bah. No time for sweet. I have a king to kill.*

"There they are," Danu murmured, and I looked up to see the island of Roskilde for the first time.

We had flown fast and high through the afternoon, straight across the sea as we had discussed in a beeline to the center of our enemy. We timed it so that we would arrive as the light faded from the sky and was replaced by the lonesome gleam of torches and ship lanterns. The waters beneath us had been busy, and so, not wanting to be seen too soon, we had flown as high we dared, with Danu using his warming magic to keep us from freezing.

Far larger than Malata, Roskilde was the largest of islands in the circular archipelago and sat at the northern apex of the chain of landmasses. Its mountains rose far above the glow of what must be the city, their slopes still glowing faintly purple and lighter grey as they caught the last of the setting sun.

So, this was my home? I thought, finding myself curiously unmoved by the sight. It was too big, for starters. What would a ruler do with so much land? How on earth could they rule well? It was impossible not to compare the dark form that spread across the horizon to Malata (*now gone...*). Roskilde had mountains and ports. It had the glitter of towns and villages, but Malata was home. My only real home.

Were we Sea Raiders so simple in how we lived? I thought as I gazed at the fat trading boats and their accompanying patrol galleons moored in their home port. The place was so big, I felt staggered by it. *Big and...sophisticated? Is this how they lived in Torvald, too – where every building is built of stone, with slate-tiled roofs and cobbled streets?* I thought about our journey, as on our flight we had seen many such vessels clipping their way across the Barren Sea to and from their home port. It felt strange to be here at last, and to see so much activity. And I suddenly had a mental picture of the wide network of trading routes and ports that stretched right across the archipelago – and beyond—unfettered access to which Roskilde enjoyed. I had never conceived of the Western Isles in that way; I had thought them a wild, almost lawless place of adventurous communities, but here I saw that it was really a net of trade and alliances that had to stretch from one end of the world to the other.

And all of this wants to crush us, I thought in alarm, as I started to see the line of boats protecting their huge stone harbor, far larger than any I had seen before. I couldn't make out the buildings yet, but if the lights were anything to go by, then just their dock and warehouse district must cover the entire northern coast of Malata itself.

And there, in front of it was the Dead fleet. I shivered as a sudden chill swept through my bones, even despite Danu's magic.

They were stationed in an irregular band of tall, black galleons around the harbor, gently bobbing with the rise and fall of the waves. They had no lights on their decks, unlike the passing boats that still (carefully, I noted) passed between them. Even from this high vantage point, they seemed to exude an ominous air.

"Are you ready?" I said, my teeth chattering – and not just from the cold.

"Yes," Danu said. and the zone of warmth suddenly dropped, making me inhale sharply. "I need to concentrate on the spell..." he added, by way of an explanation. I nodded, and Crux tipped forward, to swoop down.

"Go, Crux – give them something to think about!" I said fiercely, flattening myself to his neck as I felt Crux's savage surge of enthusiasm.

"Skreyar!" He roared as he swept out of the skies towards the Dead fleet. The boats grew larger and larger in my eyes. Changing from dots no bigger than bugs to the size of stones, cats, tables, houses-

With the whoosh of flame sucking all available air to it, Crux blazed a pillar of flame at the nearest boats, straight down onto their black masts and fluttering sails.

"Now, Crux – pull up!" I shouted as figures suddenly moved from their stationary positions on their decks as if when they weren't fighting or sailing all they did was stand there, motionless, not even bothering to go aft castle or below decks. The idea made me feel even more sick, and I was glad as I saw the flames fall to catch several of the dead sailors before we were darting out across the waters, the dive giving us a terrific speed as Crux started to rise into the air once more.

"Danu?" I called, alarmed. *Could he do it?* He had told me that he would use his magic to help us – but would it backfire, as it had on Malata? *Maybe I would have been better off coming alone.* I gritted my teeth.

"No!" Crux rebuked me savagely in my mind.

"Ia Lucis!" I heard him bellow behind me, and suddenly, out of the dark skies above us there was a clap of thunder and the world lit up as lightning bolts speared down past us.

"Woah!" I screamed, half in terror and half in exhilaration. *Danu is getting stronger by the day,* I thought. I had never seen him summon lightning before.

Half of the bolts hit the water to plumes of exploding water, but the rest hit the nearest three of the Dead fleets. No single bolt was strong enough to bring it down, but I saw one completely shattered the main mast of one of the boats, and another destroy a section of gunwale.

"Well, *that* will get their attention, for sure!" I shouted, looking behind me to see the Dead fleet ships waking, several of the first 'barrier' of the Dead fleet breaking from the line and slipping towards us. Unlike any other vessel which took time to move— for orders to be relayed, understood, and acted upon— the Dead fleet had a way of responding instantly to some hidden order. Their crew acted as one in a way that the living did not – even us Sea Raiders.

Six? Seven? I counted as they started to grow smaller behind us. *Was that going to be enough?*

"We might need to come around again!" I called.

"No – I got this!" Danu bellowed, before demanding that the sky open itself up once more for him.

It did, as another fistful of lightning bolts fell from the sky in blinding flashes, landing behind our pursuers and hitting more of the stationary Dead fleet. As I watched, this sparked the sudden break of five more of the creepy ships from their guard duty.

Eleven or twelve boats – it would have to do. It was still only a small part of the greater number of Dead fleet and more regular naval vessels that Roskilde had, but it was enough to count as an armada. With just ten fully armed galleons you could lay siege to an island, and these were all the powerful and fast Dead Ships, so I guessed that was the best that we could ask for.

"Okay, Crux – up!" I called, and Crux laboriously drove his wings to draw us higher and higher out of sight.

The air grew chill, and the rush of our flight whipped my hair and clothes around me in a thunder of noise. The Dead fleet were still following us, but they were growing smaller and smaller. *Would they keep following us? Had we done enough?*

"Ia Lucis!" Danu shouted once more, and my eyes were blinded by the decent of another clutch of lightning bolts around us. I couldn't help but think that the boom of their descent wasn't as deafening as the first had been, and maybe there weren't as many in each batch as before – but he was doing his best to still present a threat to the Dead fleet, and to lure them farther south.

The air misted and clouded around us, and I leaned to one

side, giving Crux the mental picture of veering up and *over* the clouds to head back north and north-east once more. The Phoenix dragon took my suggestion instantly, beating his wings harder to throw us into the cloud cover, where I instantly not only felt freezing but damp as well.

Ugh! I thought, distracting myself from thinking about our success or failure. *We really have to get some sort of dragon cloaks for the riders.*

Another gasp of cold escaped my lips as we broke free of the cloud layer, and we skimmed atop the grey nest, with the sky above us a purpling-blue, with the first stars starting to appear.

Wow. Despite the situation, the sights that you see on the back of a dragon are still beautiful.

Crux had turned us north-east, and I could make out the dark mass of the Roskildean mountains ahead of us, their slopes now glittering with ice and snow, and shedding banks of clouds from their upper ridges. How long before we were over the island itself? I wondered, turning to see if Danu was all right.

He was slumped in the makeshift saddle, his hands braced against the tines. "Danu!?" *Dammit! I should have known that the toll of the magic would be too high!* Isn't this precisely what had happened at the Second Battle for Malata?

"Danu – please hold on, I need you!" I said, turning and unhooking my belt to scrabble towards him.

"Hgnh?" He managed to blink at me wearily. "It's getting

easier. It's just painful. Like drinking too much Raider ale..." He smiled weakly as I settled myself in around him and thumped his chest and tried to rub the life into his limbs. I managed to get him to drink some of our water as the mountains grew closer.

"Danu dragon-friend, open your heart," Crux demanded of him. *What did he mean?*

"It is forbidden for dragons to give their life-force so freely, but amongst friends, it has been known." Crux said, and before I could ask what he meant, I felt a surge of *something* pass upwards through Crux, and into the form of Danu. It was like a wave of warmth, heat and light. *Life.* I must have been caught, too, in that wave of gifted life as I was suddenly aware of a zinging energy through my muscles and bones, and the unstoppable confidence that made me *know* that I was strong enough to do this. If I closed my eyes, I could feel the heat in my chest like a fire, and one that I might be able to spit out in a flame if I wanted to...

"No, Lila. You cannot breathe the sacred flame as we do. But you have seen a little of what it is to be a dragon, and to share hearts with a child of the sun," Crux informed me, and I opened my eyes to see that the color had returned to Danu's cheeks, and his eyes were bright again.

"I feel alive!" he said with a victorious laugh, and I had to join him. "And I think I am strong enough for another act of magic. Thanks to Crux, I can try to cloak us as we descend..." he said as I scrabbled back to my seat.

"Okay, just don't collapse on me again…" I muttered as Crux dipped into the clouds and once again I was covered in the damp cloud-fog. Danu murmured something inaudible behind me, and before we had even dropped through the lower layers of the clouds I could feel the magic emanating from Danu like ripples from a dropped stone.

And everything around us looked a little *odd,* too. Like we were still inside those clouds and staring out of a veil of fog, or through a heat mirage. "Danu? This is you, right?"

"Yeah…hiding spell…" Danu's shoulders quivered with effort. "Lots of concentration…" he hissed through his teeth.

"Oh, sorry…" We had emerged over a land of muted and blurred lines; the great island of Roskilde was made soft by Danu's magic, like a watercolor painting. This was all very well and good, but I needed to be able to see the guards!

There was a glow ahead of us, which was the brightest thing for leagues around. I took that to be the city.

"It is. Although our eyes might be affected, my nose and hearing aren't," Crux confirmed.

"Well, I guess that I'll just have to trust you then…" I said.

"Do you think I make a habit of giving my life-force away to humans?" I could feel Crux's anger. Right. I probably deserved that.

The glow ahead resolved in that way that a shape focuses when coming out of the mist. The lights became many lights, streets and avenues that were broken by plazas and parks and taller buildings of state. At least two rivers ran through

Havick's city – and to my shame, I was suddenly aware that I knew so little about this place.

The capital of Roskilde is a city called Roc, I tried to dredge my memory for the titbits of information gleaned from the charts of my father. *It is a large walled city that opens out over the Roc Bay. It has four entry gates and two guard towers at each gate. Its navy is about sixty war galleons, another fifty or so guard caravels, and another fifty smaller armed clippers.* I sighed. The only information that the Sea Raiders had bothered to record about the place were facts that pertained to raiding.

"My birth parents lived here," I murmured. It made me feel odd. Below us the ground was dark, but I could make out the silvery lines of roads, the dark humps of ancient trees. It looked like it would be a prosperous place. I imagined the sun shining on corn fields, while carts and happy farmers carried their trade back and forth.

Crux had slowed his flight to a glide now, allowing us time to search for a suitable landing spot. I started to hear the sounds of the city, too. Even at night – this place made noise. The murmur of jackdaws and seagulls in their roosts, and the occasional raised voice.

"Danu?" I breathed as the city, still blurry, but much more discernible as we moved like a silent shadow over the outer walls.

"Yes, Lila?" he said through gritted teeth.

"Is this a good place?" I heard my own words and quietly

cursed myself for being stupid. "I mean, not under Havick and Ohotto of course – but before that. When…"

"When your parents were on the throne?" His voice sounded strained, and I wondered how hard it had to be to cast a magic spell and answer questions at the same time.

"Never mind. Just concentrate on getting us in there safely," I said hurriedly. How stupid could I be to distract him? I didn't want to find out about my birth parents anyway. They were long since dead and had nothing to do with my life now.

"Liar," Crux said, his voice in the back of my mind. When I thought back that I wasn't, and no – I really *didn't* care about my birth parents, honestly – I found that he had already pulled his thoughts away. Instead, he flicked his wings and we soared up a rise that stood at one end of the city. The streets below became broader, and the dark blocky houses seemed more square, taller. Shapes emerged out of the magical haze just under Crux's feet – weather vanes and statues that must sit atop their fine buildings. This city is so big.

Crux's destination became obvious, as we flew straight over a gatehouse with torches merrily blazing over of its arrow-slit windows, and over a green sward that was split by cobbled roads and girted with low buildings. *Barracks. And that meant...*

Ahead of us stood the palace castle of my parents, the ancestral home of the rulers of Roskilde.

Damn, it was big, were my first thoughts.

The palace-keep of my parents was comprised of four tall

guard towers of a cream-grey stone in front, while the rear of the keep joined with the outer walls and melded seamlessly with the cliffs overlooking the bay. The battlements weren't blocky and rectangular like I had always pictured but were instead shaped like pointed wave tops – and there, rising in the middle was one thin tower whose fluted peak gleamed gold in the hanging giant lanterns (each lantern, I guessed, had to be as big as a person).

"Where do you keep the kingdom's most precious object apart from up there?" I asked as Crux swooped up towards the battlements

"Maybe that's where you keep the witches," Danu said nervously.

With a clashing of wings that made me nervous – *surely the wall guards heard that?* – Crux settled at the rear of the palace-keep battlements, revealing a wide stone stop to the keep, with a concertina of slated rooftops beyond. It looked like the palace had been many buildings once but had been fused organically together over time into one, brute keep.

"I will wait outside the city. When you are done, I will find you," Crux said as we dismounted, and I let my hand linger on his snout for a moment, feeling his strong, encouraging warmth.

"We will return," I whispered to him, to which I received a nod and he had lifted back into the skies. For a moment I saw the way that Danu's magic shifted and blurred Crux's shape, making my eyes slide off him, and my brain tell me *it's just a cloud! It's a cloud!* I marveled again at Danu's powers, and, when I turned to look at my friend I saw that he, too, blurred at the edges somewhat like a distant picture.

He was clenching his teeth and frowning deeply as he kept muttering arcane words to keep the shields up. Not knowing how long he could keep this up, I nodded towards the nearest of the doors, amidst the maze of roof peaks here on the palace of Roc.

Luckily for us, I suppose, the nearest door was clearly some sort of entrance kept unlocked for the distant guards on the battlements to come and go. It opened onto a wide stone room where racks of crossbows and quivers of bolts were stacked on the walls around a small table where a lantern and a tureen of something hot and good-smelling sat. I would almost have considered tasting the broth, were it not for the urgency of our mission.

No doorway out, but instead a landing and wide set of stairs leading down.

"You okay?" I breathed at Danu, who nodded, keeping his eyes squinted near-shut. Taking that as good news, I drew my blade and led the way down. *We'll have to get out of this patrol area of the keep and find the way to that central tower,* I was thinking as the stairs opened onto another broad landing where I could hear the sounds of soldiers complaining and relaxing.

Open arched doorways spilled their light onto the avenue revealed. Which way? Left or right? On impulse, I chose left – at least that was heading towards the back of the keep, rather than nearer the front gates.

"I just don't like them, I tell you! I don't care what side they're on!"

"Hush – that's treason if the hags hear you saying that!"

The wash of noise filled my ears as we tiptoed carefully past the archways. They opened out onto long rooms, replete with tables, more equipment, and all manner of men and women sat drinking or mending bits of equipment as they must be waiting for their call to wall duty. My heart skipped a beat as one sharp-nosed woman turned to look out of the archway at us. I could swear that her eyes widened as she saw us, but then her glance slid away, as Danu's magic convinced her that we were nothing, just shadows in the night…

We passed the next archway without incident and the next. The primary topic of conversation was the state of the food, and how much everyone hated working with the dead. I could almost have felt sorry for them – *if they hadn't been at war with us for generations,* I thought grimly and readjusted my grip on my blade.

At the end of the landing there was a sharp turn, and this time the corridor contained many simple wooden doors. Thankfully there were no windows or openings in this one, and I could hear snoring coming from what must have been the soldiers' barracks. Strangely, even surrounded by my enemy, this made me feel a little more confident. I had spent a lot of time trying to sleep surrounded by the snores of roguish and rough Raiders. It made me feel that they were only human, after all.

The end of the corridor led to a narrow archway, and then a short staircase down to a balcony. The light and the noise were *much* louder down here, and for a moment I froze. The balcony looked over to a larger sort of banqueting hall, where there were *more* people – this time not wearing their breastplates and helmets but still in their leathers eating that victuals and listening to a flautist and his slender singing companion. There was something about the melancholy tone of the musician that cut through the laughter and ribald jokes to reach me.

"Blood is always spilling,
In the water, in the water~
How much?
Never enough, in the water~
Drown that awful past,
In the water, in the water~
Make hope last,
In the water, in the water~
The Crown that rises again,
From the water, from the water,
Is the Crown that will cleanse,
In the water, in the water."

The song was mournful and made my heart twang like a harp string. They were singing about the Sea Crown, and the prophecy, weren't they? That was almost exactly the same words as Danu had read out to me 'the Crown that rises again' from the water, which he took to be a metaphor for *me,* the heir to this place.

But it was so sad! It was a song about endless bloodshed, endless slaughter and disaster? I looked down, over the balcony to see what sort of effect that the song had on the soldiers below. Would they think it treasonous, if it was about me? But luckily most of the soldiers were already too drunk or too busy to pay much notice. Those who had been paying attention were clapping loudly, and one of them, wearing a deep blue-grey cloak suddenly stood up and raised a flagon towards the two musicians.

"Here's to the king of the Western Isles!" the cloaked man roared.

A howling shout of celebration rose from those still able, and ale cups were raised and sloshed high.

"They think that song is about Havick," I whispered to Danu. "They think that *he* is the crown that will stop the bloodshed…" I stepped back from the balcony railing, feeling suddenly uncertain. I hadn't realized quite how *strongly* that these people believed in their usurper king. Did no one here remember my real parents?

"Lila…" Danu grunted through clenched teeth. Suddenly his form swam out of the blur and was crystal sharp as his magic failed, and then slowly diffused once more around the edges.

He was losing control, and we still hadn't found the tower at all. "Okay, I get it," I said and grabbed his hand. We ran to the end of the balcony, down the next corridor (which seemed to lead to smaller store rooms and studies, which I guessed must be for the captains and lieutenants). We were still in the workers' section of the keep and we needed to get into the royal section!

Instead of following this broad corridor, I decided to take a branching corridor deeper into the keep, at least in the same direction that I thought that we had to go into. It was a little narrower, and the end of it was also occupied.

Drat! I thought, seeing a small room beside a wide iron gate across the far side – and through the gate there appeared to be another grand hall, this time dark, but I could make out the edges of wall hangings and tapestries. It was a guard station, and there was the eponymous sentry, seated on a small bench, with his halberd beside him.

He looked like the sort to be watching over the entry to the more 'official' part of the palace-keep. He was a broad-shouldered man, and he wore a finely-tooled breastplate, elaborately designed helmet, shoulder pads and greaves.

With any luck, he's a ceremonial soldier and can't fight, I thought as I tiptoed towards him. What should I do? Try to push the door open past him? What if it was locked.

I held my sword at my side and wondered if I had so little honor as to run him through when he couldn't even see me.

No. I didn't.

I reversed my grip so that I could hit him with the flat of the blade. I had just decided I would knock him out when my plan was disrupted by a whisper.

"Oh crap," Danu said, and suddenly the corridor, Danu, and I jumped into sharp focus.

"Bloody rocks!" The guard suddenly gasped as we jumped into existence. His eyes widened, and his face went pale in an instant, and, with a gasp, he collapsed to the floor. He had fainted from the shock of two fierce-looking Raiders popping into life right beside him.

"Well, that was easier than I could have hoped!" I said with a grin at Danu, seeing him clutch at his head. "Danu? How bad?"

"Better than it was before – I think. Whatever Crux did to me, it seems to have made the magic easier." He rubbed his eyes. "But it still hurts like hell."

"Here." I unclipped the unconscious warrior's breastplate and blue-grey cloak, and helped Danu put both on. Last of all, I shoved the guard's halberd into his hands. "As my first duty as regent, I appoint you, Danu Geidt, as my royal escort."

"I thought that is what I did anyway." He managed a smile. He couldn't be *that* much in pain, then. "And I have no idea how to use one of these things." He frowned at the halberd in his hands.

"I was actually thinking you could lean on it if the pain gets worse, like a walking stick," I told him. "But if we run into any trouble, you use the pointy end. Think of it like a fishing spear," I explained, before tying up the Roskildean and arranging him on the bench as if he were drunk or had decided to take a nap. It was easy to find a large ring of iron keys, and we were through the last gate and into the palace proper.

"Woah, Lila – do you see that?" Danu gasped behind me.

"Yes, Danu, I see," I muttered at what he must be looking at.

We were in a large hall, split into a larger lower area with columns and benches around the sides, and a higher, smaller alcove-area at the back, separated by a few steps, and inside of which more arched doorways led out. On our own lower level there were more doorways and in between them were tapestries hanging over statues and busts. But that wasn't what Danu was looking at, was it? We were both looking at the raised level of the hall, where the tapestries had been replaced by large oil paintings.

The largest and grandest of the paintings were all of a tall and thin man with black hair that was ferociously braided back from his head. He had a thin, weak beard (nothing like Chief Kasian's) and wore gold-edged blue-grey robes. Havick. I just knew it. Who else would have multiple pictures of themselves?

The real source of our shock were the smaller pictures, hanging all the way up to the curving rafters above. There were generations upon generations of portraits in here, of men and women, and sometimes couples, and sometimes children – all staring out of their pictures in a watery sort of way and wearing the blues, silvers, and greys of the Roskildean noble colors, with a few splashes of red and purple.

But it was more than that. They all had dark hair like mine, and many faces showed an uncanny resemblance to my own features. My sharp nose, my eyes.

"That's your family, Lila," Danu whispered, moving past me up to this portrait antechamber, his halberd clopping on the flagstones as he lurched.

"They're not my family," I said impetuously, but it was ridiculous to lie. These smaller pictures obviously were, and that thought made me angry. *What do they know of the life I have lived? When have they ever had a crew depend on them for their lives? When have they sung through the long storm nights of winter? Chopped wood for their fires? Helped pick welks from the Bone Reef?*

"This picture, I think, I think this is your birth parents, Lila," Danu whispered.

Why on earth would Havick keep those pictures? I thought in alarm – until I remembered what that courtier had said, the one who we had rescued from the boat. *Everyone thinks the Raiders killed my parents. They don't know that Havick paid them to do it.*

"He's trying to keep the people on his side," I murmured, suddenly realizing what this tribute to the Roskilde lineage was. Havick was stating that he was just the latest descendant of an embattled line…

I gazed at the picture of my own birth parents, and I instantly flushed cold. It was a smaller picture than many of the others, and it did not have the same grandeur. There was my father – a man who was tall but looked a little too lean as if he had spent too long in his study. He had slightly lighter hair, edged with grey at the temples, and he wore a deep blue braided vest with a lighter blue trim. The painter had managed to catch him smiling, as he stood with his arm around a seated woman with black hair. Black hair that would tangle as soon as the wind got at it, with skin that would tan as deep as a walnut in the warm sun.

My mother had not been captured looking out at the painter, but instead, I could see her in profile, that sharp nose, the slight turn of her lips. She was looking down at the small bundle that she held in her hands, and for a moment I wished that she was not, that she was staring straight out so that, at least once, I could look my mother in the eye.

"That must be you," I heard Danu say, pointing to the last and the smallest figure depicted in the painting. A babe in my mother's arms, which she was tenderly gazing at. It was small and swaddled in deep blue and gold silks which made it look vaguely cocoon-shaped as if I were to hatch and grow wings at any moment.

By the stars! I swore as I saw the final detail. The painter had been good, it seemed, because he had caught one of those small details that might have seemed insignificant was really precisely depicted. A square of white embroidered cloth, lacy at the edges was just slipping out of my painted chubby hands and was sliding across my blankets. It clearly showed the gold stitching (painted with minute brushstrokes) of the rising Sea Crown over a curl of waves, and the words *"Lila of Roskilde"* embroidered underneath it.

It was the exact same cloth that I had wadded in the bottom of my small carry sack right now, although mine had lost a lot of stitching and was now a faded grey, no longer the pristine white in the painting anymore. It was the same cloth that my foster-father Kasian had kept when he snatched the babe from my real mother's corpse and had delivered me to his own grieving wife, Pela.

And that is how the cloth came back to me, some nineteen years later, I thought, reaching a hand to graze the bottom of my pack.

I had known who I really was for the past year, and I had always known that I was no Raider-born but seeing this physical proof before me was like confronting that fact all over again. This was where I began. This was where my story started, I thought in revelation.

A hundred questions and demands instantly rose within me.

This is my home. How could Havick control this place? I was born here. How could Havick lie to his people so thor-

oughly? This place belongs to me. Havick is in league with the Dead!

It was hard to describe, but it was as if I had woken up and seen the world with new eyes. I suddenly felt like I had a *right* to be here, and I felt a deep *outrage* at Havick and his loyal supporters for attempting to stop me.

"Lila? Lila – we have to go. Find the Sea Crown," Danu was saying to me, as I shook my head to clear my thoughts and try to concentrate.

Havick must die. He has tricked a whole nation! Red hot anger pulsing through me.

"Lila?" Danu was looking at me oddly—I must have been grimacing.

"It's okay, Danu. We'll put an end to this travesty." I turned past him and stalked to the largest of the arched doorways that led from this raised antechamber. The grandest route must surely lead to the throne room? Or the king's compartments, mustn't they?

"The Sea Crown, Lila, remember?" Danu said from behind me.

"That's what I meant," I returned, but I didn't know whether or not he believed me at all.

The corridor was wide, now with walls that were broken by sudden alcoves displaying statues, paintings, or wall hangings.

It was the middle of the night, so the archways that opened out onto more sedate eating halls or study areas all appeared to be deserted apart from the glow of lanterns hanging on their sconces.

I passed a cursory gaze over the objects that we passed. I saw pictures of simplistic-looking figures striking out across impossibly high waves, followed by another of the same figures praising the dirt and stone shore when they had finally found safe passage.

The founding of Roskilde. It made me angry that all of my history had been denied me. *Was my family brave? Did we come from warrior stock?* How was I to know? Would *ever* know these things now?

"Halt!" someone shouted from an archway as we jogged past. I just ran faster.

"Lila – guards!" Danu gasped. "Lots and lots of guards!"

I spared a look over my shoulder to see that yes, spilling out from one of the corridors were at least five or six heavily armored guards in the same elaborate armor that the fainted one had been in. We were out of the reach of everyday soldiers and infantry it seemed, and now in the jurisdiction of the elite palace guard.

"Don't worry, Danu – if they're shouting that they don't want us to go somewhere – then we're on the right track!" I called back, feeling giddy and dangerous. *What was wrong with me?* A moment of clarity amidst my anger.

Nothing. There is nothing wrong. I just want my revenge, I told myself as we slid across the flagstones, around a corner to another wide corridor, this time with a broad set of gates in the wall at the end, and two palace guards standing at it. They must have heard the commotion as each had his halberd lowered already.

"Stop them! Intruders!" a soldier shouted from behind us as I raised my sword and, with an ululating Raider cry – charged.

"Silenci Ambit!"

Something like a gale of wind rushed past my shoulder, almost knocking me off course and two sentries were thrown backward from where they stood.

"Perves Ambit!" Danu roared, clutching his hand tight as the groaning men tried to push themselves up, somehow getting caught in their cloaks. The metal-shod greaves half slid down one's leg, and the other's helmet fell over his eyes. It was like watching the worst series of unfortunate wardrobe accidents ever.

"You did that?" I said as I skidded to a halt outside the gate.

"Never mind – better than you getting us killed! Keys!" Danu snapped, making more gestures with his hands as the two warriors ahead of us tripped, slid, and fell over each other.

I fumbled for the keys that I had just so recently stolen (*not stolen – this is my palace!*) and searched for the right one to open this gate. On the other side was a set of stairs, leading up. It must be the tower!

"Ambit!" Danu shouted, this time at the *other* set of palace guards as he threw the wind-ball at them and knocking them over like a child's game.

Wrong key. I tried the next.

But Danu was hissing as he thudded his back to the wall, still holding out one hand to control whatever arcane forces he was summoning. Some of the palace guards were still pinned to the floor, whilst others had managed to roll to the edge of the alcoves, and crouch behind statues and ornamental art.

"Crossbows to the front!" their captain ordered as that key also didn't work and I tried another.

"Lila – I can't hold them off much longer…" Danu was saying.

Click! "Yes!" The gates swung inward and we fell inside before I clanged them shut and locked them. Danu thrust his halberd against the bottom stair and the gates just as the first of the soldiers got to the other side – luckily these ones didn't have crossbows, and we jumped back as they jabbed their swords through the holes in the gate.

"Up, up!" I seized Danu by the scruff of the neck and we scrambled backwards up the stairs, as the palace guards tried unsuccessfully to batter the gate down. "That won't hold them long," I breathed as we turned up the spiral stairs.

"Better than being skewered." Danu groaned, thudding from one side of the wall to another.

"He has called on a lot of magic in little time," Crux

warned in my mind. *"He grows strong, but he cannot continue like this..."*

"Can't you send him more of your dragon-power? Like you did before?" I snapped, feeling a flash of anger at how we were so close...

"How can you ask me that? Humans are not meant to hold too much dragon-life. Do you want Danu to become like Enric? This witch Ohotto?" Crux was annoyed.

"He'll have to be fine, then!" I snarled, holding Danu's hand as I ran, two steps at a time upward, my sword in the other. *Danu will have to be fine,* I thought as I ran. *Because I am going to need him when I kill Havick...*

"What? And how will you escape, surrounded by enemies?" I could feel Crux's sudden anger. *"I can hear alarms, bells, and shouts, you know. That stone box is coming alive – and I can smell many hundreds of people in there..."*

I could feel the dragon shifting his weight from foot to foot through our connection. I caught a sudden snapshot of the night air around him in a deserted corner of a scrubby field near a stream.

He was getting ready to fly to us.

"Not yet! I need to finish this!" I begged him.

A savage growl from the dragon on the other side of my mind. *"You might die."*

"I won't," I promised him, not knowing if I could keep that promise. Right now, my anger felt like it could accomplish anything, as nineteen years of suppressed rage and heartbreak was still rushing through me. If the dragon understood that or not I didn't know because Crux did not respond. Instead, when I reached towards him I felt nothing. He had shut off our mental connection with a hot breath. I had no idea if he had decided to leave me to my foolish fate, or to damn the arrows, the bolts, the spears and the canons, and attack the palace-keep himself in order to save me.

But he wasn't cloaked! Danu hasn't hidden him with his magic! I thought in alarm. This entire stronghold against one young bull Phoenix dragon? *He will die trying to save me.*

"No." My feet slowed, staggered on the steps.

"Lila? What is it…?" Danu asked.

I felt terrible and ugly inside. Seeing Danu blink from under heavy eyes, it struck me that my thirst for revenge could well kill my closest friends. That was not what any of my parents would want, surely.

"Get to the nearest window," I said with only a little reluctance. "And then we escape. This was a fool's errand."

"What? But the Sea Crown? A way to defeat the Dead?" Danu pushed himself to standing, shaking his head at me. "If we don't find a way to stop the Dead – they will take over everything!" he said in alarm.

"Well – maybe we find another way to do it then," I said sternly. "Something that doesn't involve us losing our lives in here." My anger was fizzling out and drying up, leaving panic and fear as I considered the alternatives. *We could go back to*

Sebol. Search the library again. I could entreat Ysix and the other dragons again for their help…

"Come on, Danu, it's not much further…" I said, seeing a glow from the top of the stairs above.

The stairs ended at a wide door with carved stone lintels and doorposts depicting leaping waves and sea serpents. I just had to hope that one of these keys would work in the lock—

Click. It worked on the first go, and I swung open the door to reveal the room at the top of the central tower. I stood in wonder, for there sat a throne made of dull gold with a plush velvet cushioned seat in the center of the mosaic floor, surrounded by a circle of tall sconces.

But why was there a throne up here, where no one could reach? It just didn't make sense.

The ceiling was a vaulted dome, and I knew the outside must have been made of the gleaming gold we had seen from outside. Tall windows were set in the four cardinal points of the room and filled with stained glass depicting seascapes and small boats and in between were shelves, stacked with bottles, ornaments and maps. The only furniture in the room apart from the throne and the unlit sconces was a small side table, upon which lay a collection of maps.

"To the window," I said, my heart feeling heavy. "There's no Sea Crown here." I didn't doubt that this was just the sort of place where it might be held. It had the feel of somewhere secretive and hidden. An inner sanctum perhaps, for the despot king of the Roskildeans.

"Get up there!" We could hear the tramping of feet and the shouts of the palace guards below as they must have broken the gates down. *I have failed. All of this effort, for nothing,* I thought miserably. My foster-mother had been right. I shouldn't have come here.

"They're in the witch's tower!"

I moved to the nearest window and raised my scimitar to smash it open. "Crux?" I breathed, questing out with my thoughts towards him.

"I am coming." I could feel his powerful heartbeat through our connection, the rising sense of excitement and anger as he rushed through the skies-

"Wait, Lila – did you hear what they said?" Danu looked at me in alarm.

"That they've almost cornered us?" I said.

"Get the battering ram!" The shouts were close, and Danu heaved at one of the book shelves to topple it loudly across the door.

"That this is the witch's tower – Ohotto's tower!" Danu said, stepping back and panting to point at the floor. "This arrangement here, the throne? The torches – and look at the floor!"

I did, jumping slightly as the door shook under the first blow. There were strange marks on the floor, just inside from the torches. They looked like dried ink, dull black, or…

"Blood," I said with sudden distaste.

"I bet anything that this is dragon's blood. This is where

Ohotto summons the Darkening from – the power that animates the dead," Danu said feverishly, moving from shelf to shelf as he ransacked the room. "There must be a clue here as to what spell she used, how to undo it…"

"What's the use, without the Sea Crown?" I said, stepping back from the ugly markings to the window.

Thump! The collapsed bookshelf jumped visibly, and a crack appeared in the door.

"There must be something!" Danu said in frustration, seizing scrolls, tearing them open and discarding them in the same instant.

Thump! The crack widened. The door started to give.

"No time, Danu!" I turned and smashed the glass of the window, kicked out the larger pieces and looked out. The tower sat over the distant roofscapes of the palace keep below – and beyond that the outer wall, which melded onto the sea cliffs. It was a long way down. A *very* long way down.

"I am almost there!" Crux roared, and then I heard his draconian screech across the sky, followed by the boom of cannons and crack of arbalests as the wall guards must have seen him, too.

"Come on!" I shouted at Danu, as he turned, eyes wide, to the only piece of the room left un-searched: the small side table beside the empty throne, with its collection of papers.

"Hang on…" he muttered. "These are maps. These are *plans*."

Thump! The door broke from its hinges, as Danu seized

everything that he could and ran to my outstretched hand. I caught it tightly, feeling the warmth of his grip as the palace guards roared into the room behind us. *Phwip!* Something sparked against the wall beside my head.

I did the only thing that we could do – with Danu's hand in my own, I jumped.

CHAPTER 22
DANU, AND THE NATURE OF FEAR

I screamed as Lila basically yanked me out of the window, herself attached. The world rolled in front of my eyes. *What the hell was she doing!?* My head thumped with the pain of the magic. The peaked rooftops of the keep rushed toward us, every detail standing out in perfect relief as if time had slowed.

We are going to die…

I couldn't let go of Lila—

What spell could I use…

A roar reverberated around us, as suddenly the world went black and all of the air was knocked out of me in one burst. My stomach flipped once again, and I opened my eyes to see the blur of stone battlements, the astonished faces of guards raising their heads and then the moon-glint of waves.

I am flying. How am I flying?

There was a dragon over us, and beside me was squashed a hyperventilating Lila, both of us held in Crux's front paws as he dove towards the sea. Behind us, I heard booms and screeches as the palace keep fired its armaments at us, but we were traveling too fast. Another terrible wrench twisted my innards as Crux used his downward momentum to hurl himself upward again, raising over the bay like a cannon leaving its gun – which was ironic really, because right now there *were* the plumes of gun smoke coming from the stationed Roskildean Navy galleons as they sought to fire at us.

Fly! Fly! Fly! I willed the dragon faster, and the Phoenix dragon did not disappoint us. Peering from the edge of his claws I watched him angle his wings like a hunting hawk, making himself into a dart shape before suddenly snapping them wide open to power himself faster again. I thought I had already seen the limits of the dragon's speed, but I had clearly been wrong.

"I could go faster if I wasn't rescuing you two," Crux's voice half-jokingly growled inside my mind.

"I'm not arguing!" I said - and meant it!

"Danu?" It was Lila squashed beside me, patting one of Crux's claws for him to loosen his grip just slightly. We had cleared the line of the Dead Ships, and now Lila was pulling herself into a more comfortable position beside me as she looked at me. "You look terrible."

Oh great, thanks. But I felt ill; my limbs were aching, and my head was pounding. Was using magic always going to come with this pain?

"I would gladly give you a little of my life again, Danu, were I certain it would not corrupt you," Crux said, and immediately shook my head.

Your life, the words sunk into my heart. *Is that what he had been doing? Giving me his actual years and strength?* The thought made me feel sick. "No, you can't do that…" I managed, but somehow my thoughts had convinced him. It was already too late. A surge of warmth spread through me from the dragon holding me, and a clarity settled over my mind. I felt stronger again – not healed, as I could still feel the after-effects of the magic, but much better than before.

Disturbingly, however, Crux's wings wobbled a little unsteadily, and we dipped as if buffeted by a sudden breeze. I had a sudden thought: *did it hurt for a dragon to give their life to something?*

"It always hurts to give your life to anything," Crux said in his cryptic way, and I had no idea if this was another piece of romantic dragon wisdom or if he was speaking physically.

"Then don't do it!" I laughed. It was easy for me to see the funny side of it, now that I was full of stolen energy.

"Not stolen, Danu dragon-friend. Given. Freely," Crux said, settling into long and slow beats of his wings as he raced south-west, back across the Barren Sea and towards the other side of the Western Isles.

"I – I'm sorry," Lila said beside me, waking me from my dragon conversation.

"Oh." I remembered the feral glint in her eyes, the savage certainty that she seemed to have; that she was going to kill Havick. "It's okay," I said, but I knew that it wasn't. *Why did I care so much about what happens to Havick?* I tried to reason with myself. The man was a tyrant and a monster. He had ordered the sacking and invasion of not only Lila's home of Malata, but also my home of Sebol!

He was her uncle, I remembered the courtier saying. It made me feel unsettled and uncomfortable when I thought about it.

"I shouldn't have suggested trying to steal the Sea Crown. Everyone was right. I put all of you in danger, all in the name of revenge," she said.

My interest was piqued though. This did not sound like the fierce Sea Raider Princess that I had come to know. "What changed your mind?" I said.

"It was thinking of what would happen if I lost either of you." She looked at me with wide eyes, the distant starlight catching them so that they shone. "I have lost so much already, that I couldn't bear it if anything happened to you two as well."

She lost her home, and her father, I thought gravely, her words cutting through my heart as effectively as her scimitar could. *And still, she is willing to put down her quest for vengeance. Maybe this means she wants to finally become a princess, a liberator for the Western Isles, not just a Raider.*

"We live in dangerous times," Crux answered Lila, though I heard him too. He was repeating our conversation on the island – that Lila couldn't take it on herself when we should be in danger.

"So, you don't want your revenge?" I said.

I was rewarded with a flash of anger in Lila's eyes. "Of course I do," she said immediately before her tone softened. "But what I want more than that is justice for Malata. For Kasian. For my birth-parents." She looked out over the sea. "It was seeing that painting – the one that you pointed out to me. My real mother…"

"She looked the spit of you," I said, hoping to at least sound comforting. I realized my error as her eyes turned down and filled with tears. *Oh no. Wrong thing to say again, Danu!*

"I know," Lila said, reaching to climb out of Crux's grip and make her way up to his shoulder, and the saddle that was waiting for her.

Damn it. I would never get a word out of her now, I thought. "I'm sorry – I didn't mean to bring that up, Lila…" I said quickly as I clambered myself out of Crux's grip and up his arm to his shoulder. The wind howled around me, and it was awkward climbing with the sack of scrolls stuffed into my tunic, but I managed it, as the sea flashed past below and I finally settled and secured myself in.

"I know. It's all right Danu," Lila said distractedly.

Liar, I thought. "I guess we need to find another way to get rid of the Dead, huh?" she turned to say to me, and when she looked at me her eyes widened, and her mouth opened in horror.

"What's wrong?" I said suddenly. *Had I been hit? Hurt?*

"The Dead!" she said, pointing past me, over my shoulder and past Crux's spines to what was fast approaching on the northern horizon.

It was a heavy black cloud, and it screamed with the voices of the lost.

"Fly, Crux, fly!" Lila shouted as I stared at the power that was coming for us. I couldn't take my eyes off of it for some reason.

It was like the cloud that the witches had summoned to attack Malata – only this one was black and boiling and did not exude a silvery fog at all. It moved with an incredible speed, its thunderheads boiling up over its back unnaturally. It was like watching the smoke made from a fire – although there was no light or flame to be seen. If I stared at that dark cloud for long enough, I started to see the curl and coil of thin tendrils of the black smoke reaching out and disappearing back into itself like some strange sea anemone.

It was the Darkening, I knew it. It was just as the ancient scrolls of Sebol had described. It was the same force that the people of old had fought, and now it was under the control of the witch Ohotto and her heretics.

"I can sense it now!" Crux whistled in anxiousness, which only made me even more nervous –I had never expected Crux to be nervous about anything. *"It is evil. Blacker than night. Older than time."*

"You couldn't sense it before?" Lila shouted in alarm as she leaned low and hugged his neck.

"No. It was like the fog at the island of the Raiders. It made a shroud in my mind, which I couldn't see." I could feel the great beast's anger and confusion clearly. *"I still cannot see through it, but such a great evil cannot hide itself from me anymore."*

Then we had better fly as fast as we can, I thought, hugging myself low in imitation of what Lila was doing, and willing Crux onwards. If only I hadn't taken his life force from him – twice! He would be quicker, then, he would be able to flee this thing.

If fleeing was even possible, a dark thought snuck into my head. The cloud covered the entire northern horizon, and it was both low over the waves and high into the sky as well, eating the stars as it advanced. *It must be Ohotto, angered by our attack into her very home.*

Or maybe angry at what I stole.... The sack of stolen scrolls was still scrunched inside my tunic against my chest, and even though I wanted to look at them – I wanted to see what could be worth this tremendous act of necromancy – but

I daren't bring them out into this wind. If I were to drop them now then our entire mission, and this danger, would be for nothing.

Fly my friend, fly! I thumped my head back down onto his warm scales and scrunched my eyes tightly shut.

※

We flew through the night, with the unholy storm of the Darkening always on the horizon, fear and terror always in my soul, even through bouts of semi-feverish sleep. It was as if the dark magic itself cast a pall over our minds. I certainly felt terror and fear like I have never felt before, and on the odd times that I managed to catch Lila's eyes, her eyes were wide and her face pale just as I am sure that mine were. At one point I extended out my hand and found hers in the darkness. It was shaking with either cold or fear, but we held onto each other's fingers where we lay, both pressed down against the dragon's back.

Beneath us Crux performed a heroic feat. He beat his wings in a fast-staccato rhythm right through the night, alternating his flying styles every now and again to widen his broad wings out to fully catch as much of the currents of the wind and air as he could, before hurling himself forward once again. His breathing was like a bellows, rhythmic but extreme as he forced the air in and out of his body.

We spent hours like that, we must have, as dark shapes

flashed beneath us which I took to be the inner isles of the archipelago and then larger landmasses which had to be the westernmost islands. Still, the Darkening behind us ate up the sky as we raced towards the fading starlight.

Would we make it back to the Raiders? Should we even try? The fears and worries were as relentless as the crowd was behind us. Maybe we should just try to fly as far as possible – but where? If we flew west towards Sebol then we would be forced to directly cross the Darkening's path. Both north and south were controlled by Havick now. That only left east. Towards the mainland, and towards the Raiders.

We can't make it. It's too relentless. It's too fast, I thought, again and again as my fingers squeezed the hand of the woman ahead of me.

It was sometime during this ordeal that I came to realize that this fear that we were feeling was itself a part of the Darkening's power. Of course, we were scared of it. We had seen the living dead walk out of it! I had read legends of how it had sucked the life from ancient Middle Kingdomers as easily as a fierce gull snuffs a candle – but this heart-hammering terror that made me flinch and shiver wasn't just that. For one, the terror *kept on attacking us,* I thought.

Was that even possible? Could it be that the Darkening has the power to get into our very thoughts?

"Yes," Crux said, suddenly pushing himself into my mind, like a warm, illuminating force amidst a sea of darkness. I felt better just being in the presence of this fiery, light-filled spirit.

But the Darkening was affecting the dragon, too, for his inner fire was dimmed a little, and he seemed a little less sure of himself. I had never known the bull Phoenix to not be sure of himself!

The life force he had given me, I realized. *I* was stronger right now because Crux was weaker. Because my friend had given me some of his strength. What if he had given me too much?

"Just as dragons connect with others with our thoughts – so too can the Darkening connect with others," Crux drawled. *"It is our twin, but one made of shadow and cold."*

I wondered then if my fear and misgivings were a way that the Darkening was using to pull us from the sky. Was it even possible that it could exploit our weaknesses? Turn power-hungry men like Havick into monsters? Turn witches like Ohotto into…

No, she was pretty evil to start with, I snarled, shaking my head, and with it, my fears away. "Lila! Lila – you have to listen to me!" I shouted at her.

In response, the Princess of the Sea Raiders and the Western Isles opened her eyes a crack. She had been crying, and she looked frightened. "This is all my fault! That thing will fall on what is left of my people and that will be it. I will have doomed everyone!"

"No, it's not – now you listen to me, Lila Roskilde," I used her full and real title. "I think that Darkening, that evil magic of Ohotto's – is getting into our mind somehow. I think that it's making us *more* scared, *angrier, more* vengeful. You have to fight it!" I demanded of her.

"What?" She started to rouse herself, her eyes looking puffy and tired.

"We have to fight the darkness, Lila – tell me, what is your best memory?" I shouted.

"Uh…" Lila shook her head to mutter. "What does it matter? We're all going to die anyway."

"Just tell me. That's all that you have to do…" I begged her.

Crux's wing beats were becoming labored and unsteady. He must be tiring, I knew. How far and how fast had he flown in just one night? Had any dragon done such a task? *Maybe this is impossible. Maybe we should give up.*

No. That was the fear talking. And we weren't creatures of fear. We were creatures of fire.

"Tell me!" I gripped Lila's hands hard.

"Ow – okay, okay…" The wind whipped her hair back and forth on her head. "It was crouching on the prow of the Ariel as my father captained it, and I was flying forward over the waves…"

"Good…" I said, although Lila's eyes weren't brightening. The fear still had her in its clutches. Maybe I had been wrong. Maybe this was a stupid delusion. "That *was* your best memory?" I said in alarm.

"Yes. It's changed now." Lila suddenly looked up at me, and there was a spark of something in her eyes. *Spirit.* "It changed the very first time that Crux held me in his claws and we flew together. When we bonded." I heard her voice grow stronger as the memory, summoned just by the act of speaking it, grew in her. "Now it's flying with Crux underneath me and feeling the wind in my face." She grinned her savage, defiant grin. "It's when you are traveling faster than anything has ever traveled before. When you can see the entire world spread out underneath you, and the skies before you are open and endless…" She spoke loudly and had lost the slump that had been in her shoulders. "And it is having you at my side, Danu," she said at last and my heart soared. When she spoke the words, "And what's your best memory?" into that terrible night, I actually laughed.

"The same," I said and meant it.

"Skreych!" Beneath us, Crux bellowed his own defiance to the night and to the thing that followed us – and the three of us drew closer in that special magical bond we all shared. As we shared our joy and our resolution, so we became stronger.

It was then that something incredible happened. Or maybe it wasn't so incredible but was just about to happen all the time anyway. The sky behind the Darkening storm was lighter, and I hadn't even noticed it start to rise. In fact, the sky behind the Darkening had turned from pitch black to a watery sort of grey.

"Dawn is coming," I murmured, feeling a goofy smile spread across my face. Of course, my rational mind knew that any magic could withstand the coming of a new day – and a spell as ancient and powerful surely shouldn't care whether the sun was shining or not – but I also *knew* in that ancient heart of hearts that I shared with Lila and Crux at that moment that if the sun was rising, then the darkness must recede, at least for a little while.

As if in response, the Darkening storm slowed behind us. It did not fill the north-eastern horizon as it had done a scant little while before. Crux trumpeted his victorious call again as if to greet the coming sun as the light rose and rose. The Darkening storm was indeed growing smaller. Its contours were not so violent and black, but whisping away like morning fog on a warming summer's day.

"Maybe even Ohotto can't control it for long," Lila said, and I agreed.

It was undeniable now that we were escaping, and as the Darkening storm became nothing but a dark grey smudge on the horizon, and finally dwindled to nothing, I let out a relieved sigh and slumped back down on Crux's neck.

"Danu—what happened just then?" Lila asked, still keeping her eye on the corner of the sky where the evil spell had been.

"I think…" I started to say, wanting to tell her about the ancient legends in Sebol of the generous power of the sun, and light, friendship and warmth to always drive away fear and darkness – that since time immemorial, people have believed that all good things come about under the daylight - but a wave of exhaustion washed over me. How long had we been awake for now? A day and a half? And most of that had either been freezing or fleeing?

"I think that we kicked its butt," I murmured instead as sleep took me, a deep, natural sleep in which I would not dream.

CHAPTER 23
LILA, AND THE PLANS

We flew into the morning light, with Danu like the dead at my side. He slept deeply from that first light of morning all the way through to the late afternoon of the next day when I sighted the clouds of the southern mainland. For myself, I had managed to catch a few hours of sleep here and there but found myself waking often and abruptly, certain that danger must be following us – but seeing nothing save distant islands and endless seas.

I could tell Crux was exhausted – he had stopped racing forward and only moved his great wings with the fewest and softest moments. Most of the time he seemed content just to glide silently over the waters, gradually dipping lower and lower until his belly was barely skimming the wave tops before he would thrust his wings down again, and we would lift a little.

"Oh, Crux…." I said, putting my hands to the scales of his neck. They were barely warm, which scared me. Usually, the dragon always radiated heat from the scales on his body, as if he was only barely in charge of the fires that he contained inside, but now?

"I will be fine, wave-rider." His voice, usually brash and booming against my mind was little more than a whisper.

"We must stop!" I said, wondering why *I* was the least affected of both of my companions. Ah. The magic, I realized. Danu had used a lot of magic – an act that seemed to tax him greatly, and Crux not only had flown farther and faster than any creature that I had ever heard about – but he had also given some of his inner fire away to Danu, to heal him. They were both recovering in their own ways from their use of that precious life-stuff – while I was just nursing the pains of my own stupidity.

Why had I ever thought that breaking into the stronghold of Havick was a good idea? The dragon made no noise to correct me, but I wasn't sure how interested he would be in my own miseries at the moment anyway. Dragons are terrible when they are tired.

Stop thinking about yourself, Lila! I reprimanded myself, instead forcing my eyes to search the growing lines of the cliffs and the inlets. At least I could be useful as a scout – maybe.

My abilities in that regard were also unnecessary, however, as no sooner had I spotted the estuary I was sure led to the Raiders and the refugees, a small cloud of the Orange drakes rose on the evening airs and started to whistle and chirrup at us.

"Go away," Crux grunted as he bared his fangs at them, not even bothering to roar or call.

The smaller Orange drakes (still larger than me, but not by much, it has to be said) paid absolutely no attention to him as they flew in small gusts and gales like a flock of jackdaws on the wing. It was a wonder that they didn't smash into each other, their flight was so erratic!

"They like you," I tried to comfort Crux.

"They are idiots," the Phoenix said in return, as the Orange drakes broke off from their flight and darted back the way that they had come. I watched them wearily, the way they darted and shot near their home cliffs, before flaring their leathery wings and returning halfway to us and then flying back.

Just as if they were checking up that we were following them... the thought started to grow on me. *Almost like....*

"Something's wrong!" I said, my blood starting to pump.

"What?" Danu cracked open his eyes. He had been asleep (somehow) for more than an entire day, and I could tell that it had done him good.

"The Orange drakes, they want us to follow them. Like

they want to tell us something…" I said once more, urging Crux onward.

The bull Phoenix growled this time and managed to beat his tired wings and speed a little faster after his smaller entourage.

"What's happening?" Danu rolled his shoulders and leaned forward.

"It's the Orange drakes, they're…" I managed to say, as we rounded the headland and saw the shallow bay where we had moored our migrant boats was in turmoil.

No!

Raiders and Free Islanders ran back and forth in seeming panic across the sand. Some, I saw, were even starting to splash into the water to try and get back to the boats. *Why would they run away?* I thought as Crux became suddenly alert. A part of me knew that it wasn't like him to not notice a fight, and to not sense the panic, anger or commotion that was going on nearby. *He must be so exhausted,* I thought. *I cannot have him fight now.*

"I can fight whenever I am needed," Crux said, his misery turning into a slow-burning tetchiness.

Good, I thought coolly. Maybe we will need him angry before long…

I readied my saber and asked Crux to swoop low over the sandy beach – anywhere that he could see where it would be safe as I and Danu prepared to jump.

"And me? You just want me to fly around in circles above

you?" Crux said.

"Just see what is going on and come back," I said, not knowing whether I could dare risk him when he was in this state. Crux would usually have argued against that sentiment, but now he did not even bother as he flew low and slow over the eastern end of the beach, and Danu and I jumped off to roll in the sand.

"Pff! Pah!" I coughed out the fine stuff and pushed myself up. Danu was a whole lot slower beside me.

Maybe he will be useless too, I thought in dismay. No time – I set off back across the beach at a run, heading for where the knot of people was thickest.

"Out of the way! I have returned! What is going on?" I bellowed and shouted as I pushed and shoved Raiders, sailors and islanders out of my way. The sandy dunes and grass was hard slogging as it was, without the press of bodies.

"It's not natural!"

"I say we get out of here!"

"Where do they come from, huh? That's what I want to know!"

I could hear the shouts and angry declamations rising around me as I fought my way through the press of people – and then I smelt it. The terrible, heavy smell of grease and foul meat.

"By the stars! What is that?" I said, gagging as I held my cloak over my face and broke through the last ring of people.

There was my mother, and Elash, and Senga and Adair and Jolprun of the Islanders, and they were arguing loudly in front of a burning pyre. My eyes slid away from what was inside the wooden bonfire, but it was also unavoidable. Bodies.

"What in the name of all that is holy is going on here!?" I demanded, striding forward into the bonfire light, my eyes watering.

"There! There she is, at last!" I heard Senga shout joyously, rushing to my side as we embraced in a fierce and quick hug.

"Daughter," my foster-mother looked exhausted, in her hand, she held her own battle glaive, and I could see that its edge was dark with use. There had been a fight. A battle – but why the pyre?

"Mother – what is the meaning of this?" I whispered under my breath.

My mother looked at me with heavy eyes. "I don't think you succeeded, did you?" It wasn't a question, it was a statement. *How did she know?* I thought as I turned back to the pyre.

Oh. "They're not our own dead, are they?" I whispered.

"No, they're not. Our own are buried up on the headland," Adair stepped in to say, looking worriedly between Pela, the others and me. "It was the Dead, they came here."

"How many ships? What was it – a patrol galleon?" I said

quickly, searching my friend's eyes – but it was the Sailing Master Elash who answered me.

"We don't know, *Captain* Lila." The way that he said that final part made me want to knock his other front tooth out as well. "Because this lot came to us over the land."

"Over the land?" I repeated, feeling stupid. "But how did they get there?"

"They've landed, Lila," Senga said through gritted teeth, glaring at Elash. I did not know what hot words had been shared between them, but I knew that *I* would not want to be on the receiving end of one of Senga's glares. Besides – she had a friend who could breathe fire as well.

"Landed? Here?" Absurdly I looked up and around as if I would be able to see the Dark Ship moored just out of sight.

"A few leagues north. Two galleons," Senga answered. "But apart from a party that traveled towards us and that we ambushed with the dragons… Or tried to anyway." Her face went dark for a moment. "They just kept on coming, Lila – even after the Orange drakes had hacked and slashed at them. Even if their legs came off, they still crawled forward. We used dragon fire, but some managed to get through – they almost made it all the way to the boats before we eventually put an end to them with pitch and fire-arrows."

"Good thinking." I slapped her on the back, remembering what my father would do. "You did well. You protected your people. You should be proud."

"We lost fourteen," Pela said on my other side. "We can't

afford to lose anyone else…"

"No, we can't." I looked her in the eyes and shook my head gravely. "You say that they are a few leagues north of here? What are they doing?"

"Camping, we think?" Adair shook his head. "Which doesn't make any sense – the Dead don't eat, they don't sleep, they don't need clean water, do they? And yet on the backs of our dragons, we could see that they were building guard walls and erecting tents and digging wells…"

"They might not need to eat and sleep and rest for themselves, but that makes them the perfect workers for Havick," I said. "He must have sent them to build a fort here – and that means that he means to send living troops here as well."

"An invasion? Of the south?" Elash pulled at his straggly beard as if he were going mad. "Have you lost your mind?"

I was tired. It had already been a very long couple of days, and my friends whom I cared for needed rest. I'd had enough of Elash's lip. "Watch it, sailor." I rounded on him, even raising my scimitar blade. My father wouldn't brook any disrespect or mutiny, and neither would I. "You got something to say, you think about how you want to say it, right?" I snapped at him.

I saw the sailing master's eyes do a double-take as he looked down the edge of the blade to me. He visibly paled and stepped back slightly. Well, at least I can still put the fear of blood into him, I thought.

"It's just, *captain*, that we are here, nigh marooned on the southern coast. On the edge of the Southern Kingdom. It's never been exceptionally friendly to us Islanders – whether Roskildeans or Raiders—and it's *huge!*" he said exaggeratedly. "The Southern Princes of Vala must cover hundreds of leagues. Thousands of leagues? What on earth would Havick think he could achieve by invading Vala?"

It was then that Danu staggered his way through the ring of people and stared at everyone here with baleful eyes. His cloak was in tatters, and he looked ragged and weary with deeply haunted eyes, and in short just like the sort of half-mad witch that many feared him to be.

"Lord Havick has a new ally now – and it's not just the Dead," Danu said, his voice sounded grim and hopeless. "It's a power called the Darkening, and it hasn't been seen in these lands since the most ancient of times. It was powerful enough to bring the Torvald Kingdom to its knees, *twice!* If it hadn't been for the alliance between humans and dragons, then the whole world – both Torvald *empire* and the Western Isles would be in a soulless misery of living death."

The assembled throng went quiet at the thought of such evil. The only noise was the eerie keening of the wind above, and the crackle, hiss, and pop of the burning pyres of the dead.

Into that silence, Adair spoke to me through the side of his mouth, looking appalled. "Wow, Danu really knows how to raise your spirits, doesn't he?"

"I think you need to explain this to me. Slowly." Pela was looking at both Danu and me with the same expression that she had always used when she had caught me sneaking out on the rowboats. We stood in the command tent – a large marquee-like structure that the Raiders had apparently been using to plan what we should do next in our new home. There were old sea chests with ship's blankets hastily thrown over them to act as furniture, and an iron brazier in the center, puffing smoke from hot coals to the hole in the roof.

We weren't alone in here either. All those who had been in the center of the circle a little while earlier were also here: Elash, who was quickly becoming a secondary leader after Pela; Costa with his eyepatch, who was a trusted quartermaster and good ally to my father and mother; Jolprun, who spoke for the alliance of Free Islanders; and Senga and Adair who were speaking as Dragon Raiders. *And where did that leave me?* I thought as all eyes still looked to me and Danu. I wasn't a chief's daughter anymore. Not even second-in-command, but somehow my word mattered.

I have to speak for everyone.

"Well..." Danu took a deep breath and leaned forward from where he sat on his sea chest. He still looked haggard, but I had managed to convince him to throw one of the blankets over his shoulders, and we were nursing bowls of Pela's hot soup as we talked.

I watched the faces of those assembled as Danu proceeded to tell them everything that we had learned since we first left

Malata for the Haunted Isle of Sebol. At first, my foster-mother's face appeared skeptical—like father, she had never had a great trust in the witches, although she had a great deal of wary respect for their powers— but it was replaced by growing seriousness.

At least her eyes are alive again, I thought with a twinge of misery. Others like Elash and Costa remained fixed in frowns as I guessed that they dismissed everything that Danu said purely because it was from a witch. I was surprised to see that Jolprun seemed open to believe everything that Danu was saying.

"So, you are telling me that Havick the Pretender has summoned up some ancient evil that is threatening to destroy the world?" Pela said flatly. I couldn't tell if she was being disbelieving or not.

"Well, Ohotto and her circle of heretics have, with the help of the Sea Crown," Danu explained. "The Witches of Sebol – and the dragons, or so Crux tells us, have long had a belief that magical items were created to act as foci for magic."

"Just as the witches use dragon's remains to enhance their own magic…" Adair said with a curled lip. I was glad that she felt as much disgust and outrage at the suggestion as I did.

"Yes, precisely." Danu nodded. "There were once the Dragon Stones and the Crown of Torvald. All were used to concentrate power." His eyes found mine. For support, I thought. "What we saw in that tower throne room had all the hallmarks of a place of high magic, but at least now we have an advantage," Danu said dryly, pulling out the collection of scrolls and papers and laying them out on the floor before us, weighting them down carefully with stones, brooches and daggers. "We got these from the throne room. It's a plan of attack, I think..." Everyone leaned closer to take a look.

"That is a map of the coast." I breathed as I looked at the largest scroll. In fact, it was a map of the entirety of Torvald's north and south coast, with the wildlands to the north as well as most of the Western Archipelago. It had small markers like wings at various points – none in the southern mainland, but a cluster in northern Torvald and a couple on the nearest islands. "What are those?" I said, feeling something tickle against my memories. *I had heard of something like that before, but where...?*

"Wait a minute – there's a more detailed map of just the Western Isles," Danu said, rearranging the vellum to reveal a map of the eastern edge of the islands – the very ones that we had flown over on Crux in our flight from the Darkening.

There were the usual spires of mountains, the exaggerated tree shapes – and more of those wing shapes in red. But that wasn't all that was visible – there were blue arrows and lines, smaller ones coming from the northern edge to converge on these islands with the wing symbols, and then a much larger blue arrow leapfrogging eastward in a straight line.

"That's an attack," Elash said sagely. "Those blue lines are the routes of navies."

"And blue is the color of Roskilde," I added.

"And right about where that is…" Jolprun tapped on the map where the wing shapes sat. "Is where there is an old tower. I know this because the Free Islanders used to tell stories about them."

"They did?" I was suddenly interested. That was what the memory was – something about Queen Saffron before she became the queen and was an island girl. About living near a monastery? Or a tower...?

"Yes." Jolprun stroked his long beard. "They are said to have been built in the ancient times when mystics and healers lived at the towers – but the ones nearest to us are now watchtowers for the Empire of Torvald."

Both Elash and Costa nodded as if this made sense, and it was Costa who said, "We know that Torvald has trading routes that come west into the isles. They probably re-provision at those watchtowers, right?"

It finally clicked into place. *The Dead building their encampment on the southern shores that they wouldn't even use. The Roskildean fleet going to the watchtowers of Torvald.* "They're planning an invasion of Torvald," I said abruptly, and all eyes snapped to me. "Think about it. What do you do if you want to invade a strong force?" I pointed at the watchtowers. "You cut off any warning signs. You ambush." I looked around the room. "They're going to destroy the watchtowers so Torvald is unaware of their attack, and the Dead will already be waiting to take out any scouts that come this way before the Roskilde fleet get here."

"And the Darkening," Danu added ominously. "We have to stop them. Havick must be planning the slaughter of thousands!"

I was already nodding as Elash coughed in surprise. "Stop them? *Us?* What under the stars are you talking about?"

Danu looked at him as if he were mad. "It's obvious, isn't it? We can't let that evil infect the rest of the world..."

"*We're Raiders!*" Elash jumped up, brandishing his fist in the air. "We're not supposed to defend the damned Torvaldites! If they have a war coming to them – then I say we let them have it and go back to doing what we're already good at anyway – *raiding.*"

"You don't mean that, Elash." I stood up slowly. *How could he care so little about his fellows?*

"Of course, I do," the sailing master spat as he looked at me. "You have forgotten where you come from, Lila of Malata."

That's the thing though, isn't it? I thought as I took a step towards him. *I haven't forgotten at all.* I have found out where I come from. "I'm not *just* Lila of Malata, sailor," I growled at him. "I'm Lila of Roskilde, too."

Elash screwed his eyes up in hatred, and at his side Costa looked appalled at what I had just said. "So, you're going to side with Havick now, are you, Roskildean?" Elash spat the words at me.

I slapped him. Hard.

Elash stumbled back with a shout before rebounding and

lunging towards me, but I was ready for him. Another punch straight to the bridge of his nose. My fist stung, but I felt the satisfying *crunch* and he was flailing as he fell to the floor, swearing.

"Lila…?" Danu was at my side, fists balled at his side, and behind him I could see Pela and Senga and Adair backing us up.

"I got this," I muttered, kneeling down beside the growling Elash. Blood seeped through his fingers as he held his nose. "You get that one for free, Elash, because you were a good sailor for my father." *He knew which father I was talking about.* "But the next time you insult me like that, I'll treat you as if you had insulted my father." Everyone knew how Kasian would react to a mutiny. He wouldn't show mercy.

"Chief Kasian wasn't even your real dad!" Elash foolishly shouted, and I heard Pela hiss behind me.

"He was every kind of father that matters, Elash. I think you've said enough now, don't you?" My mother's voice was low and deadly.

I saw the argumentative sailing master look over at the only man who might have vouched for him – Costa the Quartermaster, but Costa just spared a watchful look between Pela and me, before shaking his head and stepping aside.

"We've never cared where our Raiders were born, just so long as they follow their captains." Costa nodded in deference to me.

Oh. I felt simultaneously stupid, grateful, and humbled at the brusque quartermaster's simple words. It was true, of course, nearly half of the Sea Raiders had themselves been immigrants from the other islands or the southlands – and now we had Jolprun and his council of Free Islanders as a part of our family as well – but it still brought a lump to my throat.

All this time I've been beating myself up about who I really was; a Raider or a Roskildean, and it turns out that nobody cared apart from me. I nodded my thanks to Costa, and we all turned to watch Elash lurch to his feet and back out of the tent.

"If you can't live with this, Elash – then I suggest you leave," Pela growled at my side.

"Don't worry, Pela, I will!" The sailing master turned and almost tripped in his haste to leave the main tent.

"Well." I breathed heavily into the silence.

It was Senga who broke the tension as she shrugged, "It was bound to happen sooner or later. The guy was unbearable."

"Perhaps," my mother said. "But it will mean trouble. Especially if you're going to ask the others to fight for Torvald."

"We're not fighting *for* Torvald – we're fighting for survival!" Danu pointed out. "Survival of everyone."

"That's not how the Raiders will see it," Pela said, and I was scared that she was right. Jolprun stepped forward from where he had been wisely staying out of the confrontation.

"You have us Free Islanders, Lila." He extended a hand, which I grasped to find a surprisingly strong grip. "We know the strength in community, and we know what Havick was like even before that witch came to his side."

"Thank you, Jolprun," I said and turned to the others. "Right – so I guess we need to plan a war?"

※

As it turned out (as Danu pointed out, a little surprisingly), we wouldn't have to plan an entire war all by ourselves.

"We don't need to defeat Havick, we just need to buy Torvald and Vala time to get on board – and give time for as many of the Free Islanders to join us." He nodded towards Jolprun who grinned.

"They will, when they know what is happening," the bearded islander added.

"What do you have in mind, Danu?" I said.

"We know that he's intending to silence the watchtowers, right? All we need to do is defend one long enough to send the message to the mainland," Danu said. "And meanwhile, we can be sending messengers to Queen Ysix to help, and maybe even messengers to the Trading City of Vala and Torvald itself?"

"We don't have the time to send people—even on dragons —to Torvald," I pointed out. "Not if these moon signs are right on the maps. Havick is already mobilizing. He will already have attacked the watchtowers that run through the center of the Western Archipelago."

"Then we had better pick the closest watchtowers to defend," Pela said critically, looking at the different symbols of wings. "Jolprun? Do you know anything of these islands?" She pointed to the very last islands that stood before the coast of Torvald.

The Free Island spokesman looked down at then, frowned, moving a pointing finger between one to the next. I saw him stop to consider one that stood on an atoll all alone, before shaking his head and moving to the next, nearest to the northern mainland. "This one." He nodded. "If it is the tower I have heard tell of, then it stands on a cliff overlooking the straits between its own and its sister island."

I grabbed what he meant immediately. "A bottleneck." I indicated where the islands *almost* met. "If Havick wants to bombard it from the sea, he will have to concentrate an awful lot of boats in a small area. Or if he wanted to sneak in and take it overland, then we would have the facing island to warn them from."

"It will also be our last chance," Danu murmured, indicating how close it was to the mainland. "If we don't save it, then Torvald will have no time to prepare for what is coming for them."

I looked around to general signs of agreement, and our plan was settled. We would travel as soon as we could to this watchtower on the Isle of Rhul, which was split into two 'islets' cut in half by a tiny channel of water. Thus Jolprun told us this place was called North Rhul for the top island, and

South Rhul for the one below it. We would warn the Torvald guards to send their message, and meanwhile, start evacuating what Free Islanders we could.

"The only thing, Lila, is that we don't have many boats..." Costa grumbled. "Most of our fleet is island or merchant vessels."

"The Free Islanders will have more," Jolprun said. "If we can get a favorable wind to send a fast yacht out to them, we might be able to reach them soon enough."

"Agreed." I nodded. "But it would be faster to send a dragon – Senga? How do you feel about taking Jolprun here with you on a fishing trip?"

"Gladly." Senga nodded, although Jolprun looked vaguely frightened and excited at the same time.

"I've never even been close to a dragon before," the man said with wide eyes.

"Just avoid the front end, and you'll do fine. Come on." Senga said, giving him a hand up before they hurried out of the tent.

"It doesn't matter what sort of wood is under our feet, just so long as it holds," my mother invoked the age-old Raider saying. "Whatever boats we have or can get, the Raiders can get them battle-worthy."

I grinned. I was sure that she could.

CHAPTER 24
DANU, AND THE BOOK OF ENLIL

The Raider encampment was in an uproar from the time of that council meeting onward, it seemed to me. I had spent most of my life on Sebol, where I would move from study hall to meditation hut between my duties and so I wasn't used to this frenetic cascade of activity and people.

The Raiders hurried back and forth from the boats that we had in the bay, as well as making a variety of small workspaces above the beach, where the sounds of industry could be heard day and night. Work-bands of people moved to the local thickets and copses in order to harvest timbers, and kilns and firepits were hastily built in order to tend to the making of tar and the hardening of weapon heads. I was astonished at how much the industrious Sea Raiders and their Free Islander allies managed to achieve in just such a short time.

Most of it the industry was down to Chief Pela, of course; she had transformed from a grieving widow into a matriarch of her people. She moved between groups, checking progress and giving suggestions where they were needed, as well as organizing any she could into different teams. Raiders and Islanders worked on weapons, on boat repairs, or in the ad-hoc carpentry yards, or re-sewing sailcloth, or hunting, skinning, and curing provisions for the raid.

The Raid. For that was what the coming battle had come to be called – which was an inspired choice of name on Pela's part, as no sooner had the phrase left the mouths of the Sea Raiders it was replaced with a bloodthirsty, savage grin.

"This will be the biggest raid in our history," I overheard Pela exhorting one work team at some point. "Fast in. Surprise the enemy. Revenge for Malata!"

The cheers that followed that little speech had been loud.

On the second day since our return to the coast the *Orchard* and the three Free Island boats were finally made ready, along with the *Ariel* and the *Claw* for battle. The islander boats were re-fitted with what spare guns we had, their hulls were reinforced, and their sides were built up to protect those sailors inside. Still, six ships were a pathetically small number against such a vast force. We also had a collection of our boats that had accompanied the *Orchard* on its escape from Malata – but these were little more than yachts to skiffs to even a couple of catamarans. *Maybe they would be able to dart in and attack like seagulls on a shoal,* I thought critically, but they wouldn't be able to sustain a prolonged battle.

In the dying light of the second day, however – more sails appeared on the horizon, directed towards us by Senga and Jolprun riding on the Sinuous Blue dragon Kim. It was the Free Islanders – they had come! The joyous news spread through the camp, as we welcomed a few hundred more sturdy Free Islander sailors and warriors, and the same number again in families and children. With them, they brought no less than thirty boats ranging from longboats to semi-military carracks, with as many cannons as they had to spare.

But was it enough?

"I already have a plan," Lila told me determinedly that afternoon when I had voiced these concerns to her. She didn't stop to explain her plan to me, however, as she raced off to urgent military meetings with Costa and Pela. She *did* send one of the Raider fisherwomen on a fast skiff up the coast eastwards, however – on orders to stay out of sight of the Dead encampment if she could and try to warn what communities and sailors she encountered. It was a small gesture, and the Dead fleet were already menacing the southern shores anyway, but I knew that Lila felt like she had to do *something* to try and help the innocent villagers and fisherfolk who might live here.

"And I just hope that you have a dang good plan, Lila." I sighed, finding myself anxious as I walked back to where Crux was still sleeping at the edge of the dunes.

The great Phoenix dragon raised his head to regard me as I approached, giving me a soft whistling churr in greeting. *"Your spirit looks heavy, dragon-friend,"* he greeted me as always, straight to the point.

"It is," I agreed. "But I am glad to see that my friend looks much recovered." I patted him on the snout as I produced the strips of cured fish that I had brought for him. He whistled happily as I threw them to him, noting with pleasure how his eyes were much brighter now, and that even his scales seemed to have regained their luster. The journey back from Roskilde had taken a heavy toll on his 'inner fire' he had explained to me, but it seems that rest and food were the answer. I wondered if it was his giving of life to heal me that cost the most, with more than a little twinge of guilt.

"Freely given, Danu." Crux turned to preen his scales, scaring an Orange drake that had been settled near to him. There were several such smaller dragons nested in the dunes nearby, looking between us expectantly.

"They seem to have taken a shine to their Uncle Crux," I teased him with a wan smile. In return to that comment, all I got was a tail lash from the Phoenix dragon.

"What bothers you, Danu? We are about to ride into battle against our enemies. We are about to hunt as one great family. What greater thing is there under the skies?"

"Oh, I don't know – dying horribly, maybe?" I said a little peevishly, earning another tail lash from Crux.

"I have been thinking, Crux, about how little I can do to

help Lila and the others. All I can do is a bit of magic, and then it almost kills me…" I shrugged.

"*A little magic!?*" Crux snorted as if he found the suggestion hilarious. *"You have not judged your own strength well, Danu dragon-friend. Very few mages were able to hide themselves as you did or call the winds to serve them. That is a feat that only the ancient wizards and archmages could do!"* he said.

"It is?" I was baffled.

"Yes. I think your magic is stronger with me, I think that our bond makes it so," Crux said.

I nodded. It was the same conclusion I had reached. "Still, I don't want to borrow your life for my magic during the battle to come. We will need you to be as strong as you can be."

"Just as Lila needs you to be as strong as you can be," Crux argued.

It was hopeless. What could I do? *Unless….*

"There is something that might be able to help, Crux," I said, thinking furiously. "When I was called to Sebol, Afar and the others managed to reach out to me just through their magic, mind to mind." I remembered the feverish state that I had been in.

"Yes, I remember. It was as dragons talk to other dragons. Only very clumsy." Crux opened his maw wide and lolled his tongue.

"Well – I have not been taught that technique yet, but I know that Afar can do it. Is there a way that you can help me, *now*, to reach out to Afar and the others, so I can call on their aid for the battle?" I had vague hopes that the good witches of Sebol might be able to send magic across the oceans to attack Havick's ships, or counter the Darkening, or might even be able to teach me some powerful spell or rite that I could use. *We need all the help that we can get,* I knew.

"You wish to call on the witches as I call on the other dragons?" Crux regarded me with his large eyes. I nodded, knowing that Crux had been spending the previous sunrises and sunsets on the cliffs above the bay singing his long, ululating song out to the sun – it was a way for the dragons to communicate to each other, from what I gathered – but we hadn't heard a reply yet.

"Why don't you reach out to them like, uh, like we talk?" I asked the bull Phoenix, tapping my forehead.

"Believe me, I have tried, human!" Crux opened his maw which could have been a laugh or a warning. Even Crux's nerves might be a bit on edge. *"I believe it is the Darkening obscuring the message. A dragon's ears are almost as strong as our minds— they may yet hear my song on the eastern wind and respond. But it takes time for the message to be passed on,"* The Phoenix had explained just this morning to me. *"And then Queen Ysix will want a dragon-meet with the seniors of her brood."*

Whatever the delay was – it was taking too long! We needed aid *now*.

"I will do it, Danu." Crux put out a paw to thump onto the

sandy earth in front of me. *"Lie in my talons. Our connection is always stronger when we are in contact."*

I knew he was right and I settled my cloak around me as I uncurled myself in the great dragon's claws and concentrated on staring deep into his golden eyes. Instantly, I could feel the connection between us. The bond, as he called it – it was like a surging ocean of warmth, and one that I could dip myself into at any time. I knew instinctively too, that this was a great source of power and that I could and had been using it to power my magics.

"Now you know why the mages and witches of the world seek us out," Crux said, at the same time proud and reserved.

"I am sorry," I said, speaking not only for how I had been using him but also for all of the ways that dragons had been abused by my kind.

"Abused? Only when it is not freely sought, and freely given, young Danu. Like now, between us." I heard Crux's words as that sea of warmth opened up to me. It was like being blinded – but not uncomfortably so— and of being burned – but with no pain. When the glare dimmed I could see, with my mind's eye, the vast curve of the sky – which was crazily filled with every sort of cloud and weather. As soon as I concentrated on one section of clouds, my focus zoomed in to see them in intricate detail, to feel the currents of the air that pushed and held them where they were, to hear and smell and see the drifts of seabirds that flew at their head.

The revelation continued as I looked down at the shapes of

islands and continents, mountains and deserts. Everything was laid out in a panorama which was at the same time familiar as well as strange. It was like everything was *in detail*, at the same time as being a vista – and my small human mind couldn't take it.

"Steady yourself, Danu – it is not easy learning dragon sight," Crux's humorous voice brushed against my own.

"This is how you see all the time?" I said in awe.

"No, of course not. But this is where my mind can go, if I choose," the Phoenix dragon informed me. *"It is the space that I inherit and add to through my blood. It has the flights of my den mother and her mother before her, and so on into time."*

"So, you know everywhere in the whole world?" I spluttered out, amazed.

"Ha! No. Memory is not the same as actuality, Danu!" the dragon informed me, but would not go any further on that topic. Instead, he focused his attention on me alone. *"You wish to speak to your den mother?"*

"My...? Oh – you mean Chabon?" I said. I guessed that a Matriarch was a little like a den mother, wasn't it? If I can even reach her, that is. Her soul was failing her, her body was dying somewhere far away – if she hadn't already died. "Can you take me to Afar, my teacher on Sebol?"

"I will help you reach out to her, as I reach out to other dragons. First – you must concentrate on who she is."

I recalled Afar in my mind, her strong stare, her height and straight back, her coolly appraising eyes and her braids.

"No! Not what she looks like – who she is, to you," Crux said cryptically.

I tried again, recalling the details of my life with Afar. That she was my tutor. That she had been the one to teach me and look after me in all my years on the island. She had brought me hot milk the first few nights when night terrors had kept me awake. She was kind as well as stern – expecting the best of my attention and giving it in return. She might not have been a very affectionate woman, not really knowing how to look after a growing boy, but she tried. She had a sense of humor that was dry, cutting and hilarious all at the same time.

The dragon sight around me changed as if I were flying across the surface of the world at incredible speed. The land below me turned to seas, islands, and then more seas until I came to a place that was shrouded in fogs.

"Sebol," Crux whispered at the back of my mind. *"It is always hard to see, because of the witches' shields..."* he explained before his presence recoiled in agitation. *"But look, Danu – it is under attack,"* he informed me, directing my attention to the darker storm clouds that surrounded it.

"The Darkening? Is it here?" I said in alarm.

"No. Dragon sight is not as literal as eyesight. Those clouds do not represent the Darkening, but evil magics."

Ohotto and her cabal. I knew that it had to be them – hadn't Afar and the others said as much, that they suspected that Ohotto was casting foul magics at Chabon on a near-constant basis? I felt a surge of rage towards the witch Ohotto Zanna, the witch who I had even looked up to.

In an instant, the dragon-sight started speeding again, carrying me far away from the island, zipping over other islets and seas, until I saw a heavy, black mass of boiling cloud-like smoke – and, poking from its top was the tower that Lila and I had so recently infiltrated.

"No, Danu! You must stop thinking of the evil one!" Crux said, but my hatred was too strong as my vision drew closer and closer to the windows, curiously un-smashed in this strange imaginal realm.

There were torches lit in the room, and there was someone sitting in the center, on the throne. The tall and thin man from the portrait we'd seen, and upon his black hair sat a crown fashioned into leaping gold wavelets.

"Lord Havick!" I said, startled. The man looked gaunt, ill even as he sat slumped with his head back, his eyes open and unseeing. Thin tendrils of an ugly purplish light came from the Sea Crown on Havick's head, coiling lazily in the air like incense smoke, and all heading into the circle. This was some kind of spell, and Havick did not look as though he was enjoying it.

"Who is there?" another voice said in the dingy room, and a shadow moved, garbed in black.

Dragon sight is not like eyesight, Crux had said, and now I could see why. Ohotto Zanna with her long, cornflower blonde hair and large blue eyes and skin like alabaster had always reminded me of a faerie-tale princess. She was beautiful in the way that could stop the breath of the odd men who came to Sebol. But now, she appeared hunched in heavy black shadows, and her face was screwed up into one of hate.

I swear that she turned to look straight at me.

"Enough of this!" Crux scolded me, and I felt a sudden rush of dizzying perspective as my vision was once again drawn back the many leagues and days travel back to the occluded Sebol.

"Did she see us? What were they doing?" I asked in alarm.

"Neither you nor I is strong enough for a magical duel in the places between thoughts. Not with the Darkening," Crux chided me. *"Now. Did you want to try to reach out to your mentor, or not?"*

"Yes," I said, feeling very ashamed. Had it really been just my rage and curiosity that had directed our thoughts so far? I tried to calm my mind with the techniques that I had learned on Sebol. Waiting. Patience. Steady breaths, and then reached out to Afar.

"Afar?" I murmured into the clouds around Sebol. Would I even be able to break the Western Witches' enchantments? Not likely. "Afar, it is Danu, I need you!" I tried again, doing the mental equivalent of shouting.

"Danu?" The thought was small and hesitant, but it was there. I felt something reaching out to me, another mind? Instantly, my perspective changed, and I was in a dark cham-

bered room, with the glow of candles and the heavy fog of incense. There was a figure lying on a bed – Chabon herself – and at her side sat a very weary and tired Afar. My mentor looked almost at the end of her tether as she looked up in the dark corners of the room, where I was.

"Danu – it is you!" she said joyously. "I have been trying to reach you as I did before. Why are you here?"

"Crux the dragon brings me," I explained.

"You have learned the art of dragon sight?" Afar shook her head in amazement. "That is something few have ever done."

"Well, I wouldn't say that I've learned it yet…" I said sheepishly.

"We haven't got long." Afar brushed over my concerns. "It takes considerable strength to reach out through Sebol's defenses, and the island's enchantments are already under daily attack by the curses of the renegade witches."

"We saw," I confirmed. "The reason—"

"Wait." My mentor held up a hand. "Please, Danu, this is important. We have discovered more of the Darkening. Chabon regained consciousness a few nights ago, before falling once more. She says that she had in her trust something called the Dark Book of Enlil. It was given to her by the old Dragon Riders of Torvald before the Dark King came to power. It is a book of terrible spells and formula, and it is from here that Ohotto must have learned how to summon the Darkening."

"And how to use the Sea Crown to do it," I added, telling

her what I had seen and what we had found out – that some magical objects acted as reservoirs of great magical power.

"Yes. I fear that Ohotto found the Dark Book and studied it for years as she put her plan into motion. She would have known that she needed the Sea Crown, which means she had to take charge of Roskilde, which means that she could raise the Darkening," Afar explained. "That is what you must look for – but I fear that Ohotto will never let it leave her person! It is in the Dark Book that she learned to raise the dead!"

"We will concentrate all our efforts on the book and the crown," I promised, "but that is also why I am here. We face a battle tomorrow, between what is left of the Raiders, the Free Islanders, and everything that Ohotto and Havick can throw at us…" I explained the invasion plan, and how we hoped to buy just a little time for Torvald to come to our aid.

"But our numbers are small. *Tiny.* Even were we to dispel the Dead fleet, then Havick's mortal armada alone will wipe us out. We need your help, Afar."

Afar looked even more aghast. "We are working day and night to keep Ohotto's curses from completely overwhelming the island!"

"Then teach me a spell! A cantrip! A charm!" I implored her desperately. "Anything that I can use against vastly superior forces, please, Afar…"

My tutor looked down at the sleeping body of Chabon, and then at her hands, before nodding to herself. "What is left of the Western Witches will try to send aid to you, if we can do both the protection of Sebol and the distant magic you ask for. But if that fails, then there are a few things that I can teach you. They are not meant for anyone but the senior sisters and the mages, but seeing as you come to me in dragon-sight, you are ready to handle this power…"

I hoped that my mentor was right, as I listened intently to the words, invocations and gestures that the witch taught me.

CHAPTER 25
LILA & THE BATTLE FOR THE ISLANDS

We weren't ready, but we set off anyway. My frustration was enough to make me scream, were it not for the eyes that were on me all the time. The Raiders and the Free Islanders needed to know they had a leader that they could trust, that they could follow.

"They do," Crux reassured me.

"Thank you." I patted his snout as I gave the wave to the other Dragon Raiders to follow my lead, and for the boats to set their course. It was dark, not even morning – and it felt like an inauspicious time to start anything – but we had no choice.

I just hope our messenger gets through, I thought of Melissa, the stern Raider woman I had sent north-east in her skiff. My plan was a simple one, but it felt ragged. We had no time to prepare complicated ship movements, and we barely had the time to organize the crews of the boats that we had.

'Get to Rhul as fast as you can, and then your captains will give you your orders' had been the only direction I gave the sailors and fighters. I daren't spend any longer discussing or arguing over the details. I had to trust that my newly-appointed captains and quartermasters would be able to carry out my plans as well as they could.

"Danu?" I said softly as I turned to look at my friend, already in place behind me. He was pale from lack of sleep and worry, but he gave me a worried grin and a nod.

"I'm here," he said, a simple phrase but one that filled me with more confidence than I had thought possible. It was all that could be said, at the end of the day. *We are here, when you need.*

"Then let's raid," I said, and felt Crux leap forward into the sky, his wings cracking like sail cloth in a strong breeze.

❦

We flew not as fast as Crux could, but instead, we stayed in a circling formation above the boats until we could sight the watchtower of Rhul. On our wings were Kim and Thiel, Porax, Retax and Lucalia, Holstag and Grithor, Ixyl and Viricalia – all nine young dragons (other than Crux) of the Raiders who had stayed with us, and around them came a smaller flock of bright shapes – the Orange drakes. My eyes strayed to the stockier Green of Lucalia – she had been hurt during the second battle of Malata and was still a little slower than the others.

As soon as our duller human eyes could see the distant dark shape of the island like a smudged line on the far horizon, I gave the shout and the dragons peeled off from the boats, racing ahead to be the first to get to the watchtowers.

But there was something wrong.

"Those clouds," Danu shouted. "Coming fast from the north – too fast to be any normal clouds."

My friend was right. They were dark grey thunderheads, and they moved strangely. A moment of fear shuddered through me, as I prayed it wasn't the Darkening itself. *But what else could it be?*

"They'll get to Rhul ahead of us!" I said in alarm, before standing up on Crux's back and shouting as loud as I could. "Dragon Raiders! Fly fast and true! There is our enemy!"

"Skreyar!" Crux bellowed, leaping ahead of the others in the sky as his powerful body naturally took the lead. Behind us the other dragons fanned out to either side, followed by the whitters and clicks of a smaller, dispersed cloud of the Orange drakes. The mere fact that they had faced their fears to cross the ocean with us impressed and amazed me and strengthened my resolve. *We had to do this. We had to stop Havick.*

I heard a scream and turned in alarm to see that one of the dragons – Retax – had suddenly veered off course, flapping his wings oddly. *What was it? What was wrong?*

And then, a split second later, I saw the cause, as something else screamed through the skies towards us.

It looked like a jag of lightning, only it was colored ugly purple, like a bruise. It flew faster than an arrow and faster than a cannon shot, and it came from that dreadful black cloud that was racing towards us.

"Bad magic. The witches are here!" Crux informed me, swerving suddenly as another jag of the tainted lightning shot towards us.

"Dragon Raiders – defend yourselves!" I shouted, wishing that I had spent more time learning how the Riders of Torvald Academy performed in the sky. I had taught what little I knew to the other Sea Raiders on their dragon mounts, but it was all based on ship fighting. How to dart in under full sail, how to use the wind to turn, to swerve, to loop-

"Skrargh!" Another roar of surprise or pain came from behind me, but I had no time to turn to look as Crux had to dive out of the way once more.

We sped for the straights of North and South Rhul which appeared oddly bright against the wall of dark cloud that was bearing down on them. I had hoped to fill that gap with my larger, slower Free Island vessels – but how could I do that now, with magical lightning hitting the sea and the land all around?

Then I saw it – the watchtower of Rhul itself, standing high on the cliff and made of a shining white stone. Its head appeared to be a cone of metal and glass, where a mighty bonfire could be lit and concentrated to warn the other towers both further ahead into the islands, and behind it on the mainland.

Which was odd, now that I thought about it. Why had Torvald rebuilt these towers out here, so far out of their territory? Was it just to protect their shipping? What sort of messages did they relay about us islanders? But I had no time for momentary suspicions.

"Where are the guards?" I called to Danu, seeing people racing around the base of the tower. They must be trying to light the bonfire, as still more ran towards the cliffs, where a tiny avenue of stairs led down to a small pier. There were boats on that pier, and I wondered if some of the Torvald watchtower guards meant to take to the waves in order to take the message by sea, rather than risking their lives in the tower that might draw the lightning to it.

THABOW! Another crackle of lightning hit the straits, narrowly missing the cliffs.

"Those aren't Torvald guards..." Danu breathed in horror as we flew closer. He was right. The soldiers we saw were dressed in blue, and scurried along the pier, raising weapons to hack at the ropes that held the messenger boats there.

"But what about those up top?" I peered, at the soldiers clustering at the base of the tower and saw they were attempting to break their way in.

Ambush. We were too late. Havick must have seen what we did, must have recognized the potential Rhul held, and sent some of his fighters in early to kill the guards. The message would never get through if the watchtower wasn't lit!

The confusion of strategy and battle planning suddenly coalesced into one moment of clarity. I knew what we had to do. We hadn't come intending to man – but now it was clear that we would have to hold this point for as long as possible, to light the watchtower and make sure that the signal had time to be received. Hopefully, it would mean something to whoever manned the nearest tower on the mainland.

We had to hold off Havick.

"Ho!" I shouted, waving my hands, as our ships, far behind us, started to surge toward the straits between the two islands. We could keep his fleet busy in that tight space, I hoped.

BOOM! Another bolt of the magical lightning shot past us, causing Crux to duck and shriek awkwardly. The wind was picking up ahead of the unnatural storm, becoming faster like a gale, and our eight dragons were scattering under the onslaught of the storm. *It was too strong! Too fast!* I almost cried. Even Crux was having difficulty making headway in the gale.

"I know something that might help," Danu growled, and as I watched, he lowered his head and started murmuring furiously. He had told me that – somehow – he had managed to talk to Afar just a few hours ago, and that she had given him instructions for some new spell. *I just hope it's a good one*, I thought, as I fought to keep my seat on Crux.

"Fall back!" Senga shouted, with her brother Adair behind her, his teeth caught in a fierce grimace. They fought her way alongside us for just a moment. Even brave Senga couldn't see a way forward? I thought in alarm.

"We can't!" I shouted, as behind me Danu's muttering rose.

THABOOOM! Our two dragons flared apart as a trio of lightning bolts seared through the spot where we had been. We were now flying *inside* the straights between north and south Rhul, and the entire world to the west of the islands was a low wall of angry thunderheads.

"The dragons can't fly in this!" Senga was pointing back to where the other Dragon Raiders were now hundreds of meters behind us, some seeking to fly high over the gales, and others swooping low and dodging more of these thrown bolts. "We have to wait for the ships!" she shouted.

"It'll take too long!" I called back – not knowing what else to do. I only had Crux and Kim here, with Senga, Adair, me and Danu. Two dragons against the dark sorceries of Ohotto and her witch cult?

"Ia Mirablis! Doppl-Reflecio! Silver Ships of the Sea – I call thee!" I heard Danu's eerie shout, and Senga suddenly pulled back in alarm at the wave of power he unleashed. I felt it too, flowing through me like a bow wave and out into the straits ahead of us. Crux coughed flames in discomfort, and there was another crack of thunder – but this time it appeared to be natural and unaccompanied by ugly purple lightning.

The natural grey clouds over us broke and started to rain. *Is that it? Rain?* I thought in alarm, remembering the first magic trick that Danu had ever shown me when he had thought he was 'rescuing' me from the dragon atoll. He had summoned a rain cloud, and it hadn't been a very big one.

The rain fell in a sheet to the seas below, and then it fell in a hammer. It was a hard thunderstorm – but it wasn't enough to do anything other than make us all inimically miserable.

"Danu?" I shouted in exasperation as we swayed and jumped, Crux struggling to ride the clashing gale winds.

"Look, Lila – it's working!" Danu slumped back into his seat, as apparently this one didn't require him to throw his energy at it all of the time. He was pointing down to the boiling white waters of the straights between North and South Rhul. Something was happening to the froth of the waters. As the rain fell, the white grew and rose from the waves to take shape…

They were forming into boats. Silver-white boats made of boiling waters. They had no sails, but they moved through and with the waves as fast as the water that they had been, and they were heading straight towards the clouds. It was a staggering act of magic – something worthy of the most ancient sagas. The first darting silver ship hit the low wall of dark cloud and obliterated into a spray of white foam, while the dark thunderheads convulsed as if hurt.

BOOOM! Another purple lightning bolt darted out from the enemy stormfront, exploding one of the silver ships with ease. It appeared that was all that they were – just concentrated water, but they struck at the black-magic fog itself like a thrown punch. Immediately, more of the purple darts of evil energy shot out and started to pick off the suicidal silver ships – but I saw what Danu had done.

Whilst Ohotto's storm was attacking the silver ships, it wasn't attacking us.

"Come on!" I urged Crux up, fighting and struggling against the gales to swoop closer to the watchtower. We might be able to light it yet – but Crux needed a clear shot with his dragon-fire, and the hurricane-winds were fierce…

Crux bellowed as his front claws managed to punch out and grab the edge of the cliffs in the storm wings. He lowered his neck and spewed forth fire to the base of the tower. The winds caught much of the dragon fire, but still, some found its mark on those who were seeking to fight their way in. I saw bodies of the Roskildean fighters thrown back from the doors under the blast – but the doors were already knocked open.

They had already managed to fight their way in as we had struggled to stay afloat above the straits. Had they already killed all of the Torvald watchmen inside?

"Crux?" I shouted. "How many can you sense in there?" I called desperately. The Phoenix dragon snarled in frustration, shaking his head back and forth as the storm clouded his own senses. Instead, he leaned forward once more, almost surrounding the tower with his body.

"None. Look – they flee already!" he said, hissing at the

Roskildean guards emerging from the tower door and running across the cliff top.

Then there was only one thing that we could do. "Crux? Light the bonfire."

I could feel the dragons pleasure as he took a deep breath and roared his dragon-ichor and flame at the top cone of the watchtower. The glass of the windows obliterated, fire rushed through, and the entire top floors of the Torvald watchtower became a burning inferno.

"You did it! You did it!" I could hear Adair's thin voice over the storm winds, as he and Senga and Kim joined us on the cliff top, to swipe and shoot—for Senga was armed with her bow— at the retreating Roskildeans.

"We can pull back!" Senga said happily.

Yes! I thought, giving the word to Crux to lift off from the cliffs – just as our world went black.

"Think a little flame would stop us?" an unearthly voice howled in the darkness.

I couldn't even see my hands in front of my face. I knew that I was still seated on Crux, but the hurricane level winds were forcing me sideways, and beneath me, Crux convulsed as he sought to maintain his grips on the rocks below.

The magical storm cloud summoned by Ohotto and the others was all around us. It had overwhelmed the island of

Rhul entirely – and what was worse, was the fell voice on the winds.

"You cannot stop us, girl."

It was a voice made up of howlings, made up of many voices melded together. Within the blackness that engulfed us, there were flashes of movement, like tendrils of smoke moving on the wind – and I had the intense feeling that it was *these* smoke-balls that were making those noises.

Just like I had seen on Malata, when Ohotto summoned the dead to attack the island, I thought.

"You and your unschooled dragon mage and your paltry dragons..." The voice was cold and cynical.

Crux roared out at the night, flame bursting from his jaws in a sheet to wash over the cliff top. His flame caught and held to the rocks and the walls of the tower of Rhul, driving back the darkness somehow. Even though the black storm-fog was all around us, there was also light. It was a hellish vision, one of howling winds and charred ground.

And the dead.

There were figures approaching through the storm, walking as if the magical winds didn't even affect them. They had fair hair and drawn, tight skin on their faces.

The captains of the dead.

"Senga! Adair!" I shouted. Where had they gone? They had been right here at our side.

"The Darkening flows through us. The Darkening comes," the assembled Captains of the Dead all intoned, in

perfect unison. As if commanded, the atmosphere suddenly changed. The wind died down, to be replaced with a terrible, awful cold that wasn't just in the skies but was also in the mind as well.

"Lila!" Danu shouted in alarm. "We have to fly – come on!"

He was right, but both I and Crux weren't eager to flee this battle. Crux summoned his dragon flames again, even as ice started to coat his scales and spread up my legs.

It was freezing. Like being plunged into the winter sea unexpectedly. Crux groaned, coughed gobbets of flame – but not enough to reach the Dead Captains.

"All fires can be put out. Even dragon fire," the Dead said, and one in the center raised his ancient arm and pointed at the watchtower of Rhul. The ice took it, snaking up the white stone as fast as spilled milk, putting out any of Crux's fires that remained.

"You cannot win against the Darkening. So I have just one thing to ask of you – die!" The captain, Jarl Lars Oldhorn, the Bloodhammer, thrust both of his hands straight at us, and the cold frost winds flung themselves at us, knocking us from the cliff.

We fell, tumbling to the seas below.

"Crux!" I begged as we plummeted. The Phoenix dragons'

wings were coated in heavy plates of ice. He thrashed, trying to crack and shatter the ice as fast as the plates reformed.

Was this it? Was this how we died?

"NO!" I felt Danu's shout as much as I heard it, as a surge of warmth washed through both me and the dragon that I clung onto. The warmth was enough to enliven the young bull, as he threw his wings open at the last moment to soar out over the straits that were now dotted with ice and sleet. I didn't know which direction we were flying, but Crux was roaring in pain and fury as the warmth pooled around us.

Danu. It is Danu, keeping us warm – I thought as I looked down the length of the dragon to see Danu with his eyes rolled white and his hands planted on either side of Crux's spine, as white-golden waves of light flooded from him and into Crux beneath us.

THOOOM! There was another crash of sound, and ahead of us the black-hulled vessels of the Dead emerged from the wall of storm. They must have been hiding in the dark storm, just as they had before. And they were firing – but not at us.

"Get 'em, lads!" a voice shouted as we swerved around the first one, then another Dead Ship to find the *Ariel*, cutting its way into the magical stormfront and firing with all cannon at the Dead fleet, before swerving back in a spray of water out of the storm. The Raiders were attacking! They were flying *into* the Darkening and shooting at the enemy ships – and it wasn't just the Raiders either. The slower, heavier Free Islander vessels were diving straight into the ice water of the straits, their rigging and sails coating with frost in seconds, as they conducted my plan.

My stupid, outrageous plan.

The largest of the Free Islander vessels were not staffed with Jolrpun's people, but the fiercest Raiders. They had no intention of turning around, but instead, they slowed and formed a living barricade across the straights.

"Get out!" I started to shout. "Get out now!"

That had always been the second part of the plan, for the heavier vessels to form a wall, and for the lighter ships to unload their sailors and fall back. Skiffs and yachts braved the freezing, terrifying magical storm to skim the waters as Raiders leapt from the decks of the stranded vessels.

My plan was working, miraculously – but not entirely. As we flew, several of the recuse boats froze completely, while another was hit by one of the purple lightning bolts.

"*Noooo!*" I screamed. Who would be on those boats? Who had now been lost to us?

Our barricade of merchant vessels slowed the Dead fleet and the approaching Roskildean navy they protected – but it did not stop the freezing Darkening storm. As it swept around all of us, many of the fierce Raiders screamed and wailed in terror, for the Darkening had brought that unnatural fear that unmanned even the largest of us.

"No – the plan!" I shouted – although there was no way that the Raiders and islanders could hear me, I knew. But Danu and I had *told* them about what effect the Darkening has. How it freezes the heart and thoughts as well as the body.

You have to fight it with fire, Crux had said. *You have to fight it with hope,* Danu had said.

But the Raiders and islanders below seemed to be doing neither. Many were running, leaping into the freezing waters

No. Not all. Even in the loud storm winds, I saw a group of Raiders stern-faced on their smaller boat. They were working in pairs. Each pair had linked elbows and bowing their heads as they worked against the storm. They were fighting it. They were using their friendship to fight it.

THOOOM! The Dead fleet and the Roskildeans fired at the barricade, smashing the abandoned boats with ease, but only succeeded in creating more wreckage. We had held them off for a bit – but would the message get through to the mainland? Would the watchtowers there have time to light? Had Crux's dragon fire lit the bonfire for long enough? Would our warning help the people of Torvald and Vala in time?

"Lila…?" Danu gasped, still crouching over Crux's back, his hands glowing white-gold as he pumped his magic into us, while he nodded with eyes that were deep and haunted.

I looked in the direction he was looking - and swore.

There, slowing before the barricade was the largest galleon that I had ever seen, and it was as black as night. It had sails that were ragged and tall, and it dwarfed the other boats around it.

And on its prow stood my uncle, a lone living figure

amidst the army of the dead: Lord Havick the Pretender of Roskilde.

※

"Uncle!" I shouted, and Crux bellowed underneath me in shared fury as he wheeled over the retreating Raider boats. Crux shared my wish. We would end this.

"Lila – what are you doing?" Danu groaned. "I cannot keep the frost away for much longer…."

"I have to stop this!" I cried. "If I can get the Sea Crown – then maybe we can reverse this curse of the Dead. Are you with me?"

Danu looked at me with grave eyes, holding my gaze for a moment. "I'll be at your side," he said, lifting his glowing hands from Crux and snarling in pain and power as he extended them to the flagship.

Instantly, the magical frost started settling on Crux, but he was already flying fast towards Havick. I saw the flash of cannons out of the corner of my eye as the Dead fleet attempted to stop us.

Just as the Dead Captain Lars 'threw' frost at us with the magic in his hands, so Danu threw something at Havick's galleon. It looked like golden light, and when it hit the black timbers they started to smoke.

My own uncle cried out as he staggered back from the

blinding light. Behind him, the other Dead soldiers were screaming and scratching at their own blinded faces-

"Now!" Crux swooped in as I rose from the saddle—

"Stop her!" I heard the Pretender King of the Western Archipelago scream.

I vaulted, legs spinning in the air before I felt the jolt of connection with the wood of Havick's flagship. I was on the enemy ship!

Crux was flashing past the prow, light gleaming from Danu's hands—

My momentum pushed me forward as I reached out a grasping hand for my uncle's face, and the Sea Crown atop it.

Sea. Storms. Rain-winds and salt-water. The instant my fingers brushed the strange green-gold metal, something jolted into me like I had been hit by one of the witch's lightning strikes. It was like the way that I talked to Crux, but there was no intelligence behind it. No emotions. Just cold and ancient power.

Water that was as blue as the sky, or as grey as my mother's eyes – my birth mother's eyes – I had never remembered that, but now I did. My mother had eyes as grey as sea-water.

Water that was black in the depths of winter-cold, or as gleaming white with the northern ice. The waters of the world were ancient. Older even than dragon-kind, and they were eternal.

Images flashed into my head in a flickering, constant furor. *Giant cliffs made of ice, somewhere far to the north. Seas that were shallow and gleaming with corals that pulsed with color and life. Dark trenches and pits under the waves in which nothing ever dared venture.*

The water had been through it all, it had been through and around the entire world many times over – just as the warmth of the sun and the fire of the dragons were the same thing - somehow - forever giving life to the world, so the water was also an eternal force – either as hard as ice, as soft as spring water, and as enduring as memory.

With that memory of the world came power, a raw sort of power that reminded me of storm surges and thunder. It was a wild sort of power that I didn't know how to direct or control, only that it was now inside my hand, in the form of the Sea Crown. *This was it. This was who I was meant to be,* I thought. *Who my family really were. We were the guardians of the islands, and of the sea.*

Just as fast as it had arrived, the vision and its power was gone – and I was leaping past my astonished uncle. The dragon was roaring as I bounded off the railing.

"Crux!" I screamed, and the air was knocked out of me as the tip of his black scaled tail curled around my middle like a rope.

I was yanked upward into the sky, the blinding light failing as Danu's magic left him. All around us was dark black and freezing cold as we climbed and climbed. I heard the distant booms of cannons and still, we climbed.

"Hold on, dragon-sister!" Crux's words brushed through my mind as my body froze—

And then the sudden rush of clear still air as we burst out of the top of the Darkening-storm, and into blue skies.

I was shouting, although I couldn't tell if it was from the pain of freezing or from exultation at what I had achieved. I had the Sea Crown of Roskilde. I had the heritage of my family, here, in my hands. Everything that I had lost, everything that I had fought for – here it was, at last.

But at what cost?

"Look, wave-rider!" Crux called, and I turned my head to see, below us, that the black clouds of the Darkening was beginning to wisp apart, and the ice-laden winds were dying down. In its wake, the unnatural storm left half-frozen and tortured ships and churned the straits of Rhul with the froth of white water. What was happening?

"It's the crown!" Danu called to me through chattering teeth. When I turned to stare at him, I could see that his eyes were wide with astonishment. "It is one of the magical treasures of the world. Ohotto has been tapping into it to help her magic. Now, without it. Without her Sea King…."

He didn't have to spell it out. I could see the storm clouds starting to break, and clots of the Darkening separating from their mass and picking up speed as if it, too, was fleeing. But what could it be scared of – a girl with a crown?

"They are coming! The queen is here!" Crux crowed exultantly, and I could see, speeding towards us out of the western

skies were other, large shapes on the winds. They gleamed white, green, blue and red. The dragons of the islands. They had heard and answered the call.

The Darkening separated into clods of sea-hugging clouds that boiled and sped in different directions away from the oncoming roar of vengeful dragons.

"Where is Havick? Where is my uncle?" I shouted, looking back below us to see that his ghostly black galleon had vanished.

EPILOGUE
LILA, OF THE WESTERN ISLES

We sat on the headlands that overlooked the bay, my dragon and me. The skies were mostly blue, if a little grey, and there were dragons rising in the thermals – both Orange drakes and a few of the Western Isle dragons.

Below me, the burgeoning encampment of the Free Islanders and the Sea Raiders busied themselves with caring for the wounded and mourning the dead. Out in the inlet, I could see the haphazard collection of boats that had managed to limp home after the battle, some of them lying low in the waves after all the water they had taken in.

It was a marvel that any of us survived at all.

But despite our victory against my uncle and his sorcerous allies, none of us felt like celebrating. We had won the battle, but the war was still before us.

Queen Ysix and her brood had given chase to the different clouds of Darkening, but just like before after the First Battle of Malata, they could not penetrate it entirely, and it sped unnaturally fast back to the north.

We also did not find my uncle's flagship. Had it been hidden inside one of those clouds?

But without the Sea Crown it seemed the power of the Darkening and the Dead was much diminished, at least. Their arcane storm that stretched for leagues, and through which the witches could shoot their strange sorcerous darts, and which amplified the powers of the Dead, had been reduced to a dirty black sea cloud.

They escaped, Queen Ysix confirmed with Crux, and I had no doubt that they would be back.

We would not celebrate because there were still many dangers, and many had died. There were Dead still on the shores just south of us, and every moment I scanned both the seaward and the landlocked horizon for fear of seeing their lurching forms coming for us. I could not celebrate because, although we might have spared enough time for the message to get through to Torvald and Vala, none of us had managed to communicate with them yet. *What if Torvald thinks we are to blame? What if Vala believes we are invading their territory?*

There were too many questions and not enough time for answers. Some of the Raiders were advocating strongly to take to their boats and head south along the coast. Maybe end up in the spice coast. Some of the Free Islanders were suggesting that we could settle here. But how can we do that? We are water-borne people, and our home is out there, in the burning dirt of Malata.

And then there was Danu – the last reason why I could not celebrate. Even though he was not physically hurt during the raid, he was much weakened since using his magic. He gave some of his life-magic to keep us warm, just as Crux healed him with his own dragon-energy. Though Danu told me he was okay, I often caught him rubbing his joints and knuckles as though they pained him, and his eyes had taken a haunted look.

How much had I asked of these people, my friends? My family?

"No more than we ask of you," Crux murmured at my side, slapping his tail lazily.

In my hands sat the Sea Crown, stolen from the head of my own uncle. It was a fine piece of gold with a greenish sheen, but as I turned it over in my hands, I could not imagine the whole world being thrust into chaos for it.

"Danu thinks you should wear it, you know." Crux opened one eye slyly.

"I know," I whispered. "He thinks I should announce my claim to the Western Isles."

"And why don't you?" The Phoenix dragon raised his head to look at me seriously. *"You might make a good den mother, you know."*

"Pfft." I slipped the Sea Crown back into my knapsack,

unworn. "You know what, Crux? I am tired of prophecies about who I should and shouldn't be. From now on, I think we're going to have to make our own fate."

"Isn't that all that we ever did anyway?" Crux said.

"Ugh. You and your dragon-logic." I slapped him playfully on the talon. "How about we take Danu and go fishing instead?"

"Now that is fate," Crux said and pushed himself up from the ground. As we walked down the hill, I thought of my father—both my fathers. We must live while we can, I told myself. Let fate play its games, and let prophecies play out as they will. For now, we will soak ourselves in the goodness that remains to us, and then we will prepare for to the war to come.

END OF DRAGON CROWN
SEA DRAGONS TRILOGY BOOK TWO

Sea Dragons Series

Book One: Dragon Raider
(Published: March 28, 2018)

Book Two: Dragon Crown
(Published: May 30, 2018)

Book Three: Dragon Prophecy
(Published: July 25, 2018)

PS: Keep reading for an exclusive extract from the next book in the Sea Dragons Trilogy, **Dragon Prophecy.**

THANK YOU!

I hope you enjoyed **Dragon Crown**. Please don't forget to leave a review.

Receive free books, exclusive excerpts and be kept up to date on all of my new releases, when you sign up to my mailing list at AvaRichardsonBooks.com/mailing-list

Stay in touch! I'd also love to connect with you on:

Facebook: www.facebook.com/AvaRichardsonBooks

Goodreads:
www.goodreads.com/author/show/8167514.Ava_Richardson

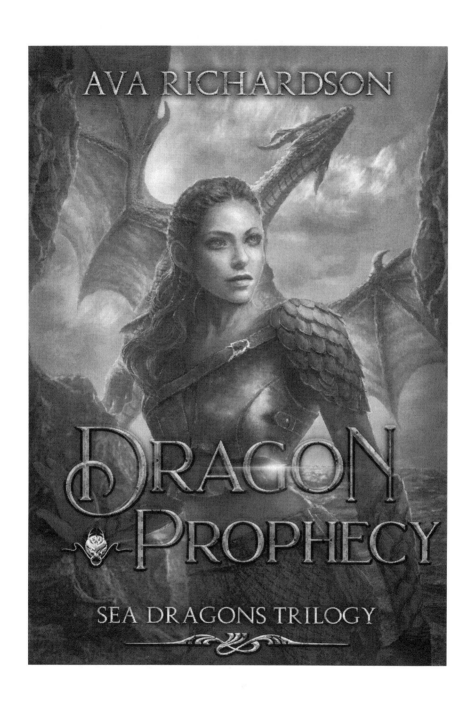

BLURB

From humble beginnings, a heroine will be forged in fire.

Forced to retreat from the Army of the Dead with her remaining force of Raiders and their dragons, Lila begins to despair that her people will ever be anything but a ragtag band. Even wielding the fabled crown of Roskilde, she cannot unite the Raiders—it seems she is not the one to fulfill Danu's cherished prophecy.

But Danu isn't giving up yet. Though he suspects the evil Havick has obtained an ancient book that will allow him unspeakable power, help may come from an unlikely source: the Dragon Riders of Torvald. These brave warriors could be their last chance to defeat the evil of Lars and Havick—but they are also the Raiders' sworn enemies. Now, Lila, Danu, Crux, and their friends have no choice but to make a perilous journey into hostile territory to seek allies against the darkness threatening to consume them all. To save her friends, Lila must become the legendary leader she was born to be.

Pre-order **Dragon Prophecy** at
AvaRichardsonBooks.com

EXCERPT

"Lila – wake up!"

I awoke in a snarl of blankets, disoriented, to the sound of Danu hissing at me urgently.

"Wha-?" *Where am I? This isn't home.* My mind scrabbled into wakefulness, noticing the stretched sails of the roof, the smell of wood smoke still hanging in the tent.

Oh yeah. We don't have a home anymore. I almost forgot – or maybe I *wanted* to forget. I was a part of the refugee group that had fled to the Southern Mainland – the last of the Sea Raiders of the Western Archipelago and what was left of the Free Islanders. We were encamped just under the bluffs that allowed us to look out into the western Storm Seas, as we regrouped after our last battle with Lord Havick.

"Lila!" This time Danu, with his messy thatch of hair, shook me.

"Ger' off!" I told him angrily, swinging my legs out from the small cot bed and planting them on the floor. *Cold.* This wasn't the colonial mansion of my family home on Malata, either. "I'm awake and I'm sitting up – what more do you want?" I groaned. My father had always said that I was "a joy" to be around in the mornings. I don't think that he was talking descriptively.

Kasian. My heart lurched at the memory. *Dad.* My Sea Raider foster-father who had fallen trying to defend our home of Malata. I gritted my teeth. It's funny how you can almost convince yourself that you have forgotten how much loss hurts, until one little memory brings grief racing back to hit you in the stomach.

"What is it?" I groan wearily, my morning grumbles replaced with the sensation of despair.

"The dragon scouts are back, and something is moving against the encampment," Danu breathed, and in a rush, my mind caught up with what my eyes had been trying to tell me. Danu was dressed in his torn and threadbare black cloak, and underneath it I could see his leather jerkin that the Raiders had loaned him. His heavy canvas trousers had a sturdy sword belted to their side, and on his feet were heavy boots. Danu was dressed for war.

"Damnit!" I seized my own things to struggle them on under my blanket, as the witch's apprentice made an embarrassed noise and turned on his heel. Whatever. You don't grow up as I did, spending most of your life close-quarters on raiding ships and still have that much modesty, I guess. In a trice, I had my breeches on and my tunic wrapped and tucked into my broad Raider's belt, already jangling with hooks and knifes and the many other small implements a life at sea requires.

"Throw me the boots, will you, Danu?" I say as I try to tame my hair back into its braid. "And tell me—what is going on?"

"Some of your mother's scouts have just come back – but not all of them. They say they were attacked about a league up the coast from here." Danu chucked first one, then the next of my calf-high boots. I listened as I strapped them on and pulled them tight.

"It was the dead, or so the survivors say. Your mother wanted to head out to meet with them, but I suggested the dragons." Danu looked tense with energy, and my heart thumped with the same. Despite our dire situation, every time I thought about flying on Crux, it gave me the same sense of excitement.

"We hunt?" Crux said in my mind, barrelling into my thoughts with all of the strength and fire that he usually did.

Morning, Wyrm, I thought as I stood up. *Yes, we are going hunting.* But first, there was one last thing that I knew that I couldn't leave unguarded here. Turning back to my small sea-chest, I opened it to pull out the heavy linen wrap that hid our great prize: The Sea Crown of Roskilde itself. For a chance moment, the linens fell away, revealing an edge of the strange green-gold treasure; its rim crafted into fluting and leaping waveforms.

Strange to think that this sat on the head of my real kin, all the way back into ancient times, I thought, as that same old shiver of unease at seeing it juddered through me. I don't know why I felt squeamish around it. It was mine by right. I was the last heir of Roskilde, Havick was my Uncle, and he had killed my blood-parents to get it. But it was also the same object that had sat on my uncle Havick's head – under whose authority the Black Fleet of the dead had been raised, and under whose direction so many of the Free Islanders had been attacked and purged.

And it is the Crown I was prophesied to wear. It was the prophesy that had spurred Danu on his original mission to find me in the first place. It foretold that I would one day wear the Sea Crown again, that I would rise from the waters, and that I would bring in my wake blood, fire, and the dead.

Well it seemed that I was already fulfilling at least one part of that prophesy, wasn't I? I thought grimly. I had retrieved the Sea Crown, and here the dead are.

"Lila? What are you waiting for?" Danu said, as behind him there was the distant banging of a pot, and a muffled shout of alarm.

"Nothing. I'm coming," I said as I stuffed the Sea Crown into my backpack, slung it over my shoulder and followed Danu out into the gloom.

The camp was still in its pre-dawn dark and the assembled tents and huts were little more than deeper pools of shadow against the greying sky, as Danu and I snaked our way towards the headland where the dragons were roosting. The clouds skudded low across the horizon this morning, and I cursed under my breath. That might mean rain, which would make it harder for me to shoot my bow accurately.

"Where's mother?" I hissed to Danu, before my question was answered by the sudden clang of a pot from up ahead.

"Up and at 'em, boys and girls!" my mother bellowed from one of the small guard fires as we rounded the last tented avenue. "Up! Up and to your posts – never let it be said that the Raiders were caught in their beds by their enemy!"

Around her was already gathered a motley of Raiders and Free Islanders, hurriedly buckling on armour and lacing boots. The Raiders did so with a calm efficiency, and even the Free Islanders I saw now had that air of casual competence around swords and spears. A lot had changed since the last battle.

Ever since, the Free Islanders had really started to think of themselves as a fighting force, as opposed to fishermen and traders who happened to be fighting for their lives.

Fighting for their very survival, I reminded myself.

"Ah, Lila – you're here, good." My mother Pela was handing out unlit torches to everyone, and she threw one to me.

I looked at it in confusion. It was a simple wooden stake, with wrappings of linen and old shirts, bound tight and soaked with precious ship oil.

"The Dead don't succumb to our weapons, remember?" my mother said. "You'll need flame to kill them."

"I'll be on a dragon, ma'" I said dryly.

"Never can be too careful. Put in in your belt and give me some peace of mind, okay?" she said to me sharply, and I heard an echo of the Chieftain that she had been back on Malata, *Pela, Thunder of the Seas,* I could almost hear my father's words call her.

"What is it, Lila?" my mother paused as she looked at me with worry. She must have noticed the look of misery that crossed my features every time that I thought about my foster father, and her husband.

"Just. You remind me of dad," I told her – which I knew wasn't strictly true, but I also knew how she would take it: as a compliment. I recognized an echo in her of that same fierce spirit, seeing the light of the watch fire illuminating my mother's warrior braid and her stern face.

"Funny. I have always thought the same thing about you," my mother said. "Now. The scouts came back not half an hour ago, and they say that they were attacked inland, straight up the coastal track to the north-east of here." My mother said.

"On land?" I paused. "That means that Havick is pushing his invasion." We had already known that Havick had sent the Black Fleet of the Dead ahead of him to reach the southern mainland, but with our success in the last battle, I had somehow naturally assumed Havick would pull them back. How stupid I had been!

"Aye – and more importantly, it means that Havick – or his dead allies, at least – are right on our doorstop!" Pela nodded. "Go. I still need another hour to rouse this ungrateful lot."

"We'll buy you that time," I promised her, crossing the space to fold the fierce little woman into a hug. "And one more thing," I suddenly thought, loosening my shoulder bag and pulling out the wrapped linen bundle, with its priceless prize inside. "Take this. Keep it safe," I told her.

"No!" my mother instantly pulled back. "That's yours. You should keep it with you, look after it…"

"No, mother." I was adamant. "I'm going to be flying and

fighting. If anything happens – I need to know that this is safe, I can't risk it being captured by enemy hands again…"

If anything happens. My own words hung in the air between me and my mother as showy as if they were one of Danu's magic tricks.

"I understand," my mother nodded, accepting the heavy burden and instantly turning to put it in her own backpack of belongings. "I'll stay with the fleet, so it will be surrounded by fighting Raider guards," she promised me. And then we had no time left at all, and with a nod at my mother, Danu and I turned, and raced past the last watchfires, climbing to the headland where the dragons were already hooting and whistling.

"You have a plan?" Danu said, wheezing as we jogged up the incline to the land of rocks above.

"Burn them until they stop moving?" I hazarded, earning an eye roll from Danu. I knew what he meant. "We keep most of the dragons back to guard the camp for now, until we know we need them. For the moment it'll be us, Senga and Adair if they're ready." I said. "This is a scout and subdue mission first and foremost."

"Subdue?" Danu echoed. "It's hard enough to kill the dead anyway – let alone 'subdue them'." We crested the rise and saw our dragons were already awake and waiting for us.

"Don't worry Danu, with these guys as friends, we can do anything," I said, my heart lifting at the mere sight of the great beasts.

"Wave Rider," Crux greeted me with his usual name for me, padding forward on claws that I could easily sit inside. Crux was giant, but still only a young Bull dragon – and a rare Phoenix one at that, too. Most of the scales on his body were a midnight black to blue, that would gleam unexpectedly in any light with greens and purples. A fiery line of orange scales edged his paler belly scales, and his eyes were a lambent green as he lowered his snout to nudge me gently against the chest.

"Hello, you," I said, allowing myself to feel the warmth of his breath and the strength of his heart for a moment. Any anxiety I had about fighting the dead vanished in this simple act. It wasn't just knowing that I would be backed up by several tonnes of fire-breathing muscle, it was that Crux completed my heart in a way I could not explain. He was a constant, warming flame in the center of my being, and just being in contact with him again reaffirmed our bond.

"We go hunt now?" He chirruped at me, stamping on the ground a little with his forepaws.

"Yes, Wyrm," I teased him, dragging myself away from that shared moment and back to the chill of the pre-dawn, and to Danu's animated discussion with the two young Dragon

Raiders Senga and Adair beyond. They were almost of an age with me, and we had grown up together on my father's flagship the *Aeriel*. They were also the first two Raiders to take to the dragons I had brought to Malata, and they rode Kim, a long Sinuous Blue dragon that I could see lashing her tail expectantly.

"All right, listen up!" I called, as I made a quick headcount of the dragons we had here. Kim and her brother Thiel, Retax and Lucalia, and of course Crux with me. But so far Senga and Adair were the only riders who had made it up to what I was thinking of as 'the dragon grounds' up here on the bluff. It joined with the rocky cliffs that swept back down to the bay where the smaller Savage Orange dragons nested – who were right now chirruping and calling as they took flight in great billowing clouds.

Only four Raiders on two dragons? I thought for a moment, before pushing my alarm away. *It would be enough. Scout and subdue, remember?*

I opened my mouth. "We're going to try and slow the march of Havick's dead, but we don't know how many we will face, nor what capabilities they will have." The last time we had met them, they had been surrounded by the strange spectral clouds Danu called the Darkening – some kind of living cloud of fear, from what I could make out.

"But we have dragon fire," I said, patting Crux's leg, who belched a great flare of the stuff at my words. "We'll set lines of fire between us and them, to buy time for my mother to ready the other fighters, and the other Dragon Raiders to get up in the air."

"We're not going for a full assault?" Senga was always the fiercest between her and her brother Adair. She looked at me like she didn't think much of my plan.

"No," I said stubbornly. "Two dragons. Crux and Kim, with us. We're going to disrupt and wait for backup, okay?"

Senga shrugged like it was no big deal to her – but I could tell that she didn't agree. I gritted my teeth in frustration. I liked Senga. I didn't want to have to get into an argument with her over this, and especially not in front of the other dragons, who were now stamping and hissing in their frustration at not being asked to join the fight.

"They want to hunt with you, Wave Rider. You are First Daughter. You lead us on the hunt," Crux informed me as tactfully as a dragon can do (which meant that he barged into my mind and hissed at me).

But no, I couldn't allow them to leave the camp yet. "I need all the other dragons protecting the refugees," I stated again firmly, and I could feel Crux's confusion at this human concern.

"We all fight. Human, dragon, young, old," he stated sullenly – but he was a dragon, and he did not have the same qualms and worries that I had.

"Scout, subdue, and disrupt – for now," I repeated firmly, nodding to Danu, who pulled himself up Crux's far shoulder to slide into his position between the Phoenix dragon's great wings. I joined him, settling onto the leather saddle that we had fashioned, and attaching the guides to my belt clips. Even though I was tired, and I had only ridden Crux just yesterday, it still felt like a return to normal to be here again.

"Are you ready?" I whispered knowing that both Danu and Crux would hear me.

"I'm ready," Danu said.

"Always," Crux informed me. I turned in my saddle to see Senga and Adair finishing their pre-flight adjustments to their own belts and saddles, before Adair looked up with a broad grin, and gave me a big thumb's up sign.

"Okay, take us up, Crux," I said, leaning forward and placing my hands on his neck. In an instant I felt the surge of powerful draconian muscles, and Crux bounded forward towards the edge of the bluffs. Kim watched the Phoenix dragon with pin-point attention, starting her own run a few moments after.

There was another jolt as Crux started leaping, once, twice, and-

Up! His claws pushed out from the edge of the rocks and his wings snapped out in a wide fan on either side of us as he jumped into the pre-dawn murk. I felt my stomach drop as it always did, and that coil of terror-excitement that I always felt just before the winds caught us with a strong push.

And we were flying, gliding down the landscape in a short swoop as Crux gathered the momentum for the first big beat of his wings, executed at exactly the bottom-most point of his arc so that we shot into the sky like a speeding arrow.

"Skreach!" A call of joy resounded from behind us as the Sinuous Blue caught the wake of our air currents, and followed us, a little behind and to our right. These great beasts didn't need to be taught how to fly in formation, I marvelled, remembering the picture books that I had of the ancient Dragon Riders of distant Torvald. They were always pictured in flying diamonds, or arrows – but the wilder dragons of the Western isles naturally fell into a wide V like a bow of migrating swans.

Below us the land shot away and I saw the dark blanket of the seas beyond the coast. The lights of our encampment were on our left, more lights kindling in the dark. My mother would be down there somewhere, waking the Raiders and Free Islanders up and pushing torches and sabres into sleepy hands. As we circled higher over the land, the Phoenix Dragon underneath me gaining altitude to speed our eventual swoop north, I could see that full extent of our camp.

We had grown over the last few weeks since the battle with Havick. Of course, I had known this already – as smaller flotillas and boats arrived on a nearly daily basis full of other Free Islanders seeking the only refuge they had from Havick and the Black Fleet – but now, to my surprise, I was looking at a shanty that was almost the size of a small town. Not quite as big as Malata harbour has been – but it was close. Upturned boat hulls (the ones that had been limping, leaking, or too damaged for us to repair with our limited resources) had become small huts and halls, and there were even clearly visible "streets" now. A couple of round timber barns had been erected from the local stands of trees, and now I could see lines of people racing back and forth, carrying equipment, and groups congregating at the shoreline where our lines of small boats were staked out, ready to cast off for the larger fighting ships we had moored in the bay.

It was for them that we fight, I felt a great comfort in admitting– which was odd, now that I thought about it. *Didn't I want revenge? Didn't I want to make my Uncle's army pay for what they had done to Malata? For taking the only father I had known from me?*

Of course I did, my anger surged at the memories of everything that I had lost – only now they were also tinged with guilt, at not having thought of them first. *A Raider is supposed to take revenge,* I scolded myself. We live and die by our honor, and our swords.

But why did I feel like I was failing at being both a Raider and a leader?

"I smell them on the wind! Bleurgh!" Crux's thought broke into my mind as we turned northwards, and, for a brief moment I think I too felt an echo of that dragon sense pass between us. Something foul and horrid, overripe like fruit gone bad, before it vanished again as soon as it had arrived. I reminded myself that I would have to beg Crux sometimes, could he *not* share his mind with me on everything?

Anyway. Our dragon had sensed the enemy, and he now angled his wings to fly towards them as silently as a gliding hawk.

Pre-order **Dragon Prophecy** at
AvaRichardsonBooks.com

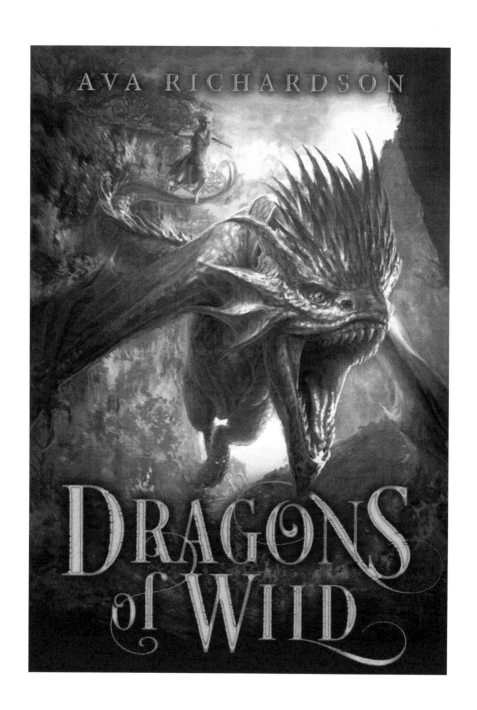

BLURB

The once-peaceful kingdom of Torvald has been ravaged by evil magic, forcing Riders to forget their dragons and their noble beasts to flee to the wilds. Now, anyone who dares to speak of dragons is deemed insane and put to death. Into this dark and twisted land, Saffron was born sixteen years ago. Cursed with the ability to see and talk to dragons, she's been forced into a life of exile and raised by wild dragons—secretly dreaming of a normal life and the family she lost. But as her powers become more uncontrollable, Saffron knows she must find her family before she hurts herself—or worse, her dragon clan.

Scholarly and reclusive, Bower prefers to spend his days reading about the legends of the Dragon Riders—even if being caught means death. But as the son of a noble house on the brink of destruction, it falls to him to fulfill a mysterious prophecy that promises to save his kingdom from the rule of the evil King Enric. When fate brings him into contact with Saffron, Bower gains a powerful ally—but one whose wild, volatile magic threatens their very lives.

Their friendship might just have the power to change the course of history, but when King Enric makes Saffron a tempting offer, their alliance will be shaken to the core.

Get your copy of **Dragons of Wild** at
AvaRichardsonBooks.com

EXCERPT

The Salamander Prophecy:

'Old and young will unite to rule the land from above. Upon the dragon's breath comes the return of the True King. It will be his to rebuild the glory of Torvald.'

(date and author unknown)

Vance Maddox

The city is in uproar. I have never seen the like—even in the old days when the wild dragons would raid from the north. Never has there been so much terror, so much bloodshed and so much anguish. Screams fill the air as people are thrown from their homes. The ringing of bells, the call of the Dragon Horns, and above it all the fire and shriek of the agonized, enraged dragons.

Another beam from the roof splinters and explodes in a shower of sparks on the flagstones at my feet. I dodge to one side. Through the gap in the tiles above I see the red and orange scales of something vast and threatening. The dragon tries once more to get at us inside—to get at me!

"Protect the prince!" I call to the guards, all of them Maddox men and women like myself: tall, light-haired and pale-skinned. They have that rangy look those of the Maddox line never seem to quite outgrow.

"Captain!" The guard chief gives me a quick, stern nod. Gone are the smiles and the fine tunics that marked this small group of bodyguards as ambassadors. We've all thrown aside finery, replacing it with the hardened steel and iron armor of my family.

A hissing roar comes from above. The red-orange dragon once again throws its weight onto the roof. We can all hear the intake of its breath like a giant bellows.

"Flame shields," I call, falling to one knee and holding up the specially-treated oval shield over my head, and not a moment too soon as a firestorm bursts into the hall from the dragon.

One of my guards is not so lucky. He screams and the stink of burning hair and flesh choke the hall. The dragon's fire is fast, incinerating him in seconds, leaving ash floating on the air.

The flames last only a brief second, but already my arm aches from the force of the dragon's breath. Maybe my brother and late father were right—how can any human live near such dangerous beasts, let alone build a city underneath their nests? This is the day that my brother, Prince Hacon Maddox, has decided to overthrow the rulers of Torvald and seize it for himself. May the storms guide me; I have sworn to help him.

"Up! Up and to the prince!" Lowering my shield, I stand and leap forward, knowing we have only a little time before the orange and red dragon will be able to breathe fire down on us again. I catch a glimpse of the charred armor of the soldier who has died, melted now into slag. I don't even know his first name.

No time for misery or cold feet now. We run through the long hall, feet pounding and armor rattling. Above us, dragons pound at the roof and walls and roar. Luckily for us, but not so lucky for Torvald royalty, this palace has been designed to withstand rogue dragon attacks. Its many halls are reinforced stone, shot through with metal bars. The king and queen's best protection will become their prison.

Turning a corner, we face the next phalanx of Torvald guards, all wearing the imperial red and purple of the Flamma-Torvald household. Scars show how many battles they have fought, and their stance is that of fighting men and women.

But Flamma-Torvald, for all of its might, for all of its fame throughout the Three Kingdoms, has grown soft. The Maddox clan hails from the furthest east some generations ago. We've fought every tribe, every bandit and every upstart warlord between here and the ends of creation. The people of the Middle Kingdom have no idea what we can do—or what strange and terrible things we have already done.

"Death to the traitors!" shouts one of Flamma-Torvald guards, throwing his longsword forward in a jab that would have skewered me were it not for my reflexes. I catch and turn the blow, spinning to step inside the man's guard.

A kick to his solar plexus sends him back. He falls, sprawling onto the floor. My second-in-command dispatches him with a solid thrust of his blade. The battle is fast and hard. I spin and parry. I hack until my sword no longer connects with armor and tissue and bone. Half my guard has been slain by the time we're done, but all the Flamma-Torvald troops have fallen under our blades. My men and women look as though they have been drenched in red by the time that we finish, and I lean on my sword, panting.

"Sir?"

Looking up, I see one of the women of my guard pointing to the brick dust and mortar raining down from above us. She is right. We don't have time for even a breath.

Ahead of us is our goal—what looks to be the ornate, wooden double-doors of the throne room. All this carnage has been planned months in advance by Hacon, my brother by our late father—and by me as well. Hacon and the Iron Guard are to be inside the throne room, seizing the king and queen, while I lead a group of soldiers through the palace halls to deal with any Dragon Riders we might meet.

Hacon has said the people of Torvald have no chance against us. I'd thought that mostly bravado. It is only now, standing outside the doors of the throne room with blood dripping down my blades that I start to believe. How long have I heard him and father rail about the day we would take the city? I never truly believed it possible.

Even now, I can hear Hacon's shouts. 'They are abominations! Dragons are evil, vile creatures—and they have enslaved the entire Middle Kingdom through their control of House Flamma-Torvald!' Our father never tired of repeating those same rants.

Why should I feel uneasy now?

The twin doors of the throne room open. Two of the Iron Guards step out, their full-plate suits looking like the scales of dragons and gleaming in the torch light. Behind them, I see the opulent throne room of House Flamma-Torvald. A ring of the Iron Guard surrounding King Mason and Queen Druella Roule.

The carpets of the throne room seem washed in blood. Bodies of the royal guards lay hacked apart. The stench is almost unbearable. Looking at the blood, my stomach clenches and turns. It wasn't meant to be like this. It wasn't meant that so many should die. What have we done?

From behind his prison of blades, King Mason shouts, "How could you? We welcomed you to the citadel! We gave you a home!" I hear tears in his voice as well as anger.

My brother, his black hair revealed with his helmet off, walks to the window. Outside, dragons swoop through the sky as the city burns. Just a scant few years ago, we came to this citadel with our Iron Guard as a fine gift for the 'glory of the dragon-king.' King Mason had been pleased then, giving us high places at court, installing our Iron Guard at every city gate and guard house. Little did he know this day would come, when our gifts would spring into action under our orders, seizing power and delivering the city to us.

Turning away from the window, Hacon smiles. His face seems sharper than ever, narrow and long. "Call off your dragons." Hacon points his sword at the queen. "Or she will be the first to die."

"Cowards!" King Mason snarls the word. "Try me first, man to man!"

He is brave, I'll give him that. I stride to my brother's side. "Hacon, let them live. We have seized the city, and with a word from this man, the dragons will retreat. There is no need to wallow in blood."

"Silence, brother!" He slashes the air with his sword and

turns to Mason again. "Call your beasts off, or your wife and child both die."

"Hacon, this wasn't part of the plan." This is a holy mission—or so I'd thought. I knew it would be ugly, but I also thought this is the right thing. "We are here to liberate the city, not kill innocent babes. Imprison these two or exile them. We have broken their power. It is enough!"

"It is never enough," Hacon hisses. "Exiles have a habit of returning, and babes grow up, brother!" With a motion and a thought, he orders the Iron Guard seize Roule, a queen no more. I knew my brother hid a cruel streak. I knew he sometimes used our family magic without wisdom or thought. But I had hoped he'd grown up over these past few months. That he had learned a little from our late father.

With a mournful call like the herons in autumn, the dragons call out. Glancing out the window, I see them disperse into the thunderclouds above the city, circling ever farther and farther. Sweat breaks out on Mason's forehead. I know he is using his unholy connection to these beasts to send them far away. Every now and then, a dragon swoops to pick up a rider—another unhappy alliance. Those that can flee are doing so, snatching handfuls of humans in their claws. But the Iron Guard raise long spears to show them never to return.

"There. It is done." Mason hangs his head and reaches out to take his wife's hand. "Leave my child and my Roule. Let us flee. You have the citadel. Take our riches, the crown, but let my family live!" He looks up, his eyes red, but his voice is firm.

Hacon's smile widens. "You really are all fools." Hacon nods. The Iron Guards lift their blades and strike down the royal couple. I turn away, sickened by the waste of it. A battle is one thing—to bring down an enemy who will take your life if you do not take his is a glorious thing. But to slaughter a man and a woman as if they were pigs meant for a feast brings no honor and tests no skill.

Hacon's voice calls me back to my duty. "The rest of you—go find the babe and destroy it." The Iron Guard lacks the intelligence to question orders. They are things, soulless and mindless, made of magic and metal. They storm out, clanking, to find the royal chambers.

I turn and slam a fist into my brother's shoulder, making him stagger. "A child? You mean murder. I don't know what you have become, Hacon, but I want no part in slaughter."

Turning, I stride from the throne room. Hacon's plans and maps are in my head and I know some backstairs the servants use. I can reach the babe ahead of the Iron Guard.

The door stands open. Bursting in, I find two Dragon Riders—man and a woman—standing between me and a crib that contains the royal babe. The man draws his sword. The woman bends over the babe.

I close and bar the door behind me. A shadow dims the light from the window. Then a flash of orange and red brightens the light. Storms protect us. Is that the same red and orange beast that attacked before? Has it bonded to the child? My throat dries, but the baby gives a gurgling laugh, and I know that allowing it to be murdered is something I cannot stomach.

Glancing at the riders, I tell them, "If you seek a glorious end, it follows just behind me! But if you seek to keep the baby alive, you must flee now! Forget the child's true name! Never speak of the parents, and you may spare its life! But go—go now!" I must look—and smell—hideous, covered as I am with blood. I can only hope they will listen.

"But the king and queen?" The man's voice shakes slightly. The woman seems to size me up with a look and seizes the baby to wrap it in her cloak. The man lifts his sword and his voice firms. "Where are they? We leave together."

The heavy clank of iron boots is muffled by the door—the Iron Guards are coming. "There is no time! Just get that child somewhere safe and never, never come back, please!"

The woman nods to the other Dragon Rider.

My brother's angry words echo outside. "Break open the door! Kill my brother if he stands in your way!"

The man glances at me, eyes side. "You are Vance Maddox?"

The door at my back shudders. A powerful fist rattles it again, shaking the hinges. It won't take much for them to get through. "Does it matter? Now please. Go. Save what you can. I will hold them as long as possible."

"Come on, this one is right. The flame must live on." The woman gives me one final look and pulls on her friend's sleeve, tugging him to the window. They flee to the waiting dragon. Its lands on the rock tower, clings there as they jump for its back. For an instant, I wonder at this horrible alliance—for an instant it almost seems an amazing thing. But I cannot think that—dragons are beasts and meant to live far from all humans.

Behind me, wood splinters. Just one more blow and they will be through. Metal hinges shriek. Turning, I step back and lift my blade. Outside, the rising mournful calls of the dragons that circled the citadel reverberate, unsure, and I wonder if they understand what is going on, or do they cry just to cry.

The door shatters, and Hacon steps through the splinters. He glances once around the room. "So, my brother—you would seek to undermine my rule?"

"It is done. You have won."

"Done?" My brother swears and shakes his head. "It will never be done until these half-humans, half-dragons never walk the land again. I will work a magic so deep and so powerful no dragon will ever remember having a human rider, and no child will ever think of dragons as anything but nightmares."

I give a shrug. "Fine. Work the magic. But the killing is done this day."

The Iron Guard step into the room. I summon the tendrils of magic within me—the ancient Maddox storm-magic that speaks to us of wolves and thunder, of the wild and forgotten places.

My brother's eyes narrow. He glances at the empty crib and back to me. "You were to be my right-hand man, my trusted adviser, my own blood who is all I can trust. Instead, you stab me in the back. You make your own plans instead of heeding mind. For this, I strip you of your name. I strip you of your family. No one shall befriend you wherever in my whole realm you go. I forbid any to feed you, to clothe you, or to shelter you. You shall be the scourge of all, and a curse I place upon your soul!"

He lifts a hand. The dark wave of his magic washes toward me. He is going to curse me into the grave, but I also have some power. I throw myself forward, the old storm magic clean and pure against his darkness. It may do me some good. But next to me, one of the Iron Guard swings a fist larger than my head. I have no time to duck the blow.

As I fall to pain and blackness, I know I have bought myself—and the Dragon Riders some time. The child survives. The flame still burns. And I can only mutter a prayer that the flame will one day purge Hacon's black heart.

Get your copy of **Dragons of Wild** at
AvaRichardsonBooks.com

Made in the USA
Middletown, DE
25 June 2018